TOLL

Nick Thorn, Chief of Vamoose PD, appraised what he could see of Harvey Renshaw's body, which was buried beneath a round hay bale. Then he hunkered down to remove Harvey's left boot. He wrapped his hand around the exposed ankle. "No pulse. He's dead."

"Told you." Amanda Hazard-Thorn slammed her mouth shut. This was not a good time to be sarcastic. She needed Thorn's cooperation, not his resentment. Furthermore, she didn't want a conflict over this murder case to seep into their recent marriage.

"Here's how I see it, Haz," Thorn said after he checked the broken hydraulic hose on the front of the John Deere tractor. "Renshaw kept the bale elevated so he could remove the nylon strings that were wrapped around the hay. One of the hydraulic hoses on the lift burst loose and wham! A ton of hay fell on Harvey. End of story."

"Maybe that's how you see it, but that isn't what happened," Amanda said.

"All right, I'll bite. How do you think it happened?"

"Someone purposely jerked the hydraulic hose loose so the bale would fall on Harvey. That unknown person, and his unidentified vehicle, were sprayed with hydraulic fluid. When I find the person with greasy clothes and boots driving an oily vehicle, I'll know who did it."

"Damn it, Hazard!" Thorn exploded. "You aren't a qualified detective, you're a magician who tries to pull clues and theories out of thin air. This isn't a murder, it's an accident!"

Accident, my eye! thought Amanda. She was going to prove Thorn wrong, and he was going to be very sorry indeed that he doubted her!

DEAD IN
THE HAY

CONNIE
FEDDERSEN

Kensington Books
Kensington Publishing Corp.

http://www.kensingtonbooks.com

KENSINGTON BOOKS are published by

Kensington Publishing Corp.
850 Third Avenue
New York, NY 10022

First Printing: October, 1999
10 9 8 7 6 5 4 3 2 1

Printed in the United States of America

This book is dedicated to my husband Ed and our children—Jon, Jeff, Kurt, Jill, and Christie—with much love. And to our grandchildren, Brooklynn, Kennedy and Blake. Hugs and kisses!

CHAPTER ONE

"Welcome back, boss!" Jenny Long said. Her eyes popped when Amanda Hazard-Thorn sailed through the office door. "Wow! You look like a sun goddess with your golden tan and sun-streaked hair. Your honeymoon in the Bahamas must have agreed with you."

Amanda smiled at her secretary, who was decked out in a plum-colored business suit that downplayed her well-endowed bust line. "I highly recommend a getaway to the tropical islands. Fabulous cuisine, balmy breezes, white sand, and clear-blue water."

"And steamy nights," Jenny put in wickedly.

Amanda wasn't in the habit of discussing the steamy nights spent with her new husband. But sexy country cop Nick Thorn in fact did steam up the nights.

"I brought fresh-baked cinnamon rolls and coffee to celebrate your return," Jenny said as she wheeled toward the supply room.

Amanda salivated. Jenny's award-winning cinnamon rolls

were out of this world. It was a shame Amanda didn't have Jenny's culinary thumb. If all facets of her recent marriage were going to function properly, Amanda needed to devote time and effort to improving her cooking skills. Nick Thorn was a big eater and he wasn't thrilled with Amanda's specialty of creamed tuna on toast.

"Here you go, boss." Jenny handed Amanda a roll and steaming coffee.

Amanda's taste buds rioted at first bite. The melt-in-your-mouth cinnamon rolls were delicious. "Mmm," she murmured appreciatively.

"Good?" Jenny asked.

"Mmm." Amanda swallowed. "Wonderful."

"Thanks. I knew they were your favorite."

Amanda strode off to fetch another roll—She couldn't eat just one. "How have things been going during my absence?"

Jenny frowned. "Things have been slow around here. Since you're such a noted celebrity in Vamoose, your clients want their accounts handled by you personally. Even though I have explained that I'm taking all sorts of accounting classes in night school, they don't believe I can handle complex situations."

"Then I shall immediately begin my campaign to inform the public that you are my top-notch assistant," Amanda declared, then gobbled up the delicious pastry. "You are as alphabetically organized and conscientious as I am."

Jenny beamed with pride. "Thanks, boss. That means a lot coming from you. After all, you're my idol."

Amanda didn't want to be anybody's idol, she simply wanted a highly functioning accounting office—and more time to spend with her hunk-of-a-husband. She and Thorn were getting along so splendidly that Amanda didn't want anything to burst their marital bubble.

The phone jingled and Jenny plucked it up. "Hazard Accounting, Jenny speaking."

Thunder rumbled outside while Jenny took the call. Amanda

devoured the last bite of cinnamon roll, then licked icing from her fingertips.

Jenny thrust the phone at Amanda. "It's your grandpa."

Amanda clamped the receiver in her sticky hand. "Hi, Pops."

"Hi, Half Pint. Just wanted to welcome you home. Did you have a good time?"

"Sure did. The tropical islands are the closest thing to paradise, this side of heaven. How are you getting along, Pops? Are you settled into Salty Marcum's place?"

Although Amanda had insisted that her paternal grandfather live with her and Thorn, Pops wouldn't hear of it. He didn't want to impose on the newlyweds, so he had accepted Salty Marcum's offer to move into the secluded farmhouse located near the small community of Adios, which was just a hop, skip, and a jump from Vamoose.

"Things are going great," Pops replied. "Sure as hell beats moving back in with your mother and my son. Haven't even seen the old hag since that fiasco at your wedding, and I haven't missed her for a second."

Amanda inwardly winced. She preferred to forget about the embarrassing conflict between Mother and Thorn's mom.

"I also called to tell you that your landlady has rented the farmhouse where you were living before you got married," Pops added. "You and Thorn need to move your stuff out by the first of the month. Harvey Renshaw is renting the place for his ex-wife and her live-in boyfriend."

Amanda frowned. "Really? That's awfully generous of Harvey."

"Harv? Generous?" Pops snorted, "Not in my book he isn't. I've only been around Harv a few times, but my first impression of him was as bad as the last. He thinks he's pretty special, for reasons that escape me. Never saw an ego the size of his before. Don't know how he bears the weight of carrying it around.

"Well, I gotta go, Half Pint. Salty and I are cleaning up this old place. I've got shrubs to trim and a house to paint."

"Now, Pops, don't go overboard," Amanda cautioned. "You're supposed to be retired, you know."

"Retired? Hell!" Pops scoffed. "Salty wants to get this place shipshape and I plan to help him. Good to have you back in town, Half Pint. Tell Thorn hello for me."

Smiling, Amanda hung up the phone. She knew her grandfather was good for the crusty Vietnam vet who'd had such a hard life. And Salty was good company for Pops. The men had become good friends while Amanda investigated the dead-in-the-mud case. And for certain, the old farmhouse could use a face-lift. Salty had let the place deteriorate for years.

"Boss?"

Amanda glanced up to see Jenny poised in front of the desk.

"Now that you're back in town, I was wondering if I could ask for some time off." Jenny's gaze skittered away as she continued. "I have . . . um . . . been seeing someone. But I have been so busy here at the office, keeping up with my homework assignments for night class, and spending time with my son that . . . um . . . my boyfriend and I haven't been able to spend *quantity* time together."

Amanda took pity on her overworked secretary. Jenny had been holding down the fort for several weeks. "Sure, you deserve a vacation. Who is this new boyfriend?" And he damned well better not be anything like that worthless slug who ran out on Jenny and left her with a young son to raise!

Jenny smiled dreamily. "His name is Dave Zinkerman. He owns a farm southeast of Vamoose. Dave raises alfalfa hay and wheat and he works part-time as a security guard at Lambert Corporation in Oklahoma City."

The new boyfriend's name didn't ring a bell. "Do I know Dave?" Amanda asked.

Jenny shook her head.

"Divorced?"

Jenny nodded.

"Kids?"

"No, but my son is crazy about Dave, and he is wonderful with Timmy."

Amanda decided to reserve judgment until she met this Dave character. With Jenny's track record of a deadbeat husband and freeloader former boyfriend, Amanda wanted to ensure that her secretary wasn't getting involved with a no-account slime-bucket. Sweet though Jenny was, she wasn't a good judge of men. The only thing Jenny had done right was to date Thorn when they were in high school. Since then, Jenny's romances had gone down the toilet.

"I expect a proper introduction to Dave," Amanda insisted. "I hope this guy realizes how lucky he is. If he doesn't, I plan to tell him."

Jenny grinned broadly. "He's a keeper, boss. I'll see if I can get him to stop by this evening before we leave town."

"I'll be looking forward to it," Amanda said.

The phone rang and Amanda plunked up the receiver. "Hazard Accounting, Hazard-Thorn here."

" 'Bout time you got back. This is Harv Renshaw. Did you get the information I need for this oil well deal I have been working on?"

Information? What information? After lolling around for two weeks on her honeymoon, Amanda had to shift mental gears. Harv was one of her most demanding, impatient clients. The ex-Air Force mechanic was gruff and grouchy. Harv lived on his military pension and wheeled and dealed to make a profit on the farm he inherited after retiring from his twenty-year stint in the armed forces.

"Well, Hazard? I realize you've been on your honeymoon, but I have been waiting around for you to get back. Business is business, you know, and I've been on hold long enough. I don't want to have to take my accounts elsewhere, but I sure as hell will if you can't keep up."

Amanda gnashed her teeth. She had half a mind to tell her grumpy client to take his account and shove it where the sun didn't shine. She had plenty of clients to keep her business afloat. Yet, no matter how cantankerous Harv was, she felt a certain loyalty to him.

"You are still in the process of negotiating for a new well site on your property?" Amanda asked.

"Hell, yes. I have dragged it out and stalled while you were cruising around the Bahamas," Harv said, then grunted in disapproval. "I wasn't about to consult a lawyer. You know damn well how I feel about them. And I sure as hell wasn't going to let your dim-witted secretary handle my business in your absence!"

Amanda bristled. "My secretary is highly efficient and exceptionally competent. Jenny could have assisted you while I was away."

"Yeah, whatever, Hazard."

"Hazard-*Thorn*," she corrected him.

"Like I said, yeah whatever. I want to know if I can claim the new oil well site as damaged property on my farm instead of listing it as capital gain on my income tax forms."

Amanda clamped her hand around the receiver, pretending it was her cranky client's throat. "No, you can't, Harv. The acres taken for use by the oil company to build the access road and well site on your farm are looked upon by the IRS as a land purchase, though there is no actual transfer of deed involved."

"Well, that's a helluva note," Harv said, then scowled. "Damn oil companies anyway. They always get the best end of every deal, and I end up paying the taxes!"

"You will be receiving payment for the oil site and royalties on the producing well," she reminded him. "We have been through this each time an oil company approaches you about drilling on your property. The laws haven't changed, Harv."

Harvey Renshaw muttered several four-letter words that

Amanda didn't need to hear—words that would have offended Mother's pristine ears.

"Well, fine," Harv grumbled. "I guess I'll have to find a way to work around that stupid tax regulation. But I still need to see you PDQ, Hazard. I have some business I want you to conduct for me. This won't wait a day longer. I've already waited long enough!"

"Office hours are nine to five, Monday through Friday," Amanda said in a businesslike tone. If Harv wanted to see her, he could come to the office. Amanda wasn't going out of her way to cater to the cranky old goat.

"I don't keep accountants' hours," Harv snapped brusquely. "You cater to your elderly clients by making house calls. You should extend the same courtesies and consideration to your busy clients. Besides, this is a private matter, and I don't want your nitwit secretary, or anyone else, overhearing what I have to say. Meet me on the access road to my oil well on the north end of the pasture. I'll be there feeding my cattle."

"Sorry, but I have—"

"Be there in twenty minutes, Hazard," Harvey demanded in a crisp military tone. "I'm paying you big bucks to accommodate me!"

Harv slammed down the phone and Amanda scowled. "It's Hazard *Thorn*. Get it right, Renshaw!"

Jenny Long looked up from the tax forms on her desk and smiled consolingly. "Charming man, isn't he? My friend Dave has dealt with Harv on several occasions and he has nothing nice to say about him. According to Dave, Harvey Renshaw is manipulative and pushy. Harv talks to me as if I don't have a brain in my head. The jerk."

Amanda muttered under her breath. She had no use for those mega-macho types who treated women like second-class citizens. She knew the only reason Harv Renshaw hired her as his business consultant was because she had gained notoriety by solving six murder cases and making headlines. Harv had the aggravating tendency of maneuvering to keep the upper hand in his business dealings. He had a fetish about ensuring his associates regarded him as an intellectual superior.

Damn, thought Amanda, the Air Force had brainwashed Harv—but good. He believed that he was entitled to respect and favors, just because he'd been an officer. The man simply had not adjusted to civilian life and probably never would.

"I ought to tell Harvey to find himself another accountant," Amanda grumbled. "Two years of dealing with him is two years too long."

"You tell him, boss," Jenny encouraged.

"By golly, I think I will," Amanda decided as she bounded to her feet. "I'll meet him face-to-face, toe-to-toe, and set him straight. Harv can take his oil well sites, his royalties, his Air Force pension, and his inflated male ego and take a flying leap!"

Jenny smiled in satisfaction. "Good. I hope I don't have to listen to that man talk down to me ever again."

Squaring her shoulders, Amanda left her office on Main Street. Thunder rumbled overhead. Gray clouds piled up like heads of cauliflower on the northwestern horizon. There was enough humidity in the air to make Amanda's naturally curly hair frizz in less than a minute.

It looked as if Vamoose was about to get a dousing of rain and a fierce blast of wind.

A steady stream of traffic—mostly pickup trucks—cruised through Vamoose as Amanda strode to her jalopy truck. She waved to her acquaintances and smiled past her irritation with Harv Renshaw. Although she had thoroughly enjoyed the Bahaman getaway, it was nice to be back in small-town America. This laid-back approach to life—with the exception of Harv Renshaw—appealed to Amanda. Those years she had spent in the corporate accounting world in the big city were forgotten memories. This was where she wanted to be, married to Nick Thorn, living the good life . . . .

Amanda's thoughts screeched to a halt when Deputy Benny Sykes cruised toward her. Hastily she flagged him down.

Benny slid his mirrored sunglasses from the bridge of his nose and stared at Amanda through the open window of his squad car. "Nice to have you and the chief back in Vamoose."

"Thanks, Benny. I need to ask—"

"Bet the Bahamas was picturesque," Benny said, cutting her off. "Sure thought you'd send me a postcard while you were gone. But maybe one of these days I'll have a chance to take a luxury cruise and see the place for myself."

"You should do exactly that," Amanda recommended. "It was the best vacation I ever had.

"I need to get in touch with Thorn. Could you get him on the horn for me, Benny?"

"On the horn, right," Benny repeated as he sat up straight on the car seat. "Have you got trouble?"

"No, but my landlady has rented her farmhouse and I have been asked to move out my furniture by this weekend," she explained. "I want Thorn to know that we have to pack up some stuff this evening after work."

"Pack this evening, right," he parroted. "I'll send out the word to the chief." He pushed his sunglasses into place with his forefinger, then rolled up the window. With a salute and a smile, Benny drove off.

Serenaded by a clap of thunder, Amanda strode back to her clunker truck, with its faded paint, bad muffler, and bald tires. One of these days she was going to take time to purchase a reliable vehicle. She had tried to do just that, but when the used car dealer ended up dead in the driver's seat, she'd been too busy investigating the case to make a car deal.

When Amanda cranked the engine, the bucket-of-rust sputtered and coughed, then hummed unevenly. She switched gears and drove away. Since it was such a warm, humid day she rolled down the window to circulate air—the jalopy didn't have air-conditioning.

Amanda passed the Last Chance Cafe, Vamoose Bank, and Thatcher's Oil and Gas Station. When other motorists recognized her clunker truck, they waved enthusiastic greetings.

Ah, rural America at its finest, she thought to herself. Best place to live. The community was like an extended family that had welcomed her with open arms. If she hadn't moved to Vamoose she would have never met that handsome police chief who had the most tantalizing way of . . .

Amanda jerked the wheel when she realized she had crossed the centerline while daydreaming about Thorn. She had better save her erotic fantasies until tonight. She had to keep her mind on business and cranky ol' Harvey Renshaw.

Amanda turned off the highway and whizzed down the gravel road leading to Harvey Renshaw's farm. The rolling hills northeast of Vamoose were dotted with oil rigs and reserve tanks. She had to wonder at the justice of life when she recalled that Harvey Renshaw already had two producing wells on his red-clay farm ground. The land wasn't good for raising anything besides prairie grass, but below the surface was a valuable pit of oil and natural gas. The grouchy ex-Air Force career man was rolling in dough. He lived on a tidy pension, compliments of the government, and raked in money for royalties from producing oil and gas wells.

Personally, Amanda wasn't sure Harv deserved such financial success. But then, who was she to judge? She was just an accountant who processed numerical facts and data. It wasn't her place to decide who struck it rich in black gold and who didn't.

Amanda glanced sideways at the county intersection. The Renshaw home was nestled against a hill that blocked brisk north winds. A Jeep, a wheat truck, and a dented gray Buick sedan sat in the driveway. Amanda presumed Harv didn't want to hold a conference in the comfort of his home because he had lots of company—though who would find Harv Renshaw enjoyable company Amanda didn't know.

The jalopy truck rattled across the washboarded road and lumbered up the steep incline. Amanda applied the brake when she reached the cattle guard that led to the access path used by oil company employees. She noticed the John Deere tractor sitting in the pasture. A round hay bale protruded from the double prongs on the front end of the tractor. Twenty head of cattle had gathered around the bale, champing hungrily on the hay.

Amanda followed the path to the oil site, then veered toward the idling tractor. Thus far, she hadn't spotted Harv. He wasn't sitting in the tractor cab or circling around on foot to check his cattle.

Amanda brought her truck to a stop, then climbed down "Harv! I'm here! Where are you?"

No answer.

Amanda glanced toward the pond that glimmered like mercury, but she didn't see Harvey anywhere. She pivoted toward the oil well site, wondering if Harv had driven off with a pumper or oil company representative to negotiate the new well site that had been staked out with fluorescent orange stakes.

As far as Amanda could see, there was no sign of other human life on this 640 acre farm. She was left to stand around, watching twenty hungry cows chow down on hay.

"Damn it, Harv, my time is as valuable as you think yours is," Amanda said to the farm at large. "I have better things to do besides hang around waiting for you to show up . . . ."

Her voice trailed off when a cattle brawl broke out on the far side of the hay bale. Two white-faced cows were banging heads, trying to knock each other out of the way. The cattle shifted and bellowed, then snatched up mouthfuls of hay before circling to find a better place on the chow line.

Before Amanda knew it, a full-scale cattle riot was in progress. Thousand-pound cows were slamming into each other and mooing in complaint. The hay bale bounced on the protruding prongs, causing the tractor to rock and creak.

"That's enough of that!" Amanda shouted. Her terse demand was punctuated with a thunderclap.

She waved her arms wildly, trying to convince the herd to back away from the bale and cease its squabbling. The timid members of the herd turned tail and raced across the pasture, but the big red bull and three raw boned cows were still banging heads.

Not to be intimidated by the brainless beef-on-the-hoof, Amanda stamped forward, screeching at the top of her lungs and flapping her arms like a goose going airborne. The cattle stopped battling for position at the hay bale, stared at her, then scattered to the four winds.

"Dumb animals," Amanda muttered at the cattle that halted at a safe distance to keep an eye on her.

She circled the bale to see hay scattered on the ground. There was so much strewn straw that Amanda nearly overlooked the pair of combat boots that protruded from the bottom of the bale.

"Uh-oh." Amanda gaped at the boots—toes pointed inward.

Legs, encased in camouflage pants, disappeared beneath a ton of hay. The hum of the idling tractor, the occasional bawl of cattle, and the rumbling of thunder broke the grim silence.

If Amanda wasn't mistaken—and she didn't know how she possibly could be—Harvey Renshaw was dead in the hay. Whatever Harv intended to say privately to Amanda would go unspoken—unless Harv planned to return from The Great Beyond for an out-of-body conference.

Damn, why was she always the one around Vamoose who stumbled over dead bodies? This was getting ridiculous!

CHAPTER TWO

As had become her custom, Amanda carefully surveyed the scene with attentive eyes. When the time came for Thorn to interview her, she wanted to present a precise, accurate account of what she had seen and heard.

Amanda scanned the road. There wasn't another vehicle in sight, not another witness to be found—only a herd of cows. The nylon strings that held the round hay bale together had been pulled to the south side of the bale. One nylon string had been wrapped up and lay beside Harv Renshaw's boots. Amanda speculated that Harv had been in the process of pulling strings when the fatal incident occurred.

For the life of her, Amanda couldn't figure out how Harv had been crushed by the heavy round bale. Obviously, the hay bale had been elevated on the prongs of the tractor at some point in time.

Had hungry cattle bumped into Harvey while he was pulling strings? Had the hydraulic suspension system that kept the bale elevated malfunctioned at a crucial moment?

Frowning, Amanda stepped cautiously around the fresh cow patties to inspect the hydraulic hoses that stretched between the hay prongs and the front lift of the tractor.

Her eyes popped when she noticed that oil had splashed on the tractor hood and cab window. Apparently, Harv's hydraulic hose had sprung a leak at the worst of all possible moments. The elevated hay bale must have come crashing down when the hose broke. Harvey had been knocked down and pinned beneath a ton of hay.

Amanda carefully appraised the hydraulic fluid that dribbled down the windshield of the tractor cab. The greasy fluid pooled on the hood. Her gaze drifted to the faulty hydraulic hose that lay in the grass. Fluid dribbled from the open end of the hose . . . .

And that's when Amanda saw the faint tracks left in the grass by an unidentified vehicle.

Careful where she stepped, Amanda approached the crushed grass. Dribbles of hydraulic fluid clung to the grass, but she noticed a rectangular area—where a vehicle must have been parked—that showed no trace of hydraulic oil.

In profound concentration Amanda squatted down on her haunches to survey another oil-free area in the grass where an unidentified person might have stood.

Hmmm . . . thought Amanda. From the look of things, Harv Renshaw might have had company when the hydraulic hose burst loose. Also from the look of things, the unidentified person and vehicle had been sprayed with hydraulic oil.

Question was: Did the unidentified person cause the hose to break loose, or did he or she bail out and leave Harv Renshaw to smother beneath a ton of hay?

Pensively Amanda came to her feet, then methodically circled the area in question. Yep, she decided a moment later, someone around Vamoose had been showered with hydraulic oil—and so had his or her vehicle.

Another curious thought crossed Amanda's mind as she

tramped toward the cattle herd that was eyeing the hay bale hungrily. She was not surprised to see dollops of oil on the hides of several cows. The hydraulic hose had apparently erupted like a geyser, splattering oil on everything within range. Amanda counted seven oily cows and one greasy bull.

Wheeling around, Amanda headed for her jalopy truck. She had to notify Thorn immediately. He would not be pleased that she had happened onto a corpse so soon after their return from their honeymoon.

Furthermore, it was going to take some talking to convince Thorn that this was a possible homicide, not an accident. Amanda Hazard-Thorn definitely had her work cut out for her on this case. She predicted that Thorn would throw all sorts of roadblocks in her path while she investigated the possibility of foul play.

A flash of lightning and loud thunderclap sent the cattle darting off in all directions. Amanda scowled as she plunged headfirst into her truck.

"It better not rain and disturb this possible crime scene before Thorn has a chance to inspect it," she said to the threatening sky.

She gunned the engine and roared off. She crossed her fingers, hoping the storm was all bluff.

Sure enough, it didn't rain.

It *poured.*

Nick Thorn, Vamoose Chief of Police, lounged in his squad car, making his presence known to passing motorists. He had parked by the sign that read: "If You Like It Country Style, Then VAMOOSE." Despite the downpour, morning traffic zipped down the highway.

Nick smiled to himself. He had spent the past few hours reflecting on his honeymoon with his new bride. Now that he and Hazard had tied the knot, life was good.

Make that great, he amended. He was married to that blonde bombshell, and he was the envy of every man in town. Especially Sam Harjo, Vamoose County Commissioner. Sam Harjo hadn't given up his battle to win Hazard's affection until the vows were spoken and the ring was on her finger.

Nick didn't blame Sam for going down fighting. Hell, Nick would have done the same thing if the boot had been on the other foot. But Nick damn well intended to keep fighting to keep the prize he'd won. He was going to give Hazard no reason whatsoever to question her decision to marry him.

They were the perfect couple. Well, except for a few personality conflicts that could be worked out during their upcoming years of matrimonial bliss.

Since Nick received the message that Hazard's landlady had rented the old house, he was mentally planning to move furniture in his stock trailer the minute he got off duty, provided it wasn't still raining to beat the band. He and Hazard would sort out the best furniture to decorate his family farm home and donate the rest to the volunteer fire deparment for their semi-annual garage sale.

Once Nick and Hazard got their home in order they might consider starting a family. The pitter-patter of little Thorn feet echoing through their house—

Nick's thoughts screeched to a halt when he noticed the jalopy truck passing every vehicle in sight. The maniac driver had to be doing eighty, despite bad road conditions! Emergency lights flashed and motorists honked at the idiot behind the wheel.

"Oh, hell!" Nick jerked upright in his seat when he recognized the clunker truck that speared through pouring rain. It was Hazard making a daredevil entrance into Vamoose. "Now what?" he scowled.

The instant Hazard spotted the black-and-white she swerved off the pavement. Cars whizzed by, and irate drivers saluted

Hazard with their middle fingers when she bounded from the truck.

Oblivious to the pounding rain, Hazard darted across the highway to reach the squad car. A sense of impending doom settled in Nick's bones as his bride approached. He had the unshakable feeling the news Hazard seemed anxious to deliver was not good. Her expression was bleak. Her blond hair was plastered against her head, and her expensive three-piece silk suit was splattered with mud.

Nick glanced skyward. "Please tell me she hasn't found a dead body," he whispered. "Gimme a break here, will You? We just got back from our honeymoon."

When Hazard yanked open the passenger door and flounced onto the seat, Nick took one look at those baby blues and knew the honeymoon was over.

He and Hazard were back to business as usual.

"Thorn, I found one of my clients dead in the hay," she said between gasps of breath.

Nick cranked the engine, checked the rearview mirror, then pulled onto the highway. He was not going to get irritated, he told himself. He would calmly, artfully instruct Hazard to let him handle this situation—whatever this situation turned out to be.

"Who is it?" Nick asked as he cruised down the highway.

"Harvey Renshaw," she reported. "Go a mile north, then hang a right."

Nick nodded. "Let's hear it, Haz. I may as well know what to expect before I get there."

Hazard slumped in her seat, inhaled a deep breath that caused her ample bosom to rise and fall. "Harv called me at the office this morning to check on information about the new oil well site that has been staked out on his property."

"Harv was getting another well? He already has two on his farm."

"The third one obviously wasn't the charm," Hazard said grimly. "Harv won't be around to reap the profit from another oil well or draw his military retirement pension. I think someone might have—"

"Just the facts, Haz," Nick cut in quickly. "Just give me the facts."

Hazard sliced him a disgruntled glance. "Geez, you're starting to sound like the Joe Friday character on *Dragnet*."

Nick didn't rise to the bait. He was going to deal with Hazard's suspicions in a rational, professional manner. "You took the call from Harv Renshaw at your office, and then what?"

"Harv wanted me to meet him for a private conference. I asked him to stop by my office, but he insisted that I drive out to his farm and speak with him while he was feeding cattle. He demanded that I cater to him the same way I cater to my elderly clients. You know how obnoxious Harv can be when he wants his way."

Nick muttered under his breath. Having plenty of money had gone straight to Harv's head. In short, he was a world-class jerk.

"Harv told me that he had something important to discuss with me and that he wanted absolute privacy," Hazard went on to say. "When I arrived at the access road that led into Harv's pasture, I found him crushed beneath a round hay bale."

"You're sure he's a goner?" Nick asked as he splattered down the road, windshield wipers flapping.

Haz shot him an indignant glance. "Of course he's a goner. He's buried beneath a ton of dusty hay, Thorn. I certainly know dead when I see it."

In the distance Nick saw the silhouette of the John Deere tractor against the backdrop of scruffy gray clouds. Nick crossed his fingers, hoping and praying that foul play wasn't involved in this case. He and Hazard always got crosswise when she took it upon herself to open unofficial investigations.

Don't lose your cool, Nick told himself. *There's no need for trouble in matrimonial paradise.*

Nick veered onto the access road, clattered over the metal cattle guard, then headed toward the idling tractor.

"No!" Hazard shouted as she lunged for the steering wheel. "Don't drive on this patch of grass! Damn it, Thorn, you're destroying the evidence!"

Nick stamped on the brake. The squad car skidded on the wet grass. Hazard spewed an unladylike curse.

"What evidence?" Nick muttered in question.

"The oil."

Nick glanced at the nearby oil site and frowned. "From the well?"

"No, from the hydraulic hoses. Back up, Thorn."

Nick clamped down on his rising temper and put the car in reverse. Before he killed the engine Hazard was up and gone.

Nick came to his feet, then slammed the car door. It was the only display of temper he would allow himself. With grim resignation, he strode off to survey the scene of the accident—not murder, damn it! Not every death in Vamoose County was a homicide! How long before this amateur gumshoe wife of his figured that out?

Amanda stared unblinkingly at Thorn while he surveyed the combat boots that protruded from the hay bale. Thorn was now wearing his well schooled cop face. To his credit, though, he hadn't shooed her away and announced that he would handle this situation. But Amanda could tell by his stance, by his closed-up expression, that he expected her to keep her trap shut while he had a look-see.

Being a newlywed, Amanda tried to accommodate her husband—temporarily at least. She would let him do his thing, but if he opened and shut this case without considering her suspicions she was going to konk him on the head!

With practiced skill, Thorn appraised what could be seen of the body that was buried under the hay. He hunkered down to remove Harv's left boot.

Nick wrapped his hand around the exposed ankle. "No pulse. He's dead."

"Told you." Amanda slammed her mouth shut. This was not a good time to be sarcastic. She needed Thorn's cooperation in this case, not his resentment.

Rising to his feet, Thorn stared at the round bale and strewn hay, then paced toward the front of the tractor to study the splatters of hydraulic oil that were visible, in spite of the recent rain. When he donned a glove to inspect the hydraulic hose, Amanda waited tensely for him to deliver his verdict.

"Here's how I see it, Hazard," Thorn said as he studied the greasy couplers that connected the hydraulic hoses to the front of the tractor. "Renshaw kept the hay bale elevated so he could cut loose the nylon strings around the hay and dispose of them properly so the cattle wouldn't get tangled up in discarded string. That is a common practice for cattlemen. They clip the strings on the bale—away from the wind—then they walk beneath the elevated bale to pull the strings with the wind at their back, not in their face. It prevents ranchers from breathing mold and dust from the hay. It also prevents you from getting an eye- and mouthful of dirt and hay."

That sounded reasonable, thought Amanda. No sense of yanking strings and letting moldy, windblown hay smack you in the face.

"But why walk under the elevated bale rather than circling around it?" Amanda wanted to know.

"Because the minute you arrive in the pasture with the hay bale, cattle stampede toward the feed. It's easier to avoid being knocked down and stepped on when you walk *under* the bale to reach the wind side," he explained.

"It's also easier for a hay bale to drop on top of you," Amanda pointed out. "If you ask me, the technique of avoiding the hungry cattle is a disaster waiting to happen. In this case someone could have—"

"Ranchers use this practice constantly," Thorn interrupted strategically. "That's just the way we do it. I've done it hundreds of times myself when I'm feeding my cattle."

"Well, I suggest you find a better way to pull strings and avoid the possibility of being crushed and smothered," Amanda said. "I don't want you squished under a hay bale. I happen to like you and I intend to keep you around for the next hundred years or so."

Thorn beamed in delight. "Thanks, Hazard."

"You're welcome. Now, about that hydraulic hose that somebody could have—"

Amanda was positively certain that Thorn was trying to tap-dance around her suspicions of foul play. That was the third time he had interrupted her when she was ready to announce her theory.

"These hoses are under constant, intense pressure," Thorn informed her. "They operate the lifts on the front and back of a tractor. When the hoses burst loose from their couplers, or spring a leak, the hydraulic lift drops immediately. It's a common occurrence with heavy machinery."

Amanda frowned as she stared at the hoses. "I don't get it. Why would anyone be stupid enough to walk under an elevated hay bale if he could be crushed at any given moment?"

Thorn hitched his thumb toward the grazing cattle. "You take your chances with being trampled by livestock or crushed under the hay. Agriculture is risky business. That's why accident rates are so high. Working with heavy machinery and unpredictable livestock is a double whammy."

Amanda knew all that stuff, because she had helped Thorn with his farm chores occasionally. She also knew Thorn was about to declare this the scene of a farming *accident*. Being a part-time farmer, he was ready to shrug off the incident as a stroke of bad luck, but Amanda wasn't buying into that faulty hydraulic hose theory.

No siree, Amanda told herself. She was positive that someone had been on the scene, and that someone had *made* this so-called accident happen!

When Thorn ambled to the squad car to notify the coroner, then contact the tractor supply store, Amanda frowned. "Are you sure this is the appropriate time to replace the faulty hose? Aren't we investigating a death here?"

Thorn pivoted toward her, the radio mike still clamped in his hand. "I can't lift the hay bale off the body without a replacement hose and a new supply of hydraulic oil."

"Oh," Amanda mumbled. "I thought maybe you could unhook one of the hoses from the back of the tractor and stick it on the front."

"Wrong size, wrong length," he replied, then turned around to speak with the police dispatcher. "Janie-Ethel, call Deputy Sykes and tell him to drive out to the Renshaw farm PDQ. I want Benny to give Hazard a lift to town. She left her truck on the side of the highway."

"Now hold on, Thorn," Amanda erupted. "I have a theory to present to you. I don't think this is a farming accident. Somebody tampered with the hose."

"You always suspect foul play," Thorn grumbled. "If some youngster tripped and fell down during an Easter-egg hunt you would be instantly suspicious of the Easter Bunny."

Amanda bristled. "And may I remind you that the past six times I have cried murder *I* have been right and *you* have been wrong!"

Thorn frowned darkly. "Don't go there, Hazard. It always causes trouble between us."

Amanda went there anyway. "Do you want to argue with the statistics, Thorn? Go ahead. You know you don't have a leg to stand on. My intuition hasn't failed me yet. Yours, however, has shown consistent flaws!''

Amanda knew she had gone too far when she saw Thorn's calm veneer crack. No matter how calm, reasonable, and mature they had tried to be, the ever-present conflict over her unofficial investigations still simmered beneath the surface. To this day, despite their wedding vows and marvelous honeymoon, Thorn still did not take her well-founded suspicions seriously. He was braced to reject her theory.

Well, tough. She was going to voice her suspicions, even if she had to tie him up and force him to hear her out.

''You have a choice, Thorn,'' she began. ''You can stand here and listen voluntarily to my theory or I can handcuff you to the squad car and *make* you listen.''

Thorn sighed audibly. ''All right, Haz, I'll bite. What made you suspicious?''

Amanda stalked forward to stare Thorn squarely in the eye. ''When I arrived on the scene, I noticed that several cows had oil splattered on their heads and backs. They were bunched together, eating hay. Obviously, the herd was so closely packed that the spray of hydraulic oil fell on them instead of the ground. But over here—''

Amanda gnashed her teeth as she directed Thorn's attention to the area where he had parked the squad car.

''Yeah? What about it?'' he demanded impatiently.

''The grass was coated with oil, except in two spots,'' Amanda continued. ''I concluded that someone had been standing beside an unidentified vehicle that was parked near the tractor.''

Thorn strode around the two areas she had indicated. ''All I see is wet grass.''

Amanda scowled at the untimely rain shower and tracks left by the squad car. Damn it, the evidence had been destroyed. ''Take my word for it, Thorn, someone else was definitely here.

That someone must have been sprayed with oil. Same goes for the unidentified vehicle."

Thorn stared somberly at her. "I know you delight in pursuing murder investigations, but geez, we just returned from the Bahamas and this case is clearly—"

"Crime doesn't take honeymoons, Thorn," she cut in. "My instincts tell me that this was no accident. Someone was out to get Harv Renshaw."

"Damn it, Hazard! You are not a certified detective. You are a magician who tries to pull clues and theories out of thin air." Thorn threw up his hands in exasperation. "I refuse to argue with you, especially not in front of Deputy Sykes." He gestured toward the patrol car racing over hill and dale with lights flashing like a Christmas tree. "I have a report to write up and a tractor to repair so I can recover the body. Go do your thing at the office and we'll speak later."

"I intend to discuss this case this evening while we are moving my stuff from the rented farmhouse to your place," she insisted.

"Fine," he bit off.

"Good," she flung smartly.

Amanda stalked toward Thorn's car to retrieve her purse. Although she didn't want to ruffle Thorn's feathers so soon after they had set up their lovebird nest, she was not going to ignore the possibility of foul play in this bale of hay. Harv Renshaw wasn't her favorite client—not by a long shot—but Amanda was compelled to uncover all the facts.

Crime should never go unpunished, not in the US of A, where truth and justice were meant to prevail. Besides, Amanda's acute sense of fair play refused to be satisfied until she knew precisely how, and why, Harv Renshaw ended up dead in the hay.

CHAPTER THREE

Nick mumbled and grumbled as he unhooked the hydraulic hose from its coupling. He and Hazard were destined to butt heads over the Renshaw *accident*. There was nothing Hazard loved better than sinking her teeth into a murder investigation. But damn it, anybody with a half a brain in her head could see this was a clear-cut accident. Hell! It was as obvious as a wart on the end of one's nose!

From all indication, Renshaw ended up at the wrong place when his machinery malfunctioned. Nick had encountered similar close calls himself while working with farm equipment. It went with the territory.

The sound of an approaching vehicle caught Nick's attention. He glanced around to see the Vamoose Tractor Supply delivery truck pulling onto the access road.

"Hi, Joe," Nick called to the long-haired young man who bounded from the truck.

"Hi, Chief. Here's the hose you requested . . . ." Joe Mason pulled up short when he saw the boot and bare foot protruding from the hay bale. "Whoa, bummer. Who is that?"

"I assume it's Harvey Renshaw," Nick replied.

Joe blinked repeatedly as he pulled a pack of cigarettes from his shirt pocket, then lit up. "No kidding? Harv had a bad hose? Bummer. As I recall, Harvey just replaced his hydraulics a couple of months back. Hope his family doesn't decide to sue us or something. My dad is going to feel real bad about this."

"Not as bad as Harv feels about it," Nick mumbled.

Pensively Nick processed the information Joe volunteered, then he inspected the oily hose. No, couldn't be, he tried to assure himself. Oftentimes, even new hoses had imperfections. During his years of farming, Nick had returned new parts that didn't function properly. Renshaw had been away from the farm for twenty years. He simply hadn't noticed a bulge or crack in the hose. Twenty years ago tractors with hydraulic hoses and power takeoffs were just coming into use. Renshaw may not have been familiar with the concept . . . .

Nick's thoughts trailed off when he recalled that Renshaw had been an Air Force mechanic before being promoted in the military ranks.

Scratch the theory of inexperience and ignorance, Nick decided. Renshaw would have recognized a faulty part if he saw one. But who was to say that he *noticed* it? According to Hazard, the man was busy and had a lot on his mind. Harvey could have been distracted and neglected to inspect the hydraulic lines.

No, hydraulics were unpredictable, he reminded himself. Breaks in pressurized hoses were common. This was nothing more than an ill-fated accident.

"Here, Chief, let me help you put on the new hose." Joe smoothed his callused hand over the replacement hose. "Looks okay to me. I'll hook it to the forklift."

While Joe secured one end of the hose to the couplet, Nick

attached the other end to the tractor. Within a few minutes Joe clambered into the tractor cab and elevated the hay bale. Nick motioned for Joe to back up the tractor.

Pensively Nick appraised the position of the body. Renshaw lay facedown in the grass. The utility knife used to cut the nylon strings off the hay bale was clasped in his right hand. The bill of his ball cap was bent backward, and hay clung to his camouflage clothes.

"Oh, man," Joe wheezed as he ambled up beside Nick. His ruddy face lost color. "I never was a Renshaw fan, but it gives me the willies to see him sprawled out like that. What a way to go."

"I've seen a lot of fatalities," Nick said as he reappraised the scene. "Don't know if there's a good way to go."

"In your sleep, maybe," Joe speculated. He stared at the body with grim fascination. "If I had my druthers, that would be my choice." Squirming uneasily, he turned away . "Well, Chief, uh . . . I have some other deliveries to make. Hope you don't mind hanging around here by yourself."

"I've kept company with several stiffs in my time," Nick told him.

"Yeah, I guess you have. Don't envy you none."

Nick noticed that Joe made tracks when he left the scene. There were several facets of police work that no one envied, Nick reminded himself. This was one of them.

But somebody had to do the rotten jobs that other folks couldn't stomach. Grimly Nick got down to the business of investigating the scene of the accident.

"My gosh, boss! What happened to you?" Jenny Long croaked, frog-eyed. "Did you have a breakdown on the road and walk in the rain?"

Amanda ran a hand through the mop of wet hair plastered

to the sides of her face, then dropped her purse on her desk. "Something like that."

"How did your conference with Renshaw go? No telling what that old buzzard wanted to say in confidence."

"He had nothing to say. I found him dead in the hay."

"Oh, no!" Jenny gasped. "I swear you have the worst luck, boss. This is the sixth—"

"Seventh," Amanda corrected.

"—body you've happened onto," Jenny rattled on. "I don't know how you handle it so well." She stared sympathetically at Amanda. "The very thought gives me the heebie-jeebies."

Amanda drew a fortifying breath. She reminded herself that Thorn had dealt with these morbid incidents for years. She wondered if he had become callous, immune. Wondered if some self-protective device kicked in like adrenaline to get Thorn through the gruesome incidents that he rarely discussed.

She, on the other hand, found herself emotionally involved in these cases. She wanted to know why it happened, how the incident might have been prevented, and who might have given bad luck a nudge.

"Tell me everything you know about Harvey Renshaw," Amanda requested as she plunked in her chair. "You grew up in Vamoose. What do you know about him and his family?"

Jenny eyed her warily. "Are you suspicious again, boss?"

"You know me," Amanda said, shrugging dismissively. "I believe in considering all possibilities for fear of overlooking vital facts."

Jenny nodded somberly. "I guess your hunches have been right a lot. Better to ask questions than to ignore the unpleasant situation, I suppose." She stared at Amanda for a thoughtful moment. "Do you really think somebody bumped off Renshaw?"

"He wasn't Vamoose's favorite son, now was he?"

"Hardly. Dave told me—"

When Jenny clamped her mouth shut so fast that she nearly

clipped her tongue, Amanda frowned. "Dave? As in the new boyfriend?"

Jenny busied herself by alphabetizing the files on her desk. "I've got a lot of work to do, seeing how I'm taking some time off. I better get back to work."

"Oh, no, you don't." Amanda bolted from her chair to block Jenny's retreat. "You've aroused my curiosity. When and why did your boyfriend deal with Harv?"

When Jenny refused to meet Amanda's inquisitive gaze, she knotted her fists on her hips and took her most intimidating stance. "Out with it. You told me this morning that Dave sold hay to local farmers and stockmen. Did Dave sell hay to Renshaw?"

Jenny looked as pained as if her teeth were being pulled without anesthetic. "Dave sells hay to several farmers in Vamoose and Pronto."

Amanda's gaze narrowed. "You're hedging. Give it to me straight. Did Dave Zinkerman get into an argument with Renshaw sometime in the recent past?"

When Jenny refused to reply, Amanda locked in on her secretary like a heat-seeking missile. "The way you're acting leads me to believe that Dave had some reason to want Harvey Renshaw dead."

"Dave would never do such a thing!" Jenny squawked in Dave's defense. "He's kind and considerate and—"

Amanda waved off the unrequested character reference. "I'm sure he is Mr. Perfect with you, at least he better be or he will have to answer to me. But I need to know if Dave and Harv had a serious conflict."

Jenny wilted into her chair, but she still kept a tight rein on her tongue.

"You want this job to be here waiting for you when you get back, don't you?" Amanda questioned, then mentally kicked herself for blackmailing her secretary. It was a cheap, underhanded trick.

It was also very effective.

"You know I need this job, boss."

"Then tell me what you know." Amanda changed tact hurriedly. "If there is the least bit of suspicion surrounding Dave it will be better if he is cleared now. Otherwise, it might raise questions when Dave skips town immediately after this fatal incident."

"Omigod!" Jenny's face turned the color of Silly Putty. "I never thought of it that way." After a moment Jenny arrived at her decision and met Amanda's intense gaze. "Dave told me that he sold sixty bales of prairie hay and alfalfa to Harv, but the cheapskate refused to pay his bill. Harv claimed the hay was moldy and made the cattle sick, but Dave insisted that it was prime-choice hay and that none of the other ranchers had voiced any complaints.

"Since Harv wouldn't pay his bill, Dave decided to have partial compensation by hooking up Harvey's stock trailer to Dave's truck so he could move his cattle herd to another pasture. Since one of the wheel bearings went out on Dave's trailer, he figured Harvey owed him a favor. After all, the old goat had cheated Dave out of several hundred dollars."

"Precisely how many several hundred dollars?" Amanda wanted to know.

"Fourteen hundred," Jenny said reluctantly.

"That would be enough to annoy the boyfriend," Amanda mused aloud. "Not that I blame him."

"Neither do I," Jenny put in quickly. "We have been saving up for our four-day getaway. Renshaw's refusal to pay his hay bill put us in a money crunch."

"How did Renshaw react when he discovered Dave had borrowed the stock trailer without asking permission?" Amanda questioned.

"He went bananas. He had the gall to pull out his Air Force-issued pistol and point it at Dave."

"Have you seen Dave this morning?" Amanda wanted to know.

Jenny nodded. "We had breakfast at the Last Chance Cafe."

"What was Dave wearing?"

Jenny frowned. "Why do you want to know that?"

"I'm very clothes conscious."

"You are not. If you were, you would have gone home to change before you returned to the office," Jenny pointed out. "Yet here you are in a mud-splattered business suit."

Amanda smiled soothingly. "Now don't get all defensive, Jenny. I'm just trying to ensure that Dave is free of suspicion before the two of you leave town. Do you want Vamoosians gossiping about the possibility of Dave being a murder suspect?"

"He was wearing a short-sleeve white T-shirt and faded blue jeans," Jenny said hesitantly. "But what difference does it make what Dave was wearing?"

"Was he in boots or tennis shoes?" Amanda questioned the question.

"Tennis shoes."

Amanda didn't want to alarm her secretary, but Dave had motive—if this turned out to be a case of murder. Harvey owed Dave money, and Harv had pulled a gun on Dave. Who was to say that Dave hadn't decided to repossess his hay bales? Who was to say that Dave, who was undoubtedly familiar with tractors, hadn't jerked the hydraulic hose from its couplet at an opportune moment? And who was to say that Dave hadn't turned around and driven away, leaving Harv dead in the hay?

"What kind of vehicle does Dave drive?" Amanda grilled her secretary.

"A two-tone Chevy truck."

"What color?"

"Red and white."

Amanda hadn't seen the truck Jenny described, but that didn't mean Dave Zinkerman hadn't come and gone before she arrived on the scene. She needed to speak with Dave. She simply could not allow her secretary to fool around with a possible murderer.

"I've got an errand to run," Amanda said as she wheeled away.

"You're going to question Dave, aren't you?" Jenny flung at Amanda's retreating back.

Amanda crossed her fingers, and her eyes. "No."

"I don't believe you, boss."

Amanda pivoted around and tried to look properly offended. "Thanks a lot, Jen."

"Dave is a nice man," Jenny insisted. "I told you that he wouldn't do such a thing."

Amanda breezed out the door. She intended to see for herself how nice Dave Zinkerman was. When somebody tried to separate a man from his money all sorts of unpleasant things happened. Dave might have wanted revenge if he couldn't recover the money and he may have succumbed if opportunity was staring him in the face.

Amanda sincerely hoped Dave Zinkerman hadn't lost his temper and flattened Harvey Renshaw beneath a hay bale. If he had, he would break Jenny's heart.

Well, better to have a broken heart now than discover you had the hots for a murderer later, Amanda told herself as she drove off.

The first thing Amanda noticed when she pulled into the driveway at Zinkerman Farm was that Dave was six feet two inches of handsome man. Not as handsome as Thorn, but nothing to sneeze at.

The second thing Amanda noticed was that Dave was wearing boots—not tennis shoes—a chambray shirt—not a T-shirt— and spotless blue jeans. *Hmmm. Now, why had Davy-boy changed clothes after doing breakfast with Jenny?*

The tall blond man removed his work gloves and ambled

toward Amanda's clunker truck. "You're Jenny's boss, aren't you? I saw your picture in the newspaper. The *Vamoose Gazette* did a front-page spread on your wedding to Thorn."

Typical small town, thought Amanda. Where else in America did a hometown wedding make front page-headlines?

"I guess Jenny asked for some time off," Dave said as he leaned casually against the side of the clunker truck.

"Yes, Jenny is a hardworking, highly efficient employee. She deserves nothing but the best."

Dave lifted a thick brow and grinned. "And you took it upon yourself to stop by to check out this character she's been dating?"

It was a perfect opening. Amanda took it. "You probably think I'm being overly protective, but I'm especially fond of Jenny. I want the best for her. She is indispensable."

He flashed a knock-'em-dead grin. "I think she's incredible."

Amanda never trusted a man who had so much charm that it practically oozed from his pores. Refusing to be distracted by a great bod and handsome face, Amanda cut to the chase.

"Here's the deal, Dave. I don't want to see Jenny or her son hurt in any way, shape, or form. She has dealt with a deadbeat husband and a freeloading boyfriend already."

"Don't worry, Amanda. I have her best interest at heart," Dave was quick to confirm.

Yeah, right, thought Amanda. Dave was no dummy and he wasn't blind to Jenny's attractive assets. He planned to whisk Jenny away for a four-day lovefest.

Dave Zinkerman was one hundred percent male and he was after Jenny's body.

"So . . . what have you been up to this morning, Dave?" *Jerk loose a hydraulic hose and smash somebody under a ton of hay?*

Dave shrugged impossibly broad shoulders. "Just the usual. Stacking hay and feeding cattle."

Amanda glanced toward the two-tone truck that was shiny clean. *Hmmm. Dave has washed his pickup? Now, why would he do that so soon after a rain? It didn't happen to have hydraulic oil smeared on the grill and windshield, did it?*

"Do you always wash your truck immediately after a spring shower?"

Dave frowned, then turned up the wattage on his smile. "I'm picking Jen up after work. I want her to travel in style."

"Then buy a Lincoln," Amanda mumbled.

"Pardon?"

"Nothing. I wondered if you heard about Harvey Renshaw's unfortunate accident." Amanda gauged his reaction closely and noted that Dave's high-voltage smile burned out immediately.

"No, that's news to me."

"He's dead," Amanda reported.

Dave didn't look the least bit aggrieved. "You don't say."

"Jenny mentioned he owed you money," Amanda baited. "You'll need to file a claim against the estate if you want to collect."

Dave stepped back. His shoulders were rigid, his green eyes flickering with hostility. "Since when do accountants drive around offering free financial consultation? I may be slow, but the reason for this visit is beginning to soak in. When somebody turns up dead around here, you start searching for suspects. Word around town is that you interrogate everyone you think might be connected to the case."

"Geez, Dave, don't get paranoid. Makes me think you have something to hide."

"You're barking up the wrong tree, honey," he hissed.

"I don't bark," Amanda replied smoothly. "I simply ask pertinent questions. Such as . . . why did you change clothes after having breakfast with Jenny?"

Dave's eyes bulged with disbelief. "Damn, lady, you don't miss a trick, do you?"

"Nope, so why did you change clothes? I'd like to see the white T-shirt you had on at seven-thirty this morning."

"My clothes are in the washing machine," he bit off.

"My, aren't you efficient," she said, and smirked.

"I'm leaving on a trip soon. I wanted to have plenty of clean clothes to pack. Is there a law against that?"

Damn, the man had an answer for everything.

"If you're through grilling me, I have chores to do."

When Dave wheeled around and stormed off, Amanda studied him pensively. She had the unmistakable feeling that Dave Zinkerman knew more than he would say. He hadn't asked how or when Harvey Renshaw met his untimely end. Most folks would have asked about the events surrounding the disaster, but not Dave.

Amanda sped away. She came to the conclusion that there was no sense delaying an extensive investigation of Harvey Renshaw's death. She would make a beeline to the most reliable source of information in Vamoose. Velma's Beauty Boutique was a hotbed of gossip, and Amanda was anxious to pick the gum-chewing beautician's brain.

CHAPTER FOUR

"Hi, hon." *Snap, chomp.* Velma Hertzog's astute gaze swept over Amanda's golden tan and sun-bleached hair. "That cruise to the Bahamas must have been sensational, because you look terrific."

Several heads, capped with rollers and dripping perm solution, nodded in agreement.

Amanda smiled a greeting to the women who frequented Vamoose's one and only beauty salon. "I recommend a cruise to everyone," she announced.

"Yeah, but not all of us get to take that stud of a police chief with us." When Velma winked, her fake eyelashes stuck together. "You lucky woman you." *Crackle, pop.*

"I don't have an appointment, but I wondered if Bev could do my nails." Amanda glanced hopefully at Velma's barrel-shaped niece who was putting the finishing touches on Millicent Price's hairdo. Hair spray fogged the salon, and the clientele grabbed Kleenex to shield their nostrils. Amanda held her breath while the sticky particles floated around the room. When Beverly Hill blasted Millicent's Brillo-pad head with another coat of hair spray, Amanda wheeled around to open the door. The mist swirled around the salon, then curled upward to burn holes in the ozone.

After a round of sputters and coughs the patrons settled back into their respective places.

"Like, I'll be glad to squeeze you in," Bev said. "I always leap at the chance to work on Vamoose's most famous citizen." She gestured a chubby finger toward the manicure table. "I'll be with you in two shakes, 'Manda."

Amanda decided to open the forum for discussion while she had a full house. Everybody in the know was at Velma's this afternoon.

"I'm afraid I come bearing bad news today, ladies," Amanda said. "I was called to a conference at Renshaw Farm and I found Harvey dead in the hay."

Stunned gazes zeroed in on Amanda.

"Harv?" *Pop, crackle.* "No kidding?" Velma shook her dyed-red head. "For over a year I've been wondering how and when Harv was going to get his due, but I never expected something like this. In the hay, you say?"

Amanda nodded. "Get his due? What do you mean by that, Velma?"

Things were going splendidly, thought Amanda. Her subtle investigation into Harv's background was under way.

"Yeah, like Harv's life is a total mess," Bev put in as she accepted Millicent's payment, then tucked the money in the pocket of her Pepto-Bismol-colored frock. "A regular Peyton Place, according to Mama and Aunt Velma."

Several curler covered heads bobbed in agreement.

"What does that mean?" Amanda quizzed the hefty young beautician, whose incandescent, half-moon eye shadow glittered in the fluorescent light.

"It means Harv was a rascal," Velma said as she snipped off Claudia Swenson's bleach-blond bangs. "The man has been married four times, that I know about. For crying out loud, you'd think he was trying to top Elizabeth Taylor's record for divorces.''

"Like, my mama said that Harv married every time he was transferred to a different Air Force base," Bev inserted. "When he shipped out, he liked to travel light. He left his bride behind and took up with another woman. Like, he thought every military transfer was his chance to begin a new life."

"Shameless, absolutely shameless," Glory Frye clucked, then flicked a piece of gray hair from the sleeve of her flannel blouse.

Amanda tried to recall if she had ever seen Glory Frye dressed in anything but flannel. The rawboned farmer's wife could have been a poster model for flannel. Glory's wardrobe consisted of every color of flannel under the rainbow—pastels, plaids, and stripes included.

"Ever since Harv was just a kid chopping cotton on our farm, girls dropped by to bring him a cola and chitchat. Never could see the appeal myself," Glory added.

"Four wives?" Amanda repeated. "Then which ex-wife was Harv going to settle in the house I've been renting?"

"Must have been Wife Number One," Velma speculated as she spun Claudia in The Chair to clip hair from the crown of her head. "Talk about a marital circus!" *Chomp, crunch.* "Laverne, that's Number One, is from these parts."

"Laverne grew up in Pronto," Millicent Price informed the crowd. "Her mama ran off and left when Laverne was just a baby. Poor girl never had much of an upbringing with her daddy in charge."

"I heard that Laverne and *her* live-in boyfriend moved in with Harv and *his* live-in girlfriend, because Laverne couldn't pay her rent." *Crackle, chomp.*

Amanda's eyes popped. "All four of them were living under the same roof?"

"Yep," Bev confirmed. "Like, have you heard of anything so bizarre?"

"No, it sounds like a soap opera," Amanda said.

"I'm not sure fiction could compete with the goings-on at Renshaw Farm," Velma said, then snorted. "Word around town is that Harv's live-in, Anita Blankenship, wanted Wife Number One off the premises. There were rumors flying that Harv and Laverne were rekindling the old flame when they had a chance."

"I wouldn't be surprised if Harv decided to rent the farmhouse so he could drop by to see Laverne without Anita Blankenship finding out about it," Glory inserted.

Holy cow! thought Amanda. She was collecting the names of suspects faster than she could process the information. Amanda put on the brakes to stop her whirling thoughts, then she made a mental list of people who held grudges against Harvey Renshaw.

Dave Zinkerman couldn't get Harv to pay his debts, and Harv had pulled a gun on Dave. That was cause for ill feelings.

Anita Blankenship was Harv's live-in girlfriend. She objected to having Laverne, Wife Number One, sleeping under the same roof—and maybe not in her own bed!

"Who is Laverne's live-in boyfriend?" Amanda wanted to know.

"Johnny Phipps," Millie Price said as she tugged on the hem of her polyester skirt to cover her bony knees.

"Like, he's a loser with a capital L," Bev put in. She lumbered over to plunge Amanda's hands into the soaking solution. "Mama says Johnny couldn't hold down a job without an anchor. He's never worked at any one place for more than six months in his entire life. Mama used to clean house for Johnny's parents and he was always lounging around, doing nothing. He wouldn't even get off his lazy butt while Mama vacuumed. She had to sweep around him."

"Laverne must be hard up if she's keeping company with

that freeloader,'' Glory said before she stuck her head under the dryer. ''Either that or Laverne has been carrying a torch for Harv all these years and is trying to make him jealous.''

''Wouldn't put it past her.'' *Chomp, crackle.* ''Laverne is one of those people who can never get enough attention. She soaks it up like a sponge.''

''That poor woman never got over Harv,'' Millie interjected. ''She's been rebounding from one man to another since Harv dumped her and flew off to another Air Force base. While he was stationed in Oklahoma, Laverne went to go see him regularly. Baked him cookies and went bearing gifts, too. I'd have to say that Laverne was willing to do most anything to get Harv back.''

Amanda could not imagine what any of Harv's four wives, and countless girlfriends, had seen in him. Maybe he was more charming when he was keeping company with potential girlfriends. Harv certainly hadn't won any personality contests with his accountant.

From the sound of things, there were any number of Vamoosians who were waiting for Harv to get his due. Amanda would have to run her legs off interviewing possible suspects, while trying to keep up at the accounting office. With Jenny taking time off, she would be exceptionally busy.

''Anita Blankenship is no better,'' Bev said as she scrubbed Amanda's cuticles vigorously. Her black Shirley Temple curls bobbed around her chubby cheeks. ''Anita works at a department store in the city and she's always bringing gifts home to Harv. Like, every time she comes to Beauty Boutique she tells me about some bargain she picked up to surprise him.''

So Anita was trying to buy Harv's affection, was she? Interesting, thought Amanda. Maybe she should try that tactic with Thorn when he got irritated with her. She could select a new electric drill or circular saw as gifts. The man loved his power tools.

''I wonder if Wife Number Three is still in town.'' *Crackle, snap.* Velma frowned pensively as her meaty hands swept over Claudia's head, smoothing the wiry strands into place. "Now, there's a strange one." *Pop, chomp.* "That woman came all the way from Georgia to see Harv. I heard Harv and Number Three had a kid together and she was demanding that he fork over the unpaid child support. Can you imagine the turmoil in the Renshaw household with Number One, Number Three, and the current girlfriend underfoot?"

"I wonder who inherits now that Harv had his unfortunate accident?" Amanda mused aloud.

The patrons of Velma's Beauty Boutique looked at each other curiously.

"Maybe Number Three's kid," Glory Frye speculated. "Who else could it be? Unless Harv disinherited his own kid. Wouldn't surprise me a bit if he did. Harv never struck me as the type who cared a fig about kids."

"Like, who knows?" Bev put in. "Considering the Peyton Place Harv's life has become, the kid may not even be his. Like, none of us are in the know because the marriage took place in Georgia."

But Wife Number Three knew, Amanda reminded herself. Number Three had motive galore. If her child inherited, Number Three would gain control of a great deal of money until the child was of legal age. Harv had two producing oil wells and a third one on the way. Not to mention his farm property, machinery, cattle herd, and fleet of vehicles. The kid would also be entitled to Harv's Social Security benefits—if the kid really was Harv's child.

Hmmm, thought Amanda. *Harv may have been more valuable to Number Three if he was dead rather than alive . . . .*

Amanda sucked air when she glanced down to see what Bev had done to her fingernails. The tips of her fingers were bright orange and sparkled with glitter. *Egad!* She looked like a third-rate floozy. Orange was definitely *not* Amanda's signature color!

"Hey, hon." *Pop, pop.* "Since you've been away on your honeymoon you probably haven't heard about the chicken noodle supper and slave auction sponsored by the Methodist Women's Society."

No, it was news to Amanda.

The hens at the Beauty Boutique began to cluck excitedly.

"Like, it's gonna be a hoot!" Bev enthused as she spread clear polish on Amanda's colorful nails. "The Methodist women selected several men in town to be slaves for the day. It gives the single, divorced, and widow women a chance to get all those handyman jobs done that have been put off all year. Like, you know, repairing leaky faucets, replacing door locks, putting up new storm doors. The event will be a blast!"

"We already put Nicky on the list." *Crackle, crunch.* "Knew he wouldn't mind since he always participates in worthwhile community causes."

Amanda predicted that every unattached woman in Vamoose, Pronto, and Adios, would show up for the noodle dinner and auction. There was something very intriguing about the prospect of having a male slave for the day.

"I'm gonna buy a slave to replace a few rotting boards on my wooden deck," Millie announced, then glanced quizzically at Velma. "You did ask our local carpenter, Buzz Sawyer, to participate, didn't you?"

"Sure did." *Pop, crackle.* "Called the local plumber, Phillip Fawcett, too. And the electrician, Sparky Watts, said he was game. Thaddeus Thatcher and Toby Fitzmire agreed to become enslaved for the day. Every competent handyman in town will participate."

"I'll bet the bidding will go high for those men." Glory beamed in anticipation. "I've got two leaky faucets and a kitchen sink to replace—"

Glory's voice dried up when Velma sprayed industrial-strength hair spray on Claudia's head.

The patrons grabbed their tissues. Amanda leaped up and

dashed to the door. The dense fog whooshed off in the wind. She could almost hear the ozone layer groaning in dismay.

"Be careful that you don't smudge your nail polish. It's not dry yet, 'Manda," Bev called out. "Anita Blankenship had a hissy fit yesterday when her nails got smudged. She was in a flaming rush. Said she had things to do and places to go and she complained the whole time I was redoing her thumbnail. I went, 'Chill out, dudette, no harm done.' But Anita was in a real tizzy."

Anita Blankenship? As in Harv Renshaw's present girlfriend? Now why did Anita need to be in such an all-fired hurry? Making arrangements to do Harv in, because he let Wife Number One live in his home and fool around with him on the sly? Or was Anita peeved because Wife Number Three showed up demanding money?

"Well, I'm outta here, girls," Glory said as she levered her stout body from beneath the dryer. "I'll have to come by tomorrow for styling, Velma. Since I'm in charge of baking hot rolls for the noodle supper I need to get to the store to buy flour and yeast, then pick up the baking pans from the church before the place is locked up tight for the night."

"Sure, Glory." *Snap, pop.* "Just come by when you have time and I'll finish your 'do."

Bev blew her breath on Amanda's sparkling nails. Bev's half-moon, incandescent blue eye shadow glowed in the shadows. "Just about finished, 'Manda. I bet you're anxious to get home tonight and fix supper for your new hubby."

Supper? Amanda winced. She hadn't the foggiest notion what she was going to fix for supper. Usually, she never gave the evening meal a thought until she walked through the front door.

Besides, Amanda mused, tonight Thorn probably preferred to skip supper and chew on *her* for claiming that Harv Renshaw might possibly be a murder victim.

Amanda paid Bev, then skedaddled from the shop. She had

to swing by the office to see her secretary off for her four-day lovefest with Dave Zinkerman.

Amanda was concerned about Jenny. The woman had such pathetic taste in men. This Dave person could turn out to be another crushing disappointment.

Outwardly Dave Zinkerman appeared to be charming and attractive, but who knew what evil, fiendish tendencies lurked behind that 150-watt smile? For all Amanda knew, Dave had planned for this little vacation to coincide with Harv's "accident."

Stranger things had happened, Amanda reminded herself. And *strange* always sent her suspicions into a state of riot.

The moment Amanda parked her jalopy truck in the office parking lot, Dave Zinkerman's smile dried up and blew away. "Did you stop by to convince Jen not to leave town with me?"

Amanda decided to lay it on the line for dear ol' Dave. She marched straight toward him, standing toe-to-toe, eye-to-eye. "I have already made it crystal clear that I consider Jenny more than a business associate. She is also my friend. I will not stand idly by to see her used or hurt. If you don't treat her with the courtesy, respect, and consideration she deserves, I'll sic the IRS on you. You better be able to account for every penny of your expenditures when you're called in for an audit."

"Damn, Hazard, you like to play hard ball, don't you?"

"I play hard ball when I have to," she assured him sternly. "Don't screw this up, Zinkerman, because I promise I will be looking over your shoulder. You have been warned twice. This is the last warning you'll get. I will take action."

Dave glared at her.

Not to be outdone, Amanda glared back.

"By the way, your fingernails look ridiculous," Dave smirked.

"By the way, where were you between nine and ten o'clock this morning?" Amanda fired back.

"I'm ready!" Jenny announced as she whizzed through the office door. She glanced warily between Amanda and Dave, who were still doing visual battle. "Thanks for giving me this time off, boss."

In an attempt to defuse what looked to be a tense situation, Jenny smiled brightly. "So . . . I guess the two of you introduced yourselves . . . . Everything is okay, I hope."

"Everything is fine," Dave gritted out, still giving Amanda the evil eye.

"Couldn't be better," Amanda said without taking her penetrating gaze off the possible murder suspect.

Amanda watched Dave clasp his hand around Jenny's elbow and escort her toward his recently washed truck. Dave gallantly opened the passenger door for Jen, then shot Amanda a parting glare. She hoped her suspicions about Dave were ill-founded, really she did. But if Dave was involved in Harv Renshaw's death, Amanda wasn't cutting the man any slack, just because Jenny Long was sweet on him.

Pivoting on her heels, Amanda strode into her office to check the messages Jen left for her. She raised her eyebrows when she saw the message from Anita Blankenship, Harvey's live-in girlfriend. According to the note, Anita wanted to speak to Amanda at her earliest possible convenience.

What was up with that? Amanda wondered. Why did the live-in girlfriend need financial consultation?

Amanda dialed the number but no one answered. She glanced at her watch. Thorn was supposed to meet her at the rented farmhouse to move furniture in a few minutes. Amanda would have to wait until morning to contact Anita.

Amanda picked up the second note. It was a message from Mother: "Call home immediately." Hurriedly Amanda dialed the number, wondering what crises had descended on the Hazard household.

"Hazard here."

"Daddy?" Amanda said. "How are things in the city?"

"Fine, sugar. Glad you're home. Did you have a good time in the tropical paradise?"

"The best. Mother left an urgent message for me. Is everything okay with you?"

"Mother and I are okay, but—"

Amanda could hear Mother's voice in the background. A clatter came down the line, indicating Mother had confiscated the phone from Daddy.

"It's about time you called back, doll. I've been waiting all afternoon!"

"Good to talk to you, too, Mother," Amanda mumbled.

"What did you say?"

"Nothing important. What did you need to speak to me about in such an all-fired rush?" Amanda asked.

"We've got major problems," Mother announced.

Obviously not, thought Amanda. Mother and Daddy were alive and well. But Mother had never been able to differentiate between major and minor. Every problem was a big deal to Mother.

"Your house burned down? Your car caught on fire?"

The caustic questions were met with noticeable silence, followed by Mother's snort of irritation. "I see your new husband's sarcasm has rubbed off on you. I knew the chief of police in Sleepy Hollowville, and part-time farm boy, was going to be a bad influence on you. Not that I'm surprised he turned out the way he did, considering how his uncivilized mother behaves. My goodness! She made an absolute spectacle of herself at your wedding. I couldn't believe she had the gall to talk to me the way she did. And you should have heard the rude remarks she made about you! I had to stand up for myself, and for you, didn't I?"

Amanda didn't want to rehash the conflict that had risen between Mother and Thorn's mom at the nuptials. It was the talk of the town. Two middle-aged women going for each other's jugulars, rolling around in the aisle at church!

"So . . . what's the problem?"

"It's your brother," Mother muttered. "Or rather that useless wife of his. She refuses to let me in her house. Have you ever heard of anything so outrageous?"

"What did you do, Mother?" Amanda asked in a wary voice.

"What did *I* do?" Mother howled indignantly. "I didn't do anything except tell that delinquent grandson of mine to stop jumping on the sofa as if it were a trampoline! My annoying daughter-in-law had the nerve to tell me not to discipline her brats! Somebody has to. Their behavior is embarrassing!"

Amanda yanked the receiver away from her ear when Mother's voice hit a piercing pitch. Mother was a fine one to talk about embarrassing behavior, thought Amanda.

"You've got to straighten this mess out! She is refusing to let me see those kids whenever I please. Now, how are they going to grow up respecting property and behaving themselves if I'm not around to teach them the difference between right and wrong?"

"I don't think I should get involved in this situation—"

"Of course you have to!" Mother squawked. "It's your family duty. And speaking of family duty, it is your responsibility to keep an eye on Pops. I'm not sure it's a good idea for him to be sharing his space with that weirdo who lives out in the sticks."

"Salty Marcum is good company for Pops. Or would you prefer that Pops moves back in with you?"

"Heavens, no!" Mother yowled. "The man's main purpose, while he was living here, was to drive me crazy."

"It wouldn't have been much of a drive," Amanda mumbled.

"What?"

"Nothing, Mother."

"Now, I want you to take care of this rift." It was a direct order from Hazard headquarters. "Daddy and I are leaving to

play bingo tonight. Call me back after you've reasoned with
that moron your brother married—''

Clink, hum . . . .

Amanda replaced the receiver since Mother hung up immediately after delivering her royal command.

Great, just great. Not only did Amanda have to man her
accounting office alone, investigate a probable murder, and get
settled into Thorn's farm home, but she was expected to smooth
over the latest skirmish in the ongoing battle between Mother
and her daughter-in-law.

Grumbling, Amanda locked up the office and contemplated
her extensive list of things-to-do.

''Supper,'' she groaned on her way out the door. Thorn
would probably expect her to provide supper. She would have
to swing by the Last Chance Cafe to pick up some burgers and
fries. She would have to delay cooking her first official meal
as Mrs. Hazard-Thorn until tomorrow—or maybe next week.

Nick took one look at Amanda's gaudy orange fingernails
and frowned in disapproval. ''You've been digging up gossip
at Beauty Boutique, haven't you?'' he asked without preamble.

Flashing a peace-offering smile, Hazard extended the brown
paper bag. ''I brought supper.''

Nick took the greasy brown paper sack and set it on the table.
''Thanks. So what did you find out about Harvey Renshaw?''

Hazard shrugged. ''Nothing you would be interested in, I'm
sure. After all, you have convinced yourself that Harvey suffered a fatal farming accident.''

''It's true,'' Nick concluded. ''We farmers have a saying
that goes like this: Shit happens. I found no evidence at the
scene that indicates foul play.''

''And I suppose the medical examiner was quick to agree
with you,'' Hazard muttered sourly.

Nick nodded. ''Renshaw suffered a broken neck when the

weight of the hay bale fell on him. He smothered to death. There were no suspicious blows to the head or body that suggested a scuffle. There was no sign that Harvey was knocked unconscious, then dragged beneath the elevated bale.''

"But there was that broken hydraulic hose," Hazard was quick to remind him.

"Yes, there was that," Nick agreed.

"And you can't know beyond all reasonable doubt that the hose wasn't tampered with," she argued.

Nick kept hearing Joe Mason's words roll back to him: *"Renshaw just replaced hydraulic hoses a couple of months ago."*

Could Hazard truly be onto something? She had been correct several times before, Nick reminded himself grudgingly. He should be supportive here. After all, Hazard had saved his bacon when questions about Nick's professional conduct were raised after Frank Lemon was found dead in the driver's seat.

Maybe he should give Hazard the green light to conduct her unofficial investigation. She ate that stuff up. If it made her happy, then maybe he should accommodate her. Anything to keep peace in this two-week-old marriage!

"Just to be on the safe side, go ahead and find out what you can about Renshaw's background."

Hazard's pleased smile nearly knocked Nick to his knees. She launched herself at him, causing him to stumble off balance.

"Oh, Thorn! Bless you. You're starting to come around!"

Nick grinned rakishly as he scooped Hazard off the floor and headed toward the bedroom. "I'll come around often if that's what you want, Hazard."

For the next half hour, Nick forgot about loading furniture in the stock trailer that he'd hitched to his four-wheel-drive pickup, forgot about the incidents surrounding Renshaw's untimely demise. All that concerned him was getting his hands on Hazard's luscious body. This, he reminded himself, was one of the outstanding benefits of marriage.

CHAPTER FIVE

Nick heaved Hazard's solid oak coffee table onto one shoulder and carried it from the rented farmhouse to the trailer. Hazard's three-legged dog, Pete, and Bruno—the Border collie that had appointed himself Hazard's personal bodyguard—bounded around Nick's feet, very nearly tripping him up.

"Call these mutts before I step on them," Nick hollered at Hazard.

"They're afraid they're going to be left behind," Hazard hollered back. "They *are* going with us, aren't they, Thorn? We can't abandon them."

Nick didn't know what he was going to do with two extra canines, a spoiled house cat, a henhouse full of chickens, two smelly hogs, and a duck that left unsightly deposits on sidewalks and front porches. But he knew better than to refuse to let Hazard relocate the menagerie of animals she had inherited from one of her departed clients. Nick only hoped his Pyrenees sheepdog didn't get upset when two other canines started crowding his space.

"We'll bring your pets along, but tie those dogs up before I fall over them."

When Hazard whistled at the dogs, they came running. Nick plunked down the coffee table, then returned to the house to move the sofa.

"Grab the other end, Haz," he requested.

Hazard braced her legs and lifted her end of the La-Z-Boy sofa. "Your threadbare divan will have to go, Thorn. This one is in better condition."

Nick grinned as he levered the recliner-sofa through the door. He had no objections to replacing his worn-out furniture with Hazard's. In fact, he was making plans to fool around on this couch as soon as he had it situated in his house.

Nick and Hazard worked in synchronized precision for more than an hour. He was delighted that things were going so splendidly between them. Despite his mom's bleak predictions that the marriage would decay the moment the honeymoon was over, there had been very little cause for conflict—except the minor tiff involving Harvey Renshaw's accident. Nick couldn't have been happier . . . .

"Tell me what you know about Harvey Renshaw," Hazard said out of the blue.

Nick sighed audibly. "Can't we give that a night's rest, Haz? I told you to go ahead with your investigation."

"And I am. I'm interviewing you. Humor me, Thorn. After all, you took the vows."

Nick grabbed the mattress off the bed. "The vows stated that I was to love and *honor,* not love and *humor,"* he reminded her.

"Come on, Thorn," she coaxed him. "We can move furniture and discuss this case at the same time."

Reluctantly Nick complied, though he considered this case an accident, pure and simple. But if it made Hazard happy to portray the gumshoe, then he would play along.

"I didn't know Harvey very well. He was eight years older.

I recall that he had a brother named Harold, who lived with his mother while Harvey stayed on the farm with his dad. I'm not sure where Harvey's mother and brother lived after they left here.

"Harv and old man Renshaw scratched and clawed to make ends meet on the farm and pretty much kept to themselves. I don't have to tell you what poor farm ground the Renshaws own. You can tell that red clay doesn't produce abundant crops. It's a shame the oil wells didn't come along until after old man Renshaw was long gone."

"Do you know where Harold is now? Do you suppose he might inherit part, or all, of the estate?"

"I don't have a clue. I never met Harold and I don't think he ever came back to Vamoose after his mother got her divorce. Seems like I remember my parents mentioning that Harvey's mother never would let old man Renshaw near Harold. To tell you the truth, I don't think I would recognize Harold if I saw him. I was too young to recall what went on with the domestic problems between old man Renshaw and his wife."

"From what I learned at Beauty Boutique the whole bunch of Renshaws are strange," Hazard commented.

Nick maneuvered the mattress through the door and off the porch. "What makes you say that?"

"Did you know that Wife Number One and her freeloading boyfriend have been living in the same house with Harvey and Anita Blankenship?" Her gaze narrowed. "And for the record, I will not be kindhearted enough to allow any of your old girlfriends to move in with us at any point in the future, no matter how dire the old girlfriend's straits. I want that understood. I am not sharing you with another woman . . . ever."

Nick smiled charmingly. "Not to worry, Hazard. I'm not stupid enough to set myself up for that kind of trouble." He wedged the mattress behind the sofa that sat in the trailer. "Renshaw must have been out of his mind to take in his ex-wife. Talk about a tricky situation."

"You're darn tootin'! There must have been all sorts of conflict flying around the Renshaw house. Gossip is that Harvey and Wife Number One spent time in the sack, rekindling the old flame. Harv's girlfriend didn't like it one bit."

"Geez, that's really asking for it," he said without thinking.

"No, that is *motive* for murder," Hazard said as she followed at Nick's heels. "And to complicate a difficult situation, Wife Number Three showed up from Georgia to demand child support for her kid. At least that is what Velma thinks Number Three is doing here. No one really knows for certain."

Nick picked up the box springs. "How many ex-wives are there?"

"Four that I know of. Harv really pushed his luck."

"Didn't he, though? Talk about a four-ring circus."

"Makes me wonder if Harv would have been called on the military carpet for sexual misconduct if he hadn't retired when he did. He was probably hitting on every woman he encountered. With all the craze to clean up the armed forces he would have been a prime candidate for court-martial."

Nick had to agree that Harv's wild lifestyle—if the gossip was to be believed—raised all sorts of questions about motive in his death. But Nick wasn't going to encourage Hazard. She was already fired up, certain that murder was a strong possibility in this dead-in-the-hay case.

No, Nick would simply allow Hazard to do her thing and wait to see what she turned up. Besides, wheat harvest was rapidly approaching and Nick was going to be as busy as a bumblebee stuck in a bucket of tar. In what little spare time he had, Nick needed to service his combine and repair his wheat truck. When the grain was ripe, he had to be ready to roll.

"Toss in a couple of boxes of towels and supplies and we'll call this a full load," Nick said. "This is as much as we can unload at my house before dark."

Nick piled into the truck, and Hazard followed him in her

jalopy. He was pleased at how well he had handled his new wife's suspicions. He hadn't uttered one sarcastic remark all evening. He was learning to deal with Hazard when the investigative bug bit her . . . .

Nick inwardly groaned when he realized that he hadn't *dealt* with Hazard at all.

He had simply given in to her.

He wondered if this was a sign of things to come. He could not allow Hazard to have her way constantly, he reminded himself. He couldn't let her walk all over him. She had a reputation of being a dominant, strong willed woman. Nick refused to be labeled as the *whipped* police chief of Vamoose!

Amanda was champing at the bit to speak with Anita Blankenship. She couldn't imagine what Harv's most recent girlfriend wanted, but it provided the golden opportunity to glean a few facts for the case.

The moment Amanda walked into her office bright and early in the morning she snatched up the phone and dialed Anita's number.

"Hello?"

"Anita?"

"No!" the indignant voice blared. "This is Laverne. Anita doesn't live here anymore."

This was Wife Number One, Amanda reminded herself. Obviously, the ex-wife and girlfriend had a falling-out after Anita had called yesterday afternoon.

"Well, then, Laverne, can you tell me where I can reach Anita? She left a message for me to call her."

"You think I'm Anita's keeper? Not hardly! I don't know where she is and I could care less. Who is this anyway?"

"Amanda Hazard-Thorn."

Amanda heard Laverne's shocked gasp coming down the line. "Well, if Anita plans to tattle to you, then she will be voicing outright lies. You can't believe a thing that woman says."

"Oh? What do you think Anita plans to tell me?"

"She is most likely going to claim that I owe money to Harv's estate, which is a bald-faced lie. The money Harvey gave me wasn't a loan, and he didn't expect me to pay rent when I moved into his house, either," Laverne said in a rush.

"Did he expect you to pay your own rent when you and your boyfriend moved into the farmhouse I have been renting?"

"I don't see that it's anybody's business," Laverne snapped.

"In other words, Harv planned to foot your bills," Amanda presumed.

"I didn't say that," Laverne shouted into the phone. "I'm not stupid, you know. Everybody in this county knows you're always trying to pin a murder rap on somebody when someone around here kicks the bucket. You have your nerve badgering me while I'm grieving the loss of my ex-husband and dear friend—"

"*How* dear?" Amanda wanted to know.

"There you go again!" Laverne railed. She worked up a few crocodile tears to blubber into the phone, then continued. "Don't think I don't know that Anita spread the gossip that Harv and I were shacking up. That's totally absurd. Johnny Phipps and I have a thing going."

"Uh-huh."

"Don't use that tone with me. We do, damn it!" Laverne blared.

Wow, thought Amanda. *Wife Number One is simmering with hostility.* "I was only agreeing with you, Laverne."

"Didn't sound like it to me," she sputtered. "If you're thinking I had reason to want Harv dead, you're wrong."

"Why would I think that?"

"Because you always think the worst when someone around Vamoose turns up his toes."

Amanda frowned at the comment. Did Laverne sound like

a woman who was mourning the loss of a close friend? Nope. Amanda would bet her life savings that Laverne harbored ill feelings for Harv. But what did Laverne have to gain from Harv's demise? That was the million-dollar question.

"As Harvey's financial consultant I will need a copy of his will," Amanda said in her most businesslike voice. "It will be my duty to my client to ensure that his inheritance is distributed according to his wishes."

"Well, I don't have the will!" Laverne hissed. "If I knew where it was I'd—"

Her voice evaporated. Amanda wondered what Wife Number One refused to say. Had Laverne been rummaging through cabinets and drawers to locate the last will and testament, hoping to discover that what she had inherited from Harv could relieve her destitute situation?

"I've got things to do, arrangements to make," Laverne muttered. "I don't have time to chitchat on the phone."

"You are in charge of Harv's final arrangements?" Amanda asked, surprised.

"Well, who else would be? Certainly not Anita. She was just somebody who hung around here. She meant absolutely nothing to Harvey. He would have wanted me to see that he was put to rest properly."

Amanda recalled the beauty-shop gossip that indicated Laverne had a lousy upbringing. Amanda wasn't sure Laverne understood the concept of *proper*.

"What about the ex-wife from Georgia?" Amanda questioned strategically.

"That fraud?" Laverne snorted, disgusted. "Glenda Renshaw is only after money. You can bet your butt on that. As for her kid, I don't believe for a moment that it's Harv's."

Hmmm, thought Amanda. *Maybe Wife Number Three is running a con.* If this contested estate went to court, and Number Three won, she had a great deal to gain.

And Wife Number One had a lot to lose.

A military career man like Harvey might have had a will and life insurance—especially since he had been stationed all over the States and spent time in military conflicts overseas.

What if Harv hadn't updated his will recently? What if the women in his life were jockeying to stake their claim on his oil royalties, his property, and livestock?

"I've shot the bull with you long enough," Laverne said rudely. "I've gotta go."

Before Amanda could reply, the line went dead. Frustrated, Amanda slammed down the receiver. She needed an excuse to look around Renshaw Farm, needed to get a feel for the environment Harv lived in. She also wanted to take a gander at Harv's will—if there was one . . . .

Power of attorney! Amanda wheeled toward the file cabinet. She remembered that Harv had given her power to handle last year's income tax audit—and any future ones that might arise. With the legal document in hand, she could open doors that might otherwise remain closed.

Hurriedly Amanda thumbed through Harv's file.

"Bingo," Amanda said, then groaned. She suddenly remembered that her parents had left to play bingo last night and she had been given a direct order to smooth over the relationship between Mother and her daughter-in-law.

"Rats," Amanda muttered as she plucked up the phone.

"Hazard's house."

"Hi, it's Amanda. How are things going?"

"Did your mother tell you to call me?" Regina Hazard questioned.

"Yes," Amanda said honestly.

"Well, you're wasting your time. I am not letting that old bat in my house until she apologizes and acknowledges that this is *my* house and these are *my* kids. I have listened to all her snide remarks about how I do such a lousy job of housekeeping, about what a lousy wife and mother I am. If Hazard the

Hag wants to see her grandchildren, then she can arrange to meet with them on neutral ground. Your place, for instance.''

No way was Amanda going to invite the hostile Hazard clan to her new home. ''Let Mother take the kids to the playground,'' Amanda suggested. ''All you have to do is drop them off and pick them up. You won't have to talk to her if you don't want to.''

''No,'' Regina said stubbornly. ''It's high time I taught Mother Hazard a lesson. She has been walking all over me for years. She may try to run your life, and your brother's life, but I'm tired of her running mine! Your brother's method of handling Mother Hazard is to ignore the conflicts. But then, he isn't the one who catches hell from the old hag. Far as I'm concerned, Mother Hazard can see her grandkids when they graduate from high school, and not a year before! That's ten years from now and that is soon enough to suit me!''

Amanda found herself holding the phone with no one on the other end of the line. What was there about her, Amanda asked herself, that invited people to hang up on her?

Well, she would have to find a way to resolve this family crisis later. At the moment, she had a murder case to crack.

Snatching up the legal document, Amanda breezed out the door. If Harv kept a safety-deposit box, Amanda wanted to have a look-see. There was no telling what kind of information might turn up there.

Amanda scowled when she turned the key in the ignition of her jalopy truck and was met with a mechanical gurgle. She glanced down at the fuel gauge. Damn, the old gas-guzzler had been sucking air and she had failed to notice.

Climbing down, Amanda hiked off to borrow a gas can from Thatcher's Oil and Gas.

''You're afoot?'' Thaddeus Thatcher questioned as Amanda entered the service station.

"My jalopy must have been running on fumes," she told Thaddeus.

"I'll have Bubba Hix take care of you." Thaddeus hiked up the breeches that sagged below his paunch, then galumphed off to summon Bubba who was repairing a tractor tire.

A moment later Bubba motioned Amanda toward his old truck. Hurriedly Amanda climbed in.

"How is your family doing?" Amanda asked as Bubba veered onto Main Street.

"Doin' fine, 'Manda."

"Sis still hasn't had that baby?"

Bubba shook his bushy head. "Nope, but Doc Simms says the baby could come anytime. If Sis hasn't delivered by Friday, Doc will induce labor."

The poor woman, thought Amanda. The last time Amanda had seen Sis Hix she looked ten months pregnant. How much longer before Sis's legs gave out on her? The woman was waddling like a duck and had been for two months.

While Bubba filled Amanda's bone-dry fuel tank, she glanced up to see an old-model car zooming down the street. Sis Hix stuck her head out the window. Her stringy brown hair flapped in the breeze. Sis was waving her free hand wildly.

"Bubba! It's time—" Her voice broke off into a groan as she wheeled up beside Amanda's jalopy.

Bubba jerked upright, spilling gas on the gravel driveway. "The baby's coming?" he chirped. "The baby's coming!"

Sis nodded vigorously, then grabbed her belly. Her face turned yogurt white when an intense pain hit her. *"Ouch!* We gotta go, Bubba. NOW!" she wailed.

Bubba dropped the gas can—fuel belched upward like a geyser—and charged toward the car. His leathery face was etched with concern as he watched his wife endure a fierce contraction.

"It'll be okay, honey-bunch. Just do those breathing exercises like Doc Simms told you to do. I'll get you to the hospital on time. Don't worry, don't worry," he chanted.

Amanda smiled to herself when the burly service station attendant dissolved into mush at the sight of his wife in pain. Amanda doubted Thorn would lose his cool when she dashed off to deliver a baby. Certainly not Thorn. He was accustomed to handling crises. Nothing fazed Thorn. He was the epitome of cool, calm, and collected.

Rushing forward, Amanda opened the passenger door of the old car to lift Bubba Jr. from his car seat. "I'll take B.J. with me," she volunteered.

"We can't let you do that." *Huff, puff, gasp.* "You've done too many nice things for me and Bubba already." *Huff, huff, puff.*

"Nonsense." Amanda hoisted the little tyke onto her hip. "What are friends for? We're supposed to help each other in times of need. B.J. and I will keep busy."

"Ouch!" Sis gasped, then half collapsed on the seat.

"Hit the road, Bubba," Amanda ordered. "Not to worry, B.J. and I will grab an ice-cream cone and wait for news of the arrival."

"Ithe creeeem!" B.J. bugled excitedly.

Amanda put a tight grip on the toddler who flapped his arms enthusiastically. "Come on, kiddo. We're off to Toot 'N Tell 'Em."

CHAPTER SIX

Bubba Jr. jabbered nonstop while Amanda cruised down the street. It was going to be difficult to conduct her investigation with B.J. in tow, but Amanda was determined to help a friend in need and still make headway in the case.

While B.J. lapped up ice cream Amanda headed for Vamoose Bank. If she could talk her way into the vault to study the contents of Harvey Renshaw's safety-deposit box, she might be able to figure out who had the most to gain from Harvey's demise . . . .

"Oh, B.J." Amanda's thoughts scattered when she glanced down to see chocolate ice cream smeared in B.J.'s hair, on his striped T-shirt and training pants. "Don't you ever stay clean for more than five minutes, kiddo?"

"Ithe creeem," B.J. yammered, then trailed off into a rapid-fire language Amanda couldn't understand.

Grabbing B.J.'s sticky hand, Amanda led him into the bank. The teller, a prissy female in a starched business suit, looked down her nose at B.J. "That has to be the Hix rug rat," she said, and sniffed.

"His mother is on her way to the hospital to deliver the new baby," Amanda explained.

"Great, so there is going to be another mangy toddler around here, getting sticky fingerprints on the glass door."

Amanda thought it over and decided to give the snotty teller what she deserved. "Please baby-sit B.J. for me while I'm in the vault." She flashed the power of attorney document, then scooped up B.J. and stuffed him in Abigail Pickens's arms. "I've been appointed"—well, not exactly—"to prepare Harvey Renshaw's financial statements before the will"—if there is one—"is read and the estate is finalized."

Abigail frowned when the legal document swished past her upturned nose. "I'm not sure—"

"Not to worry," Amanda interrupted strategically. "You can handle B.J. easily. He's a lovable kid who never met a stranger. Where do I sign to get the key to Harv's safety-deposit box?"

"Well . . . No, B.J.! Don't touch that!" Abigail lurched back before the kid's foot pressed down on the computer keyboard. "Hold still!"

"Why don't you wash him up while I conduct my business," Amanda suggested, giving Abigail a nudge toward the rest room. "I'll have your assistant help me."

B.J., bless him, provided the distraction needed. He made a grab for the paper that was spitting from the printer. Abigail spun around to prevent disaster, then rushed toward the rest room before B.J. demolished the computer system.

Within a minute Amanda had the young assistant convinced that she had been authorized to open Harvey's safety-deposit box. Smiling triumphantly, Amanda accepted the key and made a beeline for the vault. She hoped she could count on B.J. to make a nuisance of himself while she studied Harv's important documents.

Inside the safety-deposit box Amanda found the deed and abstract to Renshaw Farm, a certified copy of Harv's life insurance policy, military discharge papers, birth certificate, and CD certificates. Glancing over her shoulder to ensure the coast was still clear, Amanda stuffed the contents of the box into her oversize purse so she could study the papers at her leisure.

Locking the box, Amanda strode casually from the vault. B.J. had captured the attention of every bank employee—except for the president who had taken the day off to play golf. The kid was darting from one side of the bank to the other, squealing in delight, while Abigail gave chase, mouthing several four-letter words.

"Hey, kiddo, lets go have a sucker," Amanda baited Bubba Jr.

B.J. lurched around, then ducked between Abigail's legs when she tried to snatch him up by the nape of his shirt. The little tyke raced toward Amanda, then bounded into her outstretched arms.

"I decided to return when I have more time to spare," Amanda told the harried teller. "Bye now!"

Since B.J. had been so helpful, Amanda decided to take the kid with her to Renshaw Farm. She wasn't sure what she hoped to accomplish there, but instinct told her that she might stumble over a piece of information that would give her some direction in this case.

With B.J. strapped in the seat belt, licking his giant-size lollipop, Amanda cruised down the back roads to Renshaw Farm.

The two-story farmhouse had seen better days, Amanda noted. Harvey hadn't spent a penny of his military pension on repairs. The dingy white paint was chipped and flaking. The black shutters on either side of the windows hung unevenly. The picket fence was also crying out for paint, and boards were missing in four places.

However, to Amanda's delight, there wasn't a vehicle to be

seen on the premises—except for Harv's Jeep and four-wheel-drive wheat truck. Where Harv had gone, he didn't need transportation, Amanda reminded herself. But it was up to her to discover if someone had *helped* Harv get to where he'd gone.

Amanda placed B.J. on the lawn chair that sat on the covered patio. "You stay here and eat your sucker, kiddo. If anybody turns in the driveway, come get me."

The little tyke nodded his matted blond head, then jabbered unintelligibly.

Amanda put on her most serious face. "I mean it, Beeje. You have to stay right here in this chair. Aunt Amanda is counting on you."

The boy nodded solemnly. Amanda patted his head, then strode off.

The front door was locked, but the window was open. Amanda quickly removed the screen and wedged through the opening.

"Oh, geez," she said as she glanced around the untidy living room. Dirty socks, shoes, and candy wrappers littered the yellow carpet. *Canary-yellow,* for heaven sake! What kind of person purchased yellow carpet?

Photos of Harvey Renshaw dressed in his military best lined the paneled room.

Proof enough that the man was exceptionally full of himself, thought Amanda.

She studied each photo carefully, noting there was a different woman standing beside Harv in each picture. But there was a pattern forming here, Amanda mused. Although Harv had his arm around different women, the females possessed similar physical attributes: bleach-blond hair, well-endowed chests, and clothes that accentuated their hourglass figures. Bimbos, one and all, Amanda concluded.

Nothing shallow about Harvey, she thought with a smirk. Harv liked cheap, tacky women, and he was obviously a chest man—the bigger the boobs the better he liked it. The jerk.

If Amanda suspected for even one second that Thorn had been after her body she would choke him! Surely he hadn't . . . had he?

The thought rankled. Impulsively Amanda marched toward the phone.

"Janie-Ethel, this is Amanda. I need to speak with Thorn immediately. Can you patch me through?"

"Sure thing, 'Manda. How was your honeymoon?"

"Marvelous," Amanda told the police dispatcher. "Please get Thorn on the horn, ASAP."

A few moments later the line crackled.

"Thorn here. What's the problem?"

"I'm not sure there is one, but I need to know if there might be," Amanda said.

"What the hell does that mean?"

"I want to ask you a question, Thorn, and I want the absolute truth."

She waited for Thorn to testify that he would give her the truth, and nothing but.

"I need to know if you started dating me because of my body."

Thorn must have been afraid of stumbling into an unseen trap, because he hesitated a moment, then said slowly, "That isn't a fair question. I would be lying if I said I didn't notice your gorgeous body at first glance. But if the package had come without your sharp mind and keen wit I wouldn't have been interested. Why did you call me while I'm on patrol to ask me that?"

"Because I felt the need to know, here and now."

"Why?" he persisted.

"Because I am standing in the middle of Harvey Renshaw's living room, looking at photos of him with his arm around several big-busted blondes wearing painted-on clothes. He was obviously more interested in looks than personality and intellect."

"What the hell are you doing out there?" Thorn squawked.

"Searching for clues," she replied calmly.

"If you're doing a B-and-E you can expect me to start yelling."

"I didn't break a single thing on my way through the window," she assured him, then waited for him to erupt in bad temper. Predictably, he blew a fuse.

"Get the hell out of there before someone sees you!" Thorn yelled at her. "Damn it, Hazard, you can't pull that crap now that you're my wife. I'm sworn to uphold the law, not bend it to suit my mood. Same goes for you."

"Oh, phooey, Thorn. You didn't deputize me when I married you."

"Don't get cute, Haz," he said warningly. "You know perfectly well that we can be bad reflections on each other's reputations. You don't see me trying to evade taxes to make you look bad as an accountant. Now get out of that house before somebody sees you!" he demanded a second time.

"Not to worry, Thorn. I have a reliable lookout watching the road. Rest assured that I will know the second somebody returns home."

"Who is with you?" he asked suspiciously. "It better not be County Commish Harjo! He isn't there, trying to convince you that you should have married him instead of me, is he?"

"Calm down, Thorn. It isn't Sam Harjo," she told him. "It's B.J. Hix."

"WHAT! You're kidding. You better be kidding. That kid is too young to be breaking into a life of crime. He's only eighteen months old! And what the hell is he doing there with you? Where's his mother?"

"Sis is on her way to the hospital to deliver her baby. Since I am B.J.'s honorary aunt, he has been entrusted into my care. Gotta run, Thorn. See ya, later."

"Damn it, Hazard, wait a minute—"

Amanda hung up on him. It seemed the thing to do since

she had been hung up on so often lately. It was gratifying not to be the one left holding the phone for a change.

With skillful efficiency, Amanda searched the kitchen cabinets and drawers to find bank deposit slips, two letters from Wife Number Three, and three letters from Rita Renshaw. Was that Wife Number Two or Four? Amanda didn't know, but she could guess what the woman looked like. Blond hair, big chest, skintight clothes, brain corroded from extensive use of peroxide.

Amanda also found the unsigned contract from Davidson and Daniels Oil Company that stated the legal description of the property where the new oil site was to be placed. Amanda wondered what D and D Oil would do since the land owner hadn't signed the contract agreement and couldn't be contacted without a seance.

The site couldn't be leveled, nor the access road graded, without the owner's signature. Whoever bumped off Harv had jumped the gun, because the nine thousand dollars to be paid for the well site, plus royalty for production, would not be signed over to the beneficiaries.

Amanda skidded to a halt when she entered the upstairs master bedroom. To her disgust, she saw posters of near-naked women—all blondes with silicone-enhanced chests—tacked to the walls. Amanda didn't even want to think about the repulsive poster that was stapled to the ceiling, directly above the red-velvet bedspread! It was pornography at its worst!

Harvey Renshaw was a womanizer deluxe, Amanda thought to herself. He was a discredit to his gender.

Ignoring the offensive surroundings, Amanda rifled through the clothes hamper, searching for oily garments. She found nothing. It seemed everyone around Vamoose had done their weekly wash.

After rummaging through the dresser drawers, she inspected the closet. Her gaze dropped to the closet floor to see a pair of work boots that were splattered with oil, and a wadded-up pair of blue jeans and green shirt.

Harvey's? Amanda frowned ponderously. Had Harvey replaced hydraulic hoses recently? If he had, then Amanda definitely had a case. She made a mental note to check Harv's farm receipts for replacement hoses . . . .

A loud squawk spurred Amanda into action. She dashed downstairs to the front door, then hurriedly replaced the window screen she had removed to enter the house. B.J. tugged on the hem of her shirt and made a stabbing gesture with his lollipop.

"You did good, kiddo. Really good. Definitely worth another sucker."

When a car door slammed, Amanda spun around and mustered up a greeting smile. The bleached blonde in painted-on jeans and a body-hugging cotton blouse glowered at her.

"What are you doing here?"

Amanda recognized the voice instantly. "Hello, Laverne. I came by to pick up Harv's farm expense account. I'll need them to figure his estate taxes and the Schedule D, E, and F forms for the IRS."

"Oh, all right," Laverne muttered as she wiggled and jiggled her way to the door.

Amanda stared dubiously at the paper sack and three plastic garment bags that were slung over Laverne's shoulder. Evidently, the woman had been on a shopping spree. *Now, where would a woman who can't afford to pay rent get the money to buy new clothes?* Amanda asked herself.

She decided to put the question to Laverne. "Now, where would a woman who can't pay rent get the money to buy new clothes?"

Laverne glared daggers over her shoulder as she unlocked the door. "I have to have something to wear to the funeral, don't I?"

Amanda stared consideringly at the garment bags. "How many funerals are you planning to attend? Are you expecting two other somebody elses to experience the same kind of bad luck Harv encountered?"

Laverne's cherry-red-coated lips curled in irritation. "You are definitely a pain in the—"

Amanda covered B.J.'s ears the split second before Laverne said the "ass" word. "Ignore her, Beeje. She has no class and a very limited vocabulary."

Laverne's arm shot sideways. "You better get the hell off my porch. *Right now,* lady!"

"It isn't your porch," Amanda countered. "It's Harv's, and I need his farming expense account. If you don't hand them over I will have the chief of police slap you with an obstruction of justice and due process. This is still Harvey's farm, you know."

"We'll just see who gets this farm," Laverne scowled as she barreled through the door. One minute later she returned to thrust a notebook and manila folders at Amanda. "You got what you wanted, so take a hike."

Amanda didn't budge. "Are you expecting to inherit this place?" she asked. "Don't hold your breath, Laverne. You are the first of four wives, one of whom has a child. Furthermore, Harv has a brother out there somewhere."

Laverne's eyes popped. "No shit? That's the first I've heard of it."

"You don't know how to contact the brother then," Amanda said carefully.

"Hell, no. I just told you I didn't know there was one."

"By the way," Amanda said, switching topics swiftly. "I need to know where you were yesterday morning."

"In bed, fast asleep," Laverne said sassily.

"All morning?"

"Yes, just ask Johnny. He was with me."

Rats, thought Amanda. *I shouldn't have pissed off Laverne.* Now the bimbo would coerce her boyfriend into corroborating her alibi.

"Oh, one more thing before I go. I'll need Harv's credit cards.

You can give them to me or I can simply call the companies and stop payment since I have power of attorney.''

Laverne glared at her for a long moment, her face crimson red, her mascara-caked eyes spitting fire. ''Wouldn't it be a d—''

''Don't swear in front of the kid—''

''—shame if you had an untimely accident like Harv?''

''Are you threatening me?'' She glanced down at B.J. ''Make a note of that, kiddo. If anything happens to your honorary aunt Amanda, you tell Thorn what you heard here today. Thorn will be all over Laverne like a bad rash.''

Amanda found it necessary to cover the kid's ears again. Laverne spewed a few more foul oaths. Laverne did, however, hand over two credit cards. Sure enough, they had Harv's name on them. There was no telling how much money this bimbo had spent while Harv wasn't around to stop her.

''Don't forge any checks,'' Amanda warned. ''I'm putting Harv's bank account on hold.''

''And I plan to post no trespassing signs on this property,'' Laverne seethed. ''Don't show your face at Harv's funeral Friday morning. And don't show up here again without calling first. Got it?''

Amanda smiled brightly. ''Sure thing, Laverne. Have a nice day,'' she said before she scooped up B.J. and carried him away.

Amanda broke stride when she noticed that Laverne's faded gray Buick had been washed recently. Confound it, her suspects weren't being the least bit cooperative!

With B.J. strapped in his seat belt—and Thorn would probably have a fit because Sis Hix had been in too much of a rush to unstrap the little tyke's car seat before she whizzed to the hospital—Amanda drove to the scene of the supposed accident. She wanted to take another look around, hoping a clue would leap up and call attention to itself.

While B.J. jabbered and pointed at the grazing cattle, Amanda studied the site. Had she overlooked an important piece of evidence here? A crushed cigarette butt? A wad of tobacco? Candy wrappers similar to the ones seen in Harvey's living room?

Her gaze moved instinctively toward the large pond that glistened in the sunlight. She noticed the cattle had gathered to drink from the narrow creek that fed the pond, instead of spreading out around the pond itself. Odd, she thought. But then, who could understand the behavior of cattle?

When a beat-up pickup veered onto the access road and rumbled toward the oil well site, Amanda got in her truck and followed. A burly, woolly-faced oil field pumper, who looked as if he could bench press several hundred pounds, climbed down from his truck.

"Yo!" Amanda called out. "Can I speak to you for a sec?"

"Sure, what's up?" LeRoy Ashton asked as he gave her the once-over.

Although Amanda did not appreciate being visually undressed, she ignored her irritation and cut to the heart of the matter. "I wasn't sure if you had been informed that the owner of this property died in a farming accident yesterday."

"Harv? Really?"

LeRoy didn't look shocked or saddened by the news, Amanda noted.

"Did you check this oil site yesterday morning?" she asked.

"Sure did. I check the pump every day. That's my job."

"Did you see Harv?"

"Sure did. He ate me out for driving too fast. Said I was disturbing his cattle," LeRoy said, then scowled. "Harv wasn't an easy man to deal with, you know."

"So you *did* speak with Harv yesterday," Amanda clarified.

"Yep." LeRoy pulled a cigarette from his pocket, then lit up. Amanda made note of his brand.

"Precisely where were you when you had your conversation with Harv?"

LeRoy blew smoke. "I was right here. Harv flagged me down. Why do you want to know?"

"Was he driving his tractor or his farm truck?" Amanda fired at him.

"His truck." LeRoy took a long draw on his cigarette.

"What time did you see Harv?"

"About eight-thirty. Harv wanted to know when the company was going to come by to pick up the contract and break ground on the new well site. I told him I didn't know. Harv seemed in a rush to get under way."

Why was that? Amanda wondered. Did Harv need ready cash to pay off Wife Number Three, or to set up Number One in the rented house? Or was there something else going on around here that Amanda didn't know about?

Amanda glanced down at LeRoy's dirty boots, then studied the battered truck that had enough mud stuck to it to fill a flower garden. LeRoy was a possible suspect, she mused. He had taken a verbal thrashing from Harv recently, and the pumper's boots might have oil spots under that layer of crusted mud.

There was only one problem with that theory, she reminded herself. She had yet to establish a strong motive. Damn, how was she going to pry information from this human gorilla without making him suspicious?

"Did Harv flag you down to pester you on a regular basis?"

LeRoy shrugged his massive shoulders. "What can I say? Harv was a pestering kind of guy. He was always checking production of the two wells on his property to make sure the company wasn't cheating him on royalties. Always looking over everybody's shoulder like he didn't trust us. But if you ask me, he was the sneaky one. He undercut the contract for the new well site."

Amanda frowned, bemused. "What do you mean?"

"I mean the new oil site was supposed to be located over there." He indicated the property to the north. "Corky Bishop was holding out for more money for the site and access road on his property. Harv found out how much Corky wanted and offered to make a deal for a thousand dollars less.

"Believe you me, Corky was hopping mad about it. Now that the site is scheduled to be located on Renshaw Farm, Corky won't receive the ten thousand dollars he was asking for the site and he sure as h ... er ... heck won't receive any royalty, because his land isn't in this section where production will take place."

Amanda processed the information quickly. She had dealt with enough oil companies to know that everyone who owned mineral rights on the producing section of land was paid a percentage of royalty, even if the actual site wasn't located on their property.

No wonder Corky Bishop popped his cork. Harv had finagled the neighboring farmer out of thousands of dollars.

"Did you see Corky yesterday?" Amanda asked.

LeRoy nodded his woolly head. "Yep. He was feeding cattle cubes to his herd when Harvey flagged me down."

Amanda stared over the rolling hill. For certain, Corky could have monitored Harv's coming and going from the rise of ground to the north.

When LeRoy checked his watch, Amanda knew the oil well pumper was anxious to get on with his business. "I am Harv's financial consultant. If you have any questions about the prospective oil site and contract, you can call my office." She handed LeRoy a business card.

"Hazard, huh?" LeRoy's gaze narrowed. "Aren't you the one who has solved several murder cases around Vamoose?"

Amanda knew the exact moment that realization dawned on LeRoy. His droopy eyes shot open wide and his unshaved jaw scraped his chest.

"You were interrogating me, weren't you? You think somebody killed Harv? You think *I* did it?"

"Calm down," Amanda said soothingly. "I don't exactly

know why my client ended up dead, but I believe in covering all the bases.''

"Well, I sure as hell didn't do Harv in!" LeRoy all but shouted. "I didn't like the jerk all that much, but I had nothing to gain. But Corky Bishop, that's another matter. In fact, I expect the oil company will make arrangements with Corky to drill on his property so we don't have to wait for Harv's estate to be finalized. One site is as good as another in this oil basin.''

After tossing suspicion Corky Bishop's way, LeRoy stamped off to check the pump and gauges on the reserve tanks. Amanda's shoulders sagged. Rather than eliminating possible suspects, she seemed to be collecting more names for her list.

As for LeRoy Ashton, Amanda decided to get the scoop on him the first chance she got. The man had become increasingly nervous when he realized who she was. Amanda had the unshakable feeling there was more to the relationship between LeRoy and Harv than land owner and oil field pumper. She was determined to discover if there was a serious conflict between them.

Pivoting on her heels, Amanda strode back to her clunker truck. She found B.J. propped against the door, sound asleep. The remains of his lollipop was stuck to the side of his face. Quietly as possible, she eased behind the wheel and drove to town.

CHAPTER SEVEN

By the time B.J. woke from his nap it was high noon. Amanda made a beeline to the Last Chance Cafe to feed her young investigative assistant. The diner was filled to capacity. Amanda scanned the red vinyl booths with an observant eye. When she noticed a bleached blonde sitting alone, she strode forward, fairly certain she recognized the woman.

"Hi, do you mind if we share your booth? The place is really crowded and poor little B.J. is starving," Amanda said.

As if on cue, B.J. rubbed his tummy.

The woman didn't appear the least bit concerned about the starving children in the world. *Well, too bad*, thought Amanda. She was going to park her carcass in this booth whether the bimbo liked it or not, which she obviously didn't.

"I'm Amanda," she said as she plunked B.J. in the high chair. "Are you new in town?"

"Why do you want to know? Are you the one-woman welcoming committee?"

Charming lady, thought Amanda. "Sort of. Vamoosians

make it a point to make newcomers feel welcome in our community. In fact, you might want to stop by the Methodist Church this Friday evening for the chicken noodle supper and slave auction. It's for a good cause.''

"Slave auction?" The blonde repeated curiously.

Amanda nodded. "Several men in the area have volunteered their time and skills as handymen."

"Sounds fascinating." Her bored tone indicated she couldn't care less.

Amanda decided to go out on a limb, here and now, since small talk was getting her nowhere fast. "I guess you must have been an acquaintance of Harvey Renshaw. Too bad about him."

The abrupt comment got an immediate reaction. The blonde's fake lashes fluttered up, her rose-tinted mouth drooped down at the corners. "What makes you say that? I don't even know you."

No, but Amanda knew Harv's type, after surveying the photos in his living room. "Are you Wife Number Two, Three, Four, or a previous girlfriend?"

Clearly, the woman was dumbfounded, because she gaped at Amanda.

When the waitress approached, Amanda rattled off the order without taking her eyes off the speechless blonde. "If you haven't heard yet, the grave-side service is scheduled for Friday afternoon."

"I have never heard of Harv Renshaw," the woman insisted—when she finally recovered her powers of speech.

Amanda smiled cattily. "Of course, you have. I saw your photo on Harv's wall." It was Harv's trophy case of women, she realized suddenly. "Did you have a chance to see Harvey before his untimely accident?"

Amanda realized she had thrown this woman off balance from the get go. It was an effective tactic she had developed and perfected during her previous investigations.

"Look, lady, I'm not looking for trouble," the blonde said as she nervously twisted the wedding band on her finger.

Amanda made note of the gesture.

"So . . . you're just hanging around until the will is read, is that it?" Amanda asked. When B.J. squirted catsup from the plastic dispenser and began finger-painting on the table, Amanda snatched up napkins to blot up the spill. "Patience, Beeje. Lunch will be here soon." She focused her attention on the blonde. "What's your name?"

The woman compressed her lips and stared at the far wall.

"I'm Harvey's financial consultant. I'll run across your name sooner or later, so why don't you save me some time and effort here?"

The woman's shoulders sagged as she sank back against the booth. "I'm Rita Renshaw."

Ah-ha! "Wife Number Two? From Texas, I presume, judging from your accent."

"Yeah," Rita admitted, then sipped her cola through the straw.

"I suppose you've met Laverne."

Rita waited until the waitress set two soft drinks for Amanda and B.J. on the table and walked away before replying. "Yeah, I met Laverne. A real piece of work. I can see why Harv dumped her. Can you imagine letting that sleaze bucket and her worthless boyfriend share the same house? That woman will bleed the estate dry if she's given half a chance."

"No, she won't," Amanda said with perfect assurance. "I confiscated Harvey's credit cards. Laverne's hands are tied. On my way to lunch I stopped by the bank to ensure payments on checks were stopped. If Harv's signature is questionable on outstanding checks I will know immediately. The police chief will nail Laverne if she tries to withdraw cash from the account."

"Good," Rita said spitefully. "That's what Laverne deserves. According to Harvey, she was the worst mistake he ever made. She sneaked around on him with some burly oil field worker while they were married.''

Amanda blinked, stunned. Could LeRoy Ashton have been previously—and presently—involved with Laverne? *Good grief, no wonder Harv gave LeRoy a hard time every chance he got.*

''Do you recall the oil field worker's name?'' Amanda asked.

Rita sipped her cola. ''Naw, it's been too long ago. All I remember is Harv muttering about oil field trash beating his time and that he was thankful he found a loyal woman like me.''

''What happened between you and Harv?'' Amanda questioned.

Rita smiled faintly. ''Harv was transferred from Texas to Georgia and some floozy came on to him. He claimed he'd gotten lonely, waiting for me to make arrangements to rejoin him. Hadn't meant for it to happen, he said. I was the one he loved, but that vamp got pregnant and claimed he was the kid's father. He felt obligated to marry her.

''I didn't want to grant the divorce, but Harv offered me a good settlement, and well . . . I found someone to console me while he was gone. When Harv flew back to Texas on several occasions to see me, he seemed different.''

''Different? In what way?'' Amanda inquired.

Rita shrugged. ''I dunno. Just different. He had changed somehow. He claimed he hadn't come to see me, just because he wanted a place to bed down for the night and a woman to snuggle up with. He said he had been doing a lot of thinking about *us* lately.''

''Did your relationship with the new man in your life last, what with Harvey showing up unexpectedly?''

Rita shook her head, bit into her steak sandwich, then replied belatedly. ''No, I guess I was hurt and on the rebound when Harvey left. I never got over losing him, and it was hard to give up on what we had together. I kept telling myself that I was probably wasting my heart on him, but I couldn't help myself. Harv was one of a kind.''

One of a kind? Not in Amanda's book! Womanizing jerks like Harv Renshaw were a nickel a dozen.

"So why are you in Vamoose now?" Amanda asked.

"Harvey flew in to see me last month and I . . ." Her voice trailed off.

"You considered rekindling the old flame?" Amanda said, filling in the blank. "I thought you said things were never the same, that Harv seemed different."

Rita squirmed in her chair and gobbled her sandwich.

"Well?" Amanda persisted. "Just what was the purpose of this trip?"

"I thought maybe we could start all over again. But when I got here to surprise him, I realized Harvey has been stringing me along during every pit stop he made to Texas. He had a live-in girlfriend and an ex-wife, so I told him the next time he flew to Texas and thought he might drop by, that he better think again. We were finished, this time forever.''

When the waitress returned with B.J.'s and Amanda's order, they chowed down. Before Amanda could swallow her second bite of hamburger, Rita grabbed her purse and stood up.

"See ya 'round, 'Manda."

"Wait a minute—"

Amanda choked for breath when the mouthful of beef pattie got lodged in her throat. B.J. whacked her on the back. "Thanks, kiddo," she wheezed as Rita made her swift departure.

Amanda kept her gaze glued to the parking lot, noting the model of the vehicle Rita was driving. A shiny yellow Ford zipped onto the street and sped off, headed south.

She didn't know what to think of Rita's tale. Amanda wasn't buying Harvey's line about getting lonely at the new Air Force base where he had been transferred . . . Or had he *asked* to be relocated? Whatever the case, Harvey seemed to be a rounder who left a trail of women behind him so he could double back when the mood suited him.

"B.J.! We do not *wear* mustard, we *eat* it." Amanda confiscated the mustard bottle and blotted the condiment that was smeared on the side of the toddler's head. "Now be a good boy and finish your hamburger. We have work to do this afternoon."

The kid yammered something unintelligible and then consumed his lunch.

"When I finish my work, we'll stop by the park and you can swing to your heart's content. Deal?"

The boy nodded excitedly.

Hanging onto B.J.'s gooey hand, Amanda exited the cafe. She didn't have a clue how she was going to entertain the little tyke while she studied Harv's farm expense account, phone bills, and bank receipts, but for certain, she wanted to check the financial records. A good gumshoe always followed the money trail to see what discrepancies turned up.

When Amanda reached her office, she gathered up paper and pens, hoping B.J. would while away his time doodling. However, B.J. had in mind to create a mural on the wall. Amanda finally convinced him that if he drew on the paper he could show his mom, dad, and his new sibling his masterpiece.

With B.J. sprawled belly-down on the floor at her feet, Amanda thumbed through the farm receipts. Her eyes widened in surprise when she noticed that Harv had spent very little money on hay for his cattle. She knew for a fact that Harv hadn't paid Dave Zinkerman. Who else had Harv stiffed to save on expenses? she wondered.

A frown puckered her brow when she saw the farming receipts from Tractor Supply. Harvey had replaced hydraulic hoses recently. That made her all the more suspicious about the events surrounding Harvey's death. Thorn's theory on faulty hoses causing the hydraulic lift to malfunction, while Harv was standing under the elevated bale, didn't hold water.

Definitely foul play involved here, Amanda concluded.

As Amanda sorted through the bank statements she noticed several withdrawals for cash—to the tune of five grand in the past two months. What was Harv spending money on? A settlement for Wife Number Three? No wonder Harv had undercut Corky Bishop's asking price for the oil well site. Harv must have wanted to recover the money he'd spent—on what, Amanda had no idea!

Amanda was anxious to meet Wife Number Three and grill her with questions. And then there was Anita Blankenship, who hadn't tried to make contact since the day of Harvey's death. Where was the most recent girlfriend anyway? The woman must have had something important to say, or she wouldn't have left a message for Amanda.

On impulse Amanda picked up the phone.

"Velma's Beauty Boutique. We have 'dos to die for." *Chomp, crack, pop.*

"Velma, this is Amanda. Do you know the name of the department store in the city where Anita Blankenship works? I need to contact her."

"No, but hold on a sec and I'll see if anybody in the shop has the scoop on Anita."

Amanda waited for Velma to pose the question to her clientele. The beautician came back on line with a *crackle* and *snap*. " 'It's Williams', Inc. She works in the lingerie department. But Sherry Bennett told Isabelle Franks that Anita didn't show up for work today or yesterday, and Sherry had to cover for her." *Pop, pop.* "I guess Anita is so distressed about Harv's death that she can't deal with her job."

"Does anybody know where Anita is staying? She left Renshaw Farm yesterday."

"That's news to me, hon. Hold on." *Snap, crunch.* "I'll see if there's any report from the grapevine."

Again Amanda waited for the beautician to gather and report the facts.

"Sorry, hon. We've drawn a blank in the Blankenship disappearance. Did you try the Laid Back Motel in Pronto? It's the closest rent-by-the-night in the area. Maybe Anita took a room so she didn't have to stay in the same house with Laverne.''

''I'll call the motel. Thanks, Velma.''

''No problem, hon. Oh, and I'm going to pencil you in for Thursday. We need to do something about your ... um ... sun-bleached hair. Don't want your hair to get too brittle. Those split ends can be a problem, too. Come in at two, hon.'' *Pop, snap.*

Amanda hung up the phone. By the time Velma dealt with these split ends and sun-bleached hair on Thursday, Amanda should have a long list of suspects. Perhaps Velma could provide information that would narrow down this ongoing list, Amanda thought hopefully.

As for Harv's missing girlfriend, Amanda wasn't wasting a second. She called the Laid Back Motel in Pronto.

''Laid Back Motel. How can I help you?'' The receptionist yawned in Amanda's ear.

''I would like to speak with Anita Blankenship, but I don't know what room she's in.''

''Blankenship?'' *Yawn.* ''Sorry, I don't have anyone registered under that name.''

''How about Rita Renshaw?'' Amanda asked.

''Nope, nobody here by that name.''

But who was to say Rita wasn't using an assumed name? Amanda knew Rita had driven south after lunch. Maybe Rita wanted to keep a low profile until the funeral.

Amanda replaced the receiver in time to see B.J. tugging on his training pants. ''Whoa, kiddo. Let's head to the bathroom!''

B.J. took off as fast as his short legs would carry him. Amanda was on his heels, but it was too late. B.J. had an accident, and Amanda didn't have extra training pants on hand.

Muttering, Amanda glanced around for makeshift breeches. As a last resort she wrapped the little tyke in six layers of paper towels, scooped him up, and headed for the door.

"Next time tell Aunt Amanda *before* you have to go, okay?"

B.J. clamped his arms around her neck and gave her a hug.

The phone rang before Amanda could lock the office. With B.J. wrapped around her neck like a boa constrictor, Amanda hurried to the phone. "Hazard Accounting."

" 'Manda? It's Bubba. Our little girl is here!"

"Congratulations. Did everything go okay? How's Sis doing?"

"Tired but fine," he reported. "I'm on my way home. Can you drop B.J. at the house?"

"Sure thing, Bubba. What did you name the baby?"

"Sissy," he said proudly. "See ya in fifteen minutes."

Amanda spun toward the door. "Well, B.J., you've got a little sister to take care of now. Sorry, kiddo, but we have to take a rain check on that trip to the park. Your daddy is coming home to see you."

When B.J. waved his arms wildly, he accidentally whacked Amanda in the nose. Her eyes watered, her nose turned as red as Rudolph the reindeer's, but she didn't scold the little tyke for his exuberance. After all, Beeje was excited about having a sister and he had helped her out of a scrape at the bank and on Laverne's front porch. What was a punch on the nose between pals?

Nick stirred the pancake batter vigorously. Since Hazard was late getting home, he decided to fix breakfast for supper. After the meal they would hightail it over to Hazard's rented farmhouse to gather up the last of her furniture.

When Hank, the tomcat, leaped onto the counter, Nick gave the annoying feline a nudge with his elbow. "Get down and stay down, or you'll take up residence outside and see how long you last with three dogs chasing you."

The cat openly defied Nick by making a second leap onto the counter. Scowling, Nick grabbed Hank by the hair on his neck and escorted him out the door where Bruno, Pete, and Napoleon, the Pyrenees sheepdog, were ready to give chase.

"Damned cat," Nick muttered as the hounds chased Hank up a tree. "Can't say I didn't warn you, pal."

Checking his watch, Nick poured batter onto the griddle. His pancakes had to be better than Hazard's specialty of shit on a shingle. Even the tomcat turned up his nose at that tasteless slop.

While the sausage was sizzling in the skillet, Nick flipped the flapjacks. Still no Hazard. Where the hell was she?

"Hi, honey. I'm home!"

Nick glanced over his shoulder, noting that Hazard had several stains on her powder-blue business suit, and red gunk in her hair. "Where's B.J.?"

"Bubba picked him up. And not a minute too soon. I was fresh out of training pants," Hazard said as she tossed her purse on the counter. "If we have kids, Thorn, I think we should have girls. They can't possibly be as messy as boys."

"I didn't know it was possible to pick and choose in the baby category." Nick leaned over to plant a welcome-home kiss on her lips. "We'll take what we get. So . . . what does B.J. have? A brother or sister?"

"Ten pounds and two ounces of sister named Sissy. Have you given any more thought to my theory that Harv didn't end up dead by himself?" she asked in the same breath.

Nick scooped up the pancakes and put them on the plates. "Nope."

"Thanks for nothing," Hazard grumbled. She plopped down in a chair. "I'll tell you what, Thorn, I'm not sure I can keep track of the possible suspects who had an ax to grind with Harvey. With four ex-wives, a missing girlfriend, a business associate who left town conveniently, and a neighbor who lost ten thousand dollars because Harv undercut him on an oil well site, I'm beginning to wonder how long it will take to pin down the suspect who has the strongest motive for murder."

"There is the possibility that it was just what it looked like—an accident," Nick reminded her.

Hazard pulled a face. "Always the skeptic, aren't you, Thorn? You have so little faith in my instincts. In my opinion, too many people have too much to gain from Harvey's death. I sorted through his farm expenses and bank accounts this afternoon. I discovered that Harvey had recently replaced the hydraulic hoses, because he purchased them at Tractor Supply."

Nick winced inwardly. He hadn't conveyed that information to Hazard, but it hadn't taken her long to dig that up.

"Harvey wrote three checks totaling five grand, and I seriously doubt he withdrew the cash to bury in his backyard for a rainy day."

Nick frowned when he saw the life insurance policy and abstract protruding from Hazard's oversize purse. "Don't tell me this stuff was laying around Harv's house, because I won't believe it. Where did you get it, Haz?"

"From Harv's safety-deposit box," she said, unabashed.

Nick's mouth dropped open, his midnight-black eyes rounded. "How in the hell did you manage that?"

Amanda waved off his question as she came to her feet. "I'll get the plates and syrup. Bring on the flapjacks, Thorn. I'm starved."

Nick grumbled under his breath. With each case Hazard unofficially investigated, she became increasingly bold about bending the laws. He and Hazard were definitely going to have another talk about that!

"Hazard, we need to talk."

"Sure, Thorn, what about?"

Nick placed the platter of pancakes on the table, then scooped up the sausage. "If you're going to investigate these cases, I expect you to practice SOP, standard operational procedure. You are not supposed to break one law in order to accuse somebody of breaking another one."

Hazard regarded him for a pensive moment. "Are you still

stewing about me ruining your reputation? Geez, Thorn, I'll bet you bent a few rules while you were doing undercover work for the narc squad at OCPD."

"That was different. I was dealing with the scumbags of the earth, and my life was on the line every second of every day in the trenches of the streets. Things are different in Vamoose. I'm the head cop, and I grew up here. I don't want gossip flying around that I married a loose cannon of an accountant who badgers the good citizens for the personal thrill she derives from conducting unofficial murder investigations."

"Personal thrill?" Hazard hooted indignantly. "Now listen here, buster, just because you're dragging your big feet in this case doesn't mean I intend to! I shouldn't have to tell you that a cold investigative trail is tough to follow. Murderers have a tendency to cover their tracks if no one is looking over their shoulders."

Nick sighed audibly. "Eat your flapjacks, Haz. We are not going to have an argument."

"Oh, yes, we are," she snapped. "If this marriage is going to work, then you are going to have to learn to be more supportive of my hunches. May I remind you that I have been right *six* times, and you have been *dead* wrong six times."

"Thanks for throwing that in my face," Nick muttered as he doused his pancakes with syrup.

"And don't forget who saved your bacon when Frank Lemon wound up dead in the driver's seat, and your job was on the line."

"Just shut up and eat," Nick said, and scowled.

"Fine," Hazard said smartly. "Go ahead and stick your head in the sand while I investigate. You can deal with those serious crimes like jaywalking and failure to come to a complete stop. I will handle the murder cases you ignore."

"Damn it, nobody killed Harvey!" Nick shouted. "What the hell do you expect me to do? End up squished under a hay bale when my hydraulic hose breaks, just to prove to you that accidents happen?"

"You're being absurd, Thorn. You always become absurd when you get angry. Calm down before your capillaries spring a leak. It is ridiculous to suggest I would want you squished under a hay bale. I like you just the way you are, except for your aggravating tendency to think I'm crying wolf when I cry murder."

Nick inhaled deeply, ordering himself to relax. He could handle Hazard. Despite everything, he was crazy about her and she was nuts about him. They simply had a teensy-weensy conflict when it came to her compulsive obsession with investigations.

"Okay, Haz, for the sake of argument, let's say Harv did not die of accidental causes. Who has the most to gain?"

Hazard chewed on her sausage. "I won't know for sure until I find the will and study the life insurance policy."

"Maybe Harv left his will with his lawyer. That's common practice."

Hazard shook her head. "Harv didn't trust lawyers. He informed me of that every time we had business dealings the past two years. That's why Harv hired me as his financial advisor and accountant. He didn't even bother to check his monthly bank statements. He ordered me to do it for him, then I mailed them off so he could cram them in the drawer. He never even cared how much money he had in his account because he knew there was plenty and he was always finagling to get more."

"Maybe lawyers gave him the shaft each time he went through divorce proceedings," Nick speculated. "Maybe that's why he didn't have a high regard for attorneys."

He cut Hazard a discreet glance. Her feathers were no longer ruffled and he'd calmed down considerably. They were discussing the possibilities of this case—real or nonexistent—like two rational, mature adults.

Headway, Nick thought with satisfaction.

"I don't think the divorce proceedings left him with a bad taste for lawyers," Hazard countered. "He just plain didn't like them on general principle. He said lawyers were the metamorphic stage of political bugs that needed to be stamped out for the good of the national population.

"According to Wife Number Two, there was no attorney involved, just a simple parting of the sheets as they say."

"Wife Number Two?" Nick frowned. "Where did she come from? This is the first time you've mentioned her."

"I had lunch with her today," Hazard informed him. "I recognized Rita Renshaw from a photo in Harv's living room. I'm not sure who Wife Number Four is, but I suspect she was in one of those photos on the wall.

"It really puzzles me that Harv flaunted his former marriages in pictures. How would you feel if I displayed photos of me with my arm around other men I dated?"

"I'd hate it," Nick was quick to admit.

"Yet, Anita Blankenship—"

"Who?"

"The latest girlfriend," Hazard informed him. "She was living with Harv and his trophy case of photos. Worse, Wife Number One moved into the house with the couple. According to beauty-shop gossip, Anita was crazy about Harv, despite all his shortcomings. And believe me, the man was rife with shortcomings. Why would any woman put up with that nonsense?"

"Maybe Anita was so lonely and hungry for affection that she chose to overlook Harv's flaws," Nick theorized.

"Maybe I'll know where Anita is coming from when I locate her. According to Laverne, Wife Number One, Anita left the house the day Harv died. She hasn't shown up for work since. Now, why is that, do you suppose?"

"You think it's because she has something to hide?"

"Or something to *tell,* and she's afraid Harv's killer is after her. And meanwhile, Laverne has been on a spending spree. I confiscated Harv's credit cards from her before she could max them out. I don't trust that foul-mouthed woman one bit.''

"Tell you what, Haz, I'll run a check on Laverne to see if she has been in trouble with the law. But as far as I know, all she has on her record is the speeding ticket Deputy Sykes gave her last month.''

"Check on her boyfriend while you're at it,'' Hazard requested between bites. ''Johnny Phipps is his name and dodging gainful employment is his game. He also has motive and plenty of opportunity, since he doesn't punch a time clock.''

"Phipps?'' Nick frowned. ''He's got to be at least ten years younger than Harv's first wife.''

"Really? Maybe the gossip around town is accurate. Laverne may have been using Johnny to make Harv jealous. And it must have worked, because gossip also indicated Laverne and Harv had been rekindling old flames when Anita and Johnny weren't underfoot.''

Nick glanced at the antique clock on the wall. ''We better get this show on the road, Hazard. It will take a couple of hours to load the rest of your belongings, haul them over here, and unload.''

Hazard bounded to her feet to clear the table. ''Give me five minutes to load the dishwasher and change into boots and jeans.''

Thorn couldn't help himself, he followed Hazard to the bedroom to watch her undress. He hoped that didn't label him a pervert, just because he enjoyed the feminine scenery in his bedroom. And although Nick meant what he told Hazard about appreciating her keen mind and interesting personality, he absolutely adored getting his hands on her sensational body.

As it turned out, it took more than five minutes for Hazard to change clothes . . . .

CHAPTER EIGHT

Amanda was exceptionally proud of Thorn. Although she had yet to convince him that Harv Renshaw's untimely death was outright murder, Thorn had volunteered to check police records on possible suspects. Amanda knew Thorn was still operating under that age-old male concept that plagued modern man: Women are not equal to men, mentally or physically. But Thorn, bless his heart, was trying to overcome Neanderthal conditioning.

The bottom line was that Thorn would aggressively investigate the Renshaw case if *he* had been the one who picked up suspicious evidence at the crime scene. In Thorn's defense, however, he had not been on hand to see the oil-free area of grass that indicated an unknown individual and unidentified vehicle were present at the time of the incident.

"Darn rain anyway," Amanda grumbled on her way to the office. "Thorn might have been convinced if he had seen what I saw."

Amanda climbed down from her clunker truck and unlocked

the door. She growled indignantly when she saw the ransacked condition of her office. Someone had broken in and de-alphabetized her files! Papers were strewn on the floor like casualties of war. How dare somebody violate her professional space!

Amanda immediately snatched up the phone to call Janie-Ethel, the police dispatcher. "Tell Thorn I need to see him pronto," she ordered.

"Sorry, Amanda, but the chief had to testify in court this morning."

Amanda frowned. "He didn't mention that to me before he left for work."

"He didn't know until he reported in," Janie-Ethel explained. "The domestic dispute was supposed to be settled out of court, but negotiations broke down. Do you want me to contact Deputy Sykes?"

"No, I'll wait for Thorn," Amanda said. "Tell him to call me the minute he reports in."

Scowling, Amanda stepped around the clutter and plunked down in her chair. She hoisted her oversize purse onto the desk and dumped out the important documents she had retrieved from Harv's safety-deposit box.

She was primed and ready to study the papers, but the phone rang. "Hazard's Accounting. Hazard-Thorn speaking."

"Hi, doll, it's Mother."

Amanda sighed inwardly. "Hello, Mother."

"I presume you disregarded my request to talk some sense into my wooden-headed daughter-in-law. She refuses to take my calls. I've spoken to that dang-blasted answering machine ten times in two days!"

"I did speak to Regina," Amanda informed Mother. "She is put out with you, and she hasn't cooled down enough for me to negotiate a compromise. Until further notice, you have no visitation rights."

"How dare she!" Mother howled. "Those are my grand-children—delinquents though they can be sometimes. Your daddy and I have a right to be an influential part of their lives. Heaven knows that someone who shows good sense needs to influence them.''

"According to Regina, you constantly criticize her motherly and wifely skills," Amanda said, then braced herself for Mother's indignant outburst.

Sure enough, Mother blew a gasket and her voice rose five decibels.

"I have done nothing of the kind!" Mother yowled. "I simply pointed out areas that needed improvement. I offered helpful pointers for disciplining unruly children and running a household in an organized, highly efficient manner!"

"The bottom line is that you are trying to run Regina's life and she resents it," Amanda paraphrased.

"I do not try to run anybody's life!" Mother spouted.

"Yes, you do," Amanda said firmly, directly.

"I do not! And I think you are wasting your talents in that hick town, married to that hick cop, but do I harp on the subject constantly? Of course not.''

Amanda bit back a laugh. Mother was contradicting herself all over the place.

"As for Regina," Mother went on, and on, "she simply wears her feelings on her sleeve. I don't consider it my problem that she takes offense to every little thing I say. Besides, Regina doesn't know how good she's got it. Things could be much worse. She could have Thorn's mom as a mother-in-law. Talk about a bona-fide hick, and proud of it! That vicious hillbilly doesn't know the meaning of class, style, or culture!''

"Maybe both of you need to look up the meaning of the words in the dictionary," Amanda mumbled.

"Pardon, doll?"

"Nothing, Mother. I'll have another talk with Regina when I can spare the time. Right now I really need to get to work. The honeymoon put me two weeks behind schedule in the office, and my secretary left on vacation.''

"This is a family matter and family comes first," Mother contended.

Amanda was not going to hop aboard Mother's Guilt Trip Express. She had important work to do.

" 'Bye, Mother. I'll be in touch."

Mother was still yammering about family obligation when Amanda hung up. But then, Mother always yackety-yakked about one thing or another. The woman thrived on turmoil.

"Now then," said Amanda. "Where was I?"

Ah, yes, now she remembered. She pulled the insurance policy from its colorful folder. Her eyes popped when she saw the list of beneficiaries on Harv's policy. Wives Number One, Two, and Three were to receive equal shares of the thirty-thousand-dollar policy. It wasn't an enormous amount of money, but definitely enough to give a woman a financial boost if she was down and out.

Amanda frowned as she studied the document more closely. There was no mention of Wife Number Four. There was no mention of a brother. There was no mention of a child.

Hmmm. Pensively Amanda plucked up the property deed. The deed of joint tenancy listed Harv Renshaw . . . and Harv Jr. . . .

Amanda slumped back in her chair and drummed her pencil on the edge of her desk. So Harv had acknowledged his son, despite the gossip that indicated Harv was not the biological father. Wife Number One and Two refused to believe Harv was responsible for Number Three's child, but Glenda Renshaw would inherit the real estate on behalf of her underage son, as well as a portion of cold, hard cash from the insurance policy.

Talk about strong motivation, thought Amanda. Glenda Renshaw would be sitting pretty, wouldn't she? Her son would be entitled to Social Security benefits until he was eighteen and perhaps receive military benefits for his higher education. The kid had it made. His father had seen to it.

The more Amanda thought about it, the more she decided

the bequests were apropos. Harvey Renshaw used women for his personal enjoyment, but he compensated them with cash—except for the mysterious Wife Number Four. Harv had seen to it that his flesh and blood inherited the property that had been in his family for generations . . . .

But what about the missing brother?

Amanda jerked upright in her chair. What had happened to Harvey's sibling? Why hadn't he inherited half the family farm when old man Renshaw passed on? When had Harvey inherited the family property? Had he bought out his brother's half?

Amanda began rifling through the abstract. To her surprise she noted that Harold J. Renshaw had deeded his half of the farm to Harvey more than a decade earlier. Amanda hurriedly read through the document to note that Harold J. had been paid one dollar for his 320 acres of farmland and mineral rights.

One lousy dollar? Amanda shook her head in astonishment. *Why would Harold J. settle for a dollar and relinquish mineral rights to his brother?* Nobody with any brains gave up mineral rights these days, not when oil-drilling companies were poking holes in the Oklahoma countryside left and right. And where the Sam Hill was Harold J., who had a whopping one dollar in capital gains on farm property?

The question hounded Amanda while she perused the other documents from the safety-deposit box. She located the titles to Harvey's vehicles—one Jeep, a wheat truck, and the gray Buick sedan Laverne drove.

Titles to the Jeep and wheat truck had Harvey Jr.'s name on them, Amanda noted. Oddly, Harvey had given Wife Number One the title to the Buick. *Why?* Amanda asked herself.

Amanda's frown deepened when she came across a brown envelope that contained three U.S. savings bonds. The bonds were issued to Harvey Renshaw and his three ex-wives. Each ex-wife was to receive one thousand dollars when the bonds matured.

Although Harvey used women, he took care of them financially. Why?

Quite honestly, Amanda didn't know what to make of Harvey Renshaw. The man had her befuddled.

Her thoughts trailed off when the bell over the door jingled, and Thorn, dressed in his police uniform, strode inside.

"What the hell . . . ?" He stopped short to survey the disaster.

"I had a midnight visitor," Amanda said. She gestured to the stack of documents on her desk. "I suspect the prowler was looking for the papers I crammed in my purse for safekeeping."

Dumbfounded, Thorn glanced around the office. "Hell, Hazard, somebody seems all-fired anxious to know who inherited Harvey's worldly possessions."

"Kinda makes a person wonder if somebody bumped Harvey off to get their sticky fingers on all his worldly possessions, doesn't it?"

Thorn squatted down to study the income tax forms that belched from file folders. "A through Q," he murmured.

"The R's are over there." Amanda pointed her glitter-coated orange index finger at the scattered papers on the north side of her desk. "The Renshaw forms are missing. Fortunately, I keep backup copies on computer disks—"

The thought brought Amanda to her feet. "Oh, damn, I didn't check to see if the computer disks had been disturbed."

Amanda dashed into the supply room, then sagged in relief when she noticed her fireproof file box was still locked up tight as a drum.

"This B-and-E could simply be cause and effect, chain of events," Thorn said as he propped himself against the door-jamb. "Your prowler might have wanted prior information about how much dough he and/or she would inherit."

"You think my prowler is the sort of individual who likes to be prepared? Brilliant theory, Sherlock," Amanda said, and smirked. "But I do agree with you that the prowler is not necessarily the murderer."

"I didn't say anything about mur—"

"I realize that," Amanda cut in. "After reading through Harvey's important documents I discovered that every suspect on my list has motive. Take a look-see, Thorn. Several Vamoosians will be considerably wealthy when Harv's estate is settled."

Thorn stepped around the strewn folders to study the insurance policy, U.S. savings bonds, vehicle titles, and property deed.

"Man, Harv was generous to his harem of women, wasn't he? I'm getting the impression that he never met a woman he didn't love."

The comment brought Amanda's thought processes to a screeching halt. Thorn, being a man, had gotten a handle on Harv immediately. Harvey Renshaw suffered from the Harem Complex.

Hmmm. Amanda wondered if there was Turkish blood in Harv's ancestry.

"Good work, Thorn," she praised him.

Thorn's brows furrowed. "What did I do?"

"You pinpointed Harv's MO. I hadn't been able to put my finger on it. Having four ex-wives, and countless girlfriends, was as close as he could come to actually being the master of a harem in our society." Her gaze narrowed on Thorn. "But don't you dare contemplate the concept. You spoke the till-death-do-us-part vows, and I would hate to have to kill you to make it stick."

Thorn grinned rakishly as he swaggered toward her. "Don't worry, darlin'," he said in an ultrasexy drawl. "You're more than enough woman to keep me happy for the rest of my life."

With dramatic flare Thorn bent Amanda over backward and planted a steamy kiss right smack-dab on her lips. And that, Amanda decided before she momentarily lost the ability to process thought, was one of the many reasons she had never been able to get this dynamic country cop out of her system. His spontaneity always gave her a thrill. He was the spicy variety in her methodical life.

Oh, what the hell, Amanda thought as she grabbed Thorn by the lapels of his uniform and towed him into the supply room so she could lock the door.

His thick brows elevated when he noticed the twinkle in her eyes. "Can't wait until tonight, huh?" he teased as he helped her out of her clothes.

"Nope," Amanda said, then divested Thorn of his shirt. "This is going to be the best midmorning break I've had in years . . . ."

After Thorn dusted for prints, Amanda set her office in order. When Thorn sauntered off—with a wink and a grin—to deliver his findings to the county crime lab, Amanda sank down at her desk to sift through the other envelopes from Harv's safety-deposit box. The jingling phone interrupted her before she could begin work.

"Hello? I mean . . . Hazard Accounting."

"Is this Amanda Hazard?" came a quiet, feminine voice.

"Yes."

"I need to speak privately with you."

"Anita?" Amanda guessed.

"No, this is Glenda Renshaw."

Ah, Wife Number Three. But what the heck had happened to Number Four? Would she report in eventually?

Amanda wondered if Glenda had become overanxious and rifled through the office files. "Was there anything in particular you were looking for in my office?"

"What do you mean?" Glenda asked warily.

"I think you know what I'm implying."

"No, I don't think I do," she said in her sweet, little, Melanie

Griffith-sounding voice. "Are you referring to that little spat I had with Laverne and Rita after the funeral?"

Amanda blinked. "The funeral was today?"

"Yes. Ten o'clock this morning."

Laverne had told Amanda the service would be held on Friday. Why hadn't Number One wanted Amanda to attend?

"I can meet with you after lunch, but I have an appointment at two," Amanda said. "Where do you want to meet?"

"Some out-of-the-way place," Glenda requested. "Laverne has been hovering around like a vulture. I think she has her boyfriend spying on me."

So that's why Johnny Phipps is nowhere to be found. Laverne has enlisted him for stakeouts.

"Fine, we'll meet at my grandfather's place. It's a few miles from Adios." Amanda gave precise directions to the secluded farmhouse. "Meet me at twelve-thirty. There's a two-car garage on the property. Park your car inside and we'll take a stroll through the trees."

"Thank you," Glenda said quietly. "I hope I can make it without my shadow following me."

Amanda scooped up Harv's important papers and crammed them into her purse. No way was she leaving these documents in plain sight, not with a prowler ripping her office apart.

Amanda jogged across the street to grab a bite at the Last Chance Cafe. The noon crowd had yet to descend on the diner. Only two patrons were ensconced in the booths, sipping coffee. Amanda's radar gaze zeroed in on Corky Bishop, the neighboring farmer whom Harv had undercut for acquisition on a third oil well site.

Pasting on a smile, Amanda strode toward the booth and parked herself across from Corky. The crusty old farmer glanced up from beneath his grimy ball cap. In his pin-striped Osh-Kosh overalls, Corky reminded Amanda of the male version of Popeye's girlfriend, Olive Oyl. Corky had noticeable circles under his dark eyes, a pinched expression around his mouth. It was the look of a man dealing with stress, and suffering from sleepless nights.

Now, what could be haunting this rancher? Amanda wondered.

"What do you want, Hazard?" Corky asked without preamble.

"I thought we might do lunch," she said. "I'm all by my lonesome and so are you. We could share conversation over a meal."

Corky hitched his thumb toward the other patron who was devouring a bacon cheeseburger. "Go bother Stu Humphrey. I'm not in the mood for companionship."

"Why not?" Amanda asked with pretended innocence. *Worried about someone tracking you down to question you about your involvement in Harvey's death?*

"Because times are hard on the farm and I have to mentally sort out what to do," Corky mumbled, then sipped his coffee. "Go away, Hazard."

"Geez, Corky, that's not a nice way to talk to your accountant. If you need financial consultation I'm here to help." She smiled brightly. "I'm all ears. What's the problem?"

Corky opened his mouth, then snapped it shut when the waitress arrived.

"Whatcha want Amanda? The usual?"

"No, give me the high-cholesterol special," she replied. "Fried chicken fingers, French fries, and a chocolate malt."

"Coming right up." The waitress heated up Corky's coffee, then whizzed off to give the order to the cook.

Amanda leaned forward, elbows on the table, her gaze fixed on Corky. "So what's the problem? Cattle prices down? Hay and cattle cube prices up? Wheat prices down? Fertilizer prices up?"

"Yeah, all that." He stared at the contents of his cup as if it were a crystal ball that would reveal all the answers to his troubling questions.

"And it didn't help when Harvey Renshaw undercut your negotiations with D and D Oil Drilling Company, did it?"

Amanda gauged his reaction. She saw his pupils dilate, his nostrils flare. Yep, Corky was experiencing angry resentment. It was as plain as the mole on the tip of his nose.

"Figured you would hear about that. Nothing slips past you, does it, Hazard?"

"I try very hard not to let it," she told him. "I'm an accountant, you know. I've been trained to pay strict attention to details. So . . ." Amanda took a sip of the water the waitress left for her. "You were feeding cattle cubes in your pasture when Harv flagged down LeRoy Ashton, the oil field pumper."

When Corky refused to respond, Amanda stared him down. "No sense denying it. LeRoy said he saw you at eight-thirty that morning."

Hesitantly Corky nodded. "Yeah, I saw Harv giving the pumper what for."

"And you drove your truck over to Harv's pasture to have it out with him about the proposed well site, when he returned later, driving his tractor with a hay bale stuck on the front of it."

Corky jerked up his head and thrust out his pointed chin. "I did no such thing!"

Amanda looked under the table at Corky's boots. They were worn down at the heels and splattered with mud. It was impossible to tell if grease stains coated his footwear. Regardless, Amanda decided to be persistent. In her opinion Corky had GUILTY written all over his leathery face. The man had financial problems that could have been resolved if Harv hadn't undercut the negotiated price of the new oil well site.

"I believe you did drive over to talk to Harv," she insisted. "You wanted to air your frustration. Times are hard and you need extra cash from a well site and royalty benefits from production. You wanted to tell Harvey exactly what you thought of his back-stabbing deal with D and D. What did Harv do? Make some snide comment that ticked you off? Did he gloat?''

Corky blew out his breath between clamped teeth. His hand clenched around his cup.

Amanda tightened the thumbscrews. ''He did tick you off, didn't he? He taunted, he antagonized. He reminded you that you also lost the chance to provide the water supply from your farm pond that the oil company needs during the drilling process. You lost another couple thousand dollars that would have paid mounting bills.''

''All right, yes, damn it,'' Corky burst out. ''I went to see him and he needled me until hell wouldn't have it.''

''So you gave a yank on the hydraulic hose while Harv was under the elevated hay bale, pulling off nylon strings.''

''No!'' he objected loudly.

The cook, waitress, and Stu Humphrey glanced up. Corky slumped in his seat and muttered curses.

''No,'' he repeated. ''I *did not* tamper with the hydraulic hose. I got in my truck and I left.''

Well, Hazard, what did you expect the man to do, blurt out a confession? There wasn't a jailbird in prison who claimed to be guilty. Corky was no different. He was not about to fess up to a crime, especially while he was running around scot-free—and hoped to stay that way.

When the waitress delivered the food, Corky attacked his meal, leaving no time for conversation. Amanda knew she would have to interrogate Corky in private if she hoped to wring more information from him. She would have to get him off by himself, push his anger button and hope his tongue broke loose.

Of course, there was always the possibility that he, like everybody else Amanda had pinned down in previous investigations, would try to silence her—permanently. Then she would have to rely on Thorn to rescue her from imminent disaster, and that always pissed him off. Thorn absolutely hated it when she put herself in jeopardy while solving a case.

Amanda dipped her fries in catsup and chewed thoughtfully. She asked herself if this was a crime of passion or greed. In Corky's case it could have been both. Anger might have been the triggering mechanism that spurred him to retaliate, but greed might have been his ultimate goal. Corky knew the dangers of hydraulic hoses. He knew how to leave Harvey dead in the hay and make the dastardly deed look like an accident.

Corky Bishop had opportunity and motive, Amanda assured herself. With Harvey out of the way, D and D Oil Company would renegotiate with Corky.

"Harvey's loss is your gain, isn't it?" Amanda said between bites. "The oil well pumper all but told me that the company plans to deal with you since Harvey's estate will be tied up indefinitely."

Corky sucked in his breath and choked on his foot-long chili-cheese Coney. He coughed and sputtered until his face turned blue. Quick as a wink, Amanda bounded up to perform the Heimlich maneuver. Although she made a spectacle of herself when she climbed on the seat, her legs sprawled on either side of Corky's ribs, and her arms clamped around his chest, she managed to save him from choking.

"Nice work," the cook complimented her. "You okay, Corky?"

The bean-pole-framed farmer nodded and wheezed.

Amanda untangled herself and pulled down her high-riding skirt. When she plopped down to finish her meal, Corky stared solemnly at her.

"You probably saved my life. Thanks," he gasped.

"Too bad I wasn't there in time to do the same for Harvey," Amanda said pointedly.

Corky sipped his water. "Or maybe you did the world a favor by *not* being there."

Amanda peered intently at Corky. She still wasn't certain if he had choked because he was surprised *she* knew about the oil negotiations or surprised the new site would be erected on *his* property. Corky refused to say one way or the other.

Amanda checked her wristwatch. She was running on a short clock. She gobbled her meal, left a generous tip for the waitress, and hauled butt. She would have to put the pedal to the metal to keep her private appointment with Glenda Renshaw.

"Hi, Pops, Salty," Amanda greeted her grandfather and the Vietnam vet who stood guard with his trusty shotgun.

Salty lowered the gun barrel when Amanda stepped from the shadows of the garage. "You're supposed to announce yourself when you come around here," Salty reminded her gruffly.

"You're supposed to recognize my old truck when you see it," she sassed him, then winked good-naturedly.

Salty snorted, refusing to be bowled over by Amanda's teasing smile. "I met too many enemies dressed as friendlies while I was skulking around in the armpits of the world for Uncle Sam. A man's gotta be cautious. Sometimes the first reckless mistake you make is your last."

Ignoring Salty's gruff, cynical manner—because she knew for a fact that he was a tenderhearted softy when you got past his armor—Amanda gave him a peck on the cheek, then hugged Pops.

She surveyed the three-story wood-frame house that was once obscured by overgrown weeds, untended shrubs, and a thick windrow of cedar trees.

"You guys have done a fantastic job spiffying the place up." Amanda admired the newly painted peak of the house. "I hope you didn't climb up a ladder, Pops. You were supposed to give up your acrobatics when you received your first Social Security check."

Pops steadied himself on his aluminum walker. The sunlight reflected off his bald head and his wire-rimmed glasses. "Nope, I worked from the ground. Salty is the daredevil around here."

"I came to ask a favor," Amanda said. "I need to use this place for a private conference. Do you mind?"

Pops's dentures gleamed when he smiled. "You're working a new case, aren't you? You think somebody did in that Renshaw character?"

"Wouldn't be surprised," Salty put in. "I've been around career military men a lot, but I never met one so stuck on his false sense of self-importance. Couldn't talk shop with that one. I tried once. Waste of time. As long as he spent in the service, you'd have thought he would've risen to a higher rank before he retired."

"Why do you think he didn't?" Amanda asked.

"Probably because he was a damned sight better at giving orders than taking them," said Salty. "He reminded me of soldiers I knew who had a racket going on the side, the kind of guy who was always trying to make an extra buck. It wouldn't surprise me to learn that Harv shipped that Jeep of his home in disassembled parts, then put it together. No telling how many ways Renshaw managed to screw the government out of money."

Amanda pondered Salty's comments until she heard an approaching vehicle. She pivoted to see a car racing over the hill.

"Come on, Pops." Salty gestured toward the back door. "Let's make ourselves invisible while Amanda does her thing. I'll beat your socks off at gin rummy while we're hiding out."

"Beat my socks off?" Pops snorted. "That will be the day, you whippersnapper!"

Amanda smiled fondly as the two men disappeared around the side of the house. Yes indeed, Pops and Salty were providing good company for each other. These two lonely men had become steadfast pals.

She wondered if Harvey Renshaw knew the meaning of a steadfast pal. Probably not. Loyalty and trustworthiness didn't appear to be on his list of positive character traits. If they had, maybe Harvey wouldn't have ended up dead in the hay.

CHAPTER NINE

Amanda watched the shiny green Dodge Neon cruise through the tree choked intersection, then zip into the driveway and duck into the garage. A few moments later, Harvey's wheat truck topped the hill.

Amanda squinted into the sunlight, but she couldn't ID the driver. Was it Laverne or Johnny following Glenda?

The driver—whoever it was—couldn't determine which direction Glenda had taken. Too many cedar trees lined the intersection in the boondocks of Vamoose County. The battered farm truck sat in the middle of the road for a full minute before cruising over the hill and disappearing from sight.

"I think I lost him," Glenda said as she stepped into view.

Amanda turned to appraise the busty bleached blonde who had a girlish voice. Glenda could have been Laverne and Rita's sister. All three women looked amazingly alike, dressed in the same body-accentuating attire, their heads capped with the same platinum shade of hair color, their 38D's projecting forward like headlights.

"I know you're a busy woman, Amanda, so I'll get right to the point," Glenda said. "Although rumor around here has it that I tricked Harvey into marrying me, I want you to know that Harvey Jr. is Harv's son."

Glenda opened her wallet and tapped her crimson-red acrylic nail on the photo. "You would have to be blind in both eyes not to see the family resemblance."

Amanda studied the photo intently. *Yep,* she thought. *Definitely Harv's kid. Same expression around the eyes and mouth. Same hair color.* The kid, who looked to be about six years old, was the spitting image of his father. Amanda could only hope Junior hadn't inherited Harvey's Harem Complex.

"First off, you should know that I am the one Harv really loved," Glenda said with great confidence.

Gee, where had Amanda heard that before? Same song, third verse. No doubt there was a fourth verse—if and when Wife Number Four showed her platinum-blond head in town. *Would* she show up? Amanda wasn't sure. As of yet, Amanda hadn't run across any documents indicating Number Four would inherit. Maybe Wife Number Four was the only one of the harem who realized she had been played for a fool and had cut off all communication with Harvey.

"Harvey and I were deliriously happy until his dad passed on and Harv inherited the farm. He felt obliged to return to Vamoose, but I didn't want to make the move. I grew up in Georgia. My parents were beside themselves, fearing they would lose the close connection between them and their only grandchild."

"Did Harv get along with his in-laws?" Amanda asked.

Glenda's gaze dropped to the toes of her Reebok tennis shoes. "No, Harv and Daddy were always crosswise of each other. Daddy retired from the Air Force and still does consultation at the base. He and Harvey seemed to have a conflict of military philosophy."

"So Harv decided to take his retirement and move to

Vamoose," Amanda presumed. "Was he going to send for you and the boy?"

Glenda was still studying the toes of her shoes. "That's what he said, but I was reluctant to leave my job and uproot little Harvey. A month passed, then two. Every time I called Vamoose I received the message that the phone had been disconnected. An entire year passed and Harvey never called, never wrote, not even to his son."

Glenda looked up. An onrush of tears caused her mascara to bleed black rivers on her cheeks. "Then one day out of the blue Harv showed up in Georgia."

"When was this?" Amanda questioned.

"About eight months ago, then again four months ago, and then two months ago. Harv flew into the Air Force base to tell me he wanted a divorce, though he still loved me, would always love me. He said he knew little Harvey would be better off in Georgia, the grandson of military high echelon. There was something odd about his behavior the past few months, an uneasiness, restlessness, or something. I didn't know what was going on and he wouldn't say."

"So you decided to check out the situation in Vamoose and see if you could tolerate living in this small rural community?" Amanda questioned, still baffled that Glenda had waited so long to check out the situation. "Did you expect to find your husband shacking up with his latest girlfriend and allowing Wife Number One and her boyfriend to share the residence?"

The blunt remark caused Glenda's watery eyes to glitter. Outrage and humiliation had raised their unruly heads, Amanda guessed. Soft-spoken Glenda had probably come unhinged when she saw, firsthand, that she had been replaced by two look-alikes.

"Harv told me that loneliness drove him into the situation and he hadn't known how to extricate himself," Glenda said.

"Did you suggest ordering Wife Number One and the new girlfriend off the premises?"

"Of course I did. Harvey and I are still married."

Amanda blinked. "You are?" Then how could Harv have married Number Four . . . unless he committed bigamy. *Damn, Harv had royally screwed up his personal life!*

"Of course we are!" It was the first time Glenda had raised her voice. The high-pitched sound was like fingernails scraping a blackboard. Amanda's sensitive ears tingled and gooseflesh pebbled her skin.

"Don't tell me, let me guess," Amanda insisted. "Harv claimed that he didn't deserve you, that he had shamed you, and himself, by sinking so low when loneliness and despair overcame him—or something to that effect."

"Yes, he did. How did you know?"

"Wild guess. So, you drove out to speak privately with him the morning he died," Amanda speculated. When Glenda didn't respond, Amanda became persistent. "You must have met Harv on the access road to the oil site, because the house was entirely too crowded for a private conference."

"No, I went to the house."

Amanda was stunned. Glenda had more gumption than her timid, girlish voice indicated. Either that or she was lying, because she didn't want any connection between herself and the crime scene.

"Where were Laverne and Johnny?"

Glenda sniffed distastefully and swiped at her tears. "They were lounging at the kitchen table, sipping coffee. I'm not sure but I would swear they were nursing hangovers."

"They weren't in bed, fast asleep?" That was what Laverne had said when Amanda asked.

Glenda shook her head. Her brittle blond hair never moved. It must have been coated with industrial-strength hair spray.

"Definitely not. Laverne was decked out in a skimpy red negligee, and Johnny was in boxer shorts with Valentine hearts and Cupids printed on them."

"And Anita Blankenship?" Amanda quizzed Glenda. "Was she there, too?"

Glenda shifted uncomfortably. "She was on her way out the door when I stepped onto the front porch. She really blew up when she saw the wedding ring on my hand. Harv tried to, but he never got her calmed down before she left the house."

Amanda imagined the shit had hit the fan when Number Three showed up, and Number One was still lounging around in her sexy nightgown.

"What time did you arrive at the house?"

"About seven-forty-five, I guess. Anita kept carrying on about how she was the one Harv really wanted, needed, and loved, and how Laverne and I were trying to break up their perfect relationship. She said she knew Harv had met with Rita, too, and that he was also seeing someone else that Harv didn't think she knew about."

"Who was that?" Amanda asked curiously.

Glenda shrugged. "Anita didn't name names. She became hysterical so Harv shoveled her out the door and off to work. Anita kept railing about how she would be the one who held onto Harv until the end."

"The poor woman freaked out," Amanda diagnosed.

"In a big way. We could hear her gunning the engine of her car as she blazed off."

"Were you allowed to speak privately with Harv?"

Glenda sighed audibly. "Not at first. Laverne refused to leave the room, but she sent Johnny off to the bedroom to sort his socks."

"And he went dutifully?"

"He complained loudly and told Harv he was going to pay dearly for keeping everybody's life in upheaval. But then he left, because Laverne lit into him with that whiplash tongue of hers and berated him in front of us."

Amanda no longer wondered how Johnny Phipps felt about all the females Harv kept at his beck and call. It must have

been difficult to stomach, even if Johnny was getting all the
hot sex he wanted while Laverne was using him in an attempt
to win Harv back. And who was to say that Johnny actually
retired to the bedroom? He could have gone outside to eavesdrop on the conversation, then followed Harv to the pasture.

Now for the burning question, Amanda mused. "Did Harv
offer you cash compensation for the hurt and humiliation he
had caused you?"

Amanda was dying to know if the five grand Harv had
withdrawn from his bank account was meant for Glenda and
little Harvey.

"No, he didn't give me any money."

"No?" Well, that theory had just been shot to hell . . . unless
Glenda was lying through her pearly whites.

"I tried to convince Harv to come back to Georgia with me
and turn his life around. I told him we could get back together
and make it work. Laverne kept shouting that I could get down
on my bony knees and beg all I wanted, but Harv never really
wanted me in the first place, that I had tricked him into marrying
me. It wasn't until Harv hauled her into the bathroom and
jammed the lock on the door that we could talk freely.

"Harv said he would get away from Vamoose and give our
marriage another try, as soon as he could, but that he had a
few business arrangements to make before he left."

"Did you believe he was going to come back to you?"

Glenda's lower lip trembled, but she didn't cry. Good thing,
too. Her mascara couldn't withstand another onslaught of tears.

"He said he would, *promised* he would. I wanted him to,
but then he suffered that terrible accident."

Accident? My eye, thought Amanda. She studied Glenda
astutely. It would be easy to fall for this soft-spoken tale. For
sure, Glenda made her story sound convincing, but an entire
year had passed since she had heard from Harvey, then came
another two years of separation. Surely this woman hadn't

carried a torch that long. No, Glenda was after money. Amanda would bet on it.

Amanda could not overlook the fact that Glenda had very strong motivation. She was going to walk away with a helluva lot of money, and her son would own the farm—unless the missing will stated otherwise.

Furthermore, Amanda just couldn't picture Glenda standing there, watching the circus at Renshaw Farm, meeting the two other women Harv was shacking up with, without blowing her stack.

Amanda frowned pensively. She had been operating under the theory that whoever broke into her accounting office wanted to find the will, hoping to determine what he/she had to gain. But what if the prowler intended to confiscate the will, then dispose of it, because it would be to her advantage if the document no longer existed?

Who had the most to gain if there was no will? Aside from Corky Bishop, who would have instant cash in his pockets now that Harvey wasn't around to sign the contract for the proposed well site, Amanda qualified.

Amanda mentally tabulated the cash inheritance and property that Glenda would control. She would be sitting pretty if there was no will to override the bonds and property in joint tenancy.

"This is all very interesting," Amanda said as she ushered Glenda to her car. "I'll be in touch when I have Harv's estate in order." She took a shot in the dark, inspired by a suspicious hunch. "By the way, who did you hire to follow you around so I would think you were as much the victim as Harv?"

Glenda recoiled as if she had been slapped. "I did no such thing! How dare you make such an accusation!"

The abrupt change in Glenda's voice startled Amanda. Fortunately, Haz recovered quickly. "Look, lady, I'm not the one jockeying for position as prime beneficiary. And secondly, if specifically indicated in the will—" provided there is one— "the property, insurance, and saving bonds will be dispensed

according to Harv's most recent wishes. Tell your friend that
he is wasting his time driving around in Harv's truck in an
effort to convince me you're in danger. I'm not buying it.''

Glenda's face exploded with color. She compressed her lips
and clenched her fists. Amanda thought Glenda looked as if
she was ready to throw a punch. The blonde with the Melanie
Griffith voice was no shrinking violet, that was for sure.

"Just try laying a hand on me, and Salty Marcum will be
out here with a loaded shotgun," she cautioned. "You never
want to piss off Salty or my grandfather."

Glenda's furious gaze darted toward the house. No doubt,
she wondered if Amanda was lying. Amanda decided to save
Glenda's calculating brain from short-circuiting.

"Salty! Pops!" she hollered. "Come quick!"

The back door flew open. Glenda cursed when she found
herself staring at the spitting end of a shotgun. Flinging Amanda
a murderous glare, Glenda stalked into the garage and roared
off in her car.

"Having trouble, Half Pint?" Pops asked as he poked his
bald head around the doorjamb.

"Not anymore. I was being treated to a private theatrical
performance and the actress stepped out of character and got
all huffy."

Salty lowered his shotgun. "What the hell are you talking
about?"

"I'll explain later, I have a beauty appointment in fifteen
minutes."

Pops snorted. "Don't let that scissor-happy beautician scalp
you again. And for God's sake, get rid of those gaudy orange
nails. You look like a two bit harlot!"

"Will do, Pops," Amanda called as she headed for her
clunker truck.

And to think Amanda had almost been taken in by Glenda's
sweet, little voice, the trembling lips, the wash of tears. Geez,
Glenda had Amanda going, right up until that part about Harv

coming back to Georgia to give the marriage another shot. That was not how Harv operated. He had no intention of doing anything besides visiting his harem occasionally. The man had a history of burning his matrimonial bridges behind him. More than likely Harv had told Glenda that he had gone too far to turn back and that he wanted a divorce. That was exactly what Harvey meant. He had used a similar line on Wives Number One and Two.

Glenda must have fabricated the part about Harvey promising to return to Georgia to patch up their marriage. That simply wasn't the way Harvey operated.

That gentle Southern-belle routine just didn't fly. The other wives were brassy and tacky. Why would Glenda be any different?

Who was to say that Glenda hadn't hung around, watching from a discreet distance, waiting until she got Harv completely alone. And who was to say that Glenda, in that same fit of temper that exploded a few minutes earlier, hadn't yanked the hydraulic lines loose and flattened Harv like a shadow?

Yet, there was something in Glenda's story that niggled at Amanda—a few shreds of truth among the lies that coincided with information she had gleaned from other interviews.

Oh, how Amanda wished Anita Blankenship would turn up to present her version of the encounter with Laverne and Glenda. Where was that woman? Why was she lying low? Because of intense fear? Guilt?

On impulse Amanda drove past Renshaw Farm. She saw Johnny Phipps parking the wheat truck in the shed. The green Dodge Neon was idling in the driveway. Johnny jogged to the car and climbed in with Glenda.

Well, well, isn't that interesting! Glenda and Johnny are definitely in cahoots.

On the way to the beauty shop Amanda mulled over what she had seen, then reflected on her conversations with Wives Number One, Two, and Three. What really stumped her was the identity of Wife Number Four. Velma the beautician was the one who said Harv had married four times. Could Velma have been wrong?

Amanda had every intention of finding out if a fourth wife was lurking around Vamoose.

Amanda breezed into Velma's Beauty Boutique. The salon was packed, as usual. Velma was a flurry of flying hands and hairbrush. She circled The Chair, fluffing up Marjorie Lawson's outdated beehive hairdo.

"I'll be with you in a jiffy, hon," Velma called. She grinned broadly, making her jowls wrinkle like an accordion. "I have a surprise for you. Can't wait to spring it on you." *Snap, pop.*

Amanda dropped into the only vacant chair in the room and inwardly cringed. She hated surprises, especially from gung-ho beauticians.

"Like, have you ever seen such an influx of bleached blondes roosting in one place?" Beverly Hill chattered while she removed nail polish from Millie Price's nails. "Since Harv's accident Vamoose looks like the return of the swallows to Capistrano."

Interesting comparison.

"You're right about that, Bev," Velma agreed. "I touched up Laverne's dark roots before the funeral. Of course, I was surprised she had the cash to pay me."

Amanda wasn't. She suspected Laverne had raided Harv's piggy bank when he wasn't around to stop her.

"Then that Rita woman from down Texas-way dropped in late yesterday afternoon for a touch-up. Then Glenda from Georgia was here bright and early this morning. All those peroxide fumes are starting to clog my brain." *Crunch, crackle.*

"Well, that accounts for three of Harv's ex-wives," Amanda put in strategically. "I wonder if Number Four will show up soon."

All conversation died a quick death. A half-dozen pair of eyes swung to Amanda.

"*What?*" she asked the shop at large.

"Girlfriend, if Harv's fourth wife shows up, like, that would be something I'd rather not see." Bev shivered unpleasantly. "Real bummer, far as I'm concerned."

"Why? What's wrong with Wife Number Four?" Amanda wanted to know.

"She's dead," Velma informed Amanda.

Amanda swallowed. "When was this? *Who* was this?"

Millie Price leaned forward, her wrinkled features set in a bleak expression. "First off, she was a foreigner," she imparted. "Strange woman, very strange."

"Foreigner? Where was she from?" Amanda questioned.

"*Not* Oklahoma," Velma put in as she ratted and teased Marjorie's brittle hair.

Now Amanda understood. In rural, small-town Vamoose, anyone who wasn't born and raised with Midwestern values and viewpoints was a foreigner.

"West Coast," Bev reported as she buffed Millie's nails. "Like, talk about radical clothes and wild hairdos! Don't know where Harv picked up that piece of art, but Mama said she was a walking scandal."

"I swear that woman was on something," Velma said. "She always had that dazed look about her." *Crackle, snap.* "Called herself Flower Child and wore a fluorescent pink stripe down the middle of her bleached hair. Reminded me of an old hippie trying to keep a dead movement alive."

"But believe you me, that woman was no child. She had more miles on her face than my 1979 Ford has!" Millie put in. "Looked as if she'd been around several blocks in her life, and on bad roads."

"If you ask me she was one of the *original* flower children of the late sixties." *Chomp, chomp.* "She had to have been a good eight to ten years older than Harvey Renshaw. Flower

Child overdosed on some really bad stuff. At least that's what Deputy Sykes and the coroner decided.''

Amanda frowned. ''Didn't Thorn investigate the case?''

''No, that was during those two weeks Nicky took off to help his brother with an investigation with the OSBI. Something about pinning down a thug Nicky had trailed while he was on the narc squad,'' Velma explained. ''The accident took place two years ago, not long after Harv and his wacky wife moved to Vamoose. Flo—that's what we called her—must have been so high she thought she could walk on water. Harv found her floating half naked in his farm pond. She had needle marks from syringes up and down her arms.''

''Like, Mama said Harv and Flo had only been in town a couple of months before she flipped out.'' Bev shook her head. Black Shirley Temple corkscrew curls jiggled around her ears. ''Nobody saw much of Harvey for a few months after that. He just kept to himself on the farm.''

Amanda couldn't help it. She was suspicious by nature and she had the unshakable feeling Flower Child's shocking demise wasn't cut and dried. At this late date it might be difficult to investigate, but she wasn't so sure that someone other than the victim, who had a history of addiction, hadn't given the lethal injection. Too bad Harvey Renshaw wasn't around to question about his involvement in his wife's death.

Which woman in the string of photos in Harv's home was Flo? Amanda wondered. Well, she would simply have to take another look around the house, just to satisfy her curiosity.

''Now, then, hon, hop up here,'' Velma commanded. ''Bev, bring me the surprise from the storeroom.''

''You bet, Aunt Velma.'' Bev bounded up and galumphed away. ''This is gonna be mega cool!''

Amanda gaped when Bev returned moments later with strands of blond hair. Her startled gaze flew to Velma. ''I thought you said you wanted to trim my split ends.''

''Surprise, hon!'' *Snap, crunch.* ''We ordered hair extensions for you, to compensate for that minor hair disaster that occurred before your wedding.''

Minor *disaster*? Amanda scoffed to herself. That particular visit to the beauty shop would go down as one of the worst moments of Amanda's life!

''I've been wanting to dabble with these extensions for ages.'' *Chomp, pop.* ''Since you've always been such a good sport to let us experiment, we knew you'd agree to be our guinea pig again.''

''Actually, I'd—''

Velma whirled The Chair around so quickly that Amanda's neck whiplashed.

''I don't want you to see what I'm doing till I'm done,'' Velma insisted. ''This won't take long, hon. You once said Nicky liked your long hair best, so we're gonna give your length back.''

''Like, this is gonna be awesome,'' Bev enthused as she dangled the blond locks from her meaty fist. ''You'll probably set a new trend in town. Like, we'll be ordering extensions by the truckload!''

Amanda clamped her hands around the armrest of The Chair. Velma and Bev huddled around her like surgeons performing a delicate operation. Amanda decided to take her mind off the inevitable cosmetic catastrophe and focus on her investigation.

''I met Glenda Renshaw this afternoon,'' she announced. ''I don't suppose anyone has seen her around town with a companion.''

Bev snickered. ''You mean a companion of the male gland? *That* kind of companion?''

Amanda tried to nod, but Velma jerked on her head.

''Hold still, hon!'' *Snap, pop.* ''You gotta hold real still so we can add the attachments.''

''Haven't you heard?'' Marjorie Lawson said as she dug into her purse to pay for the style and set. ''Laverne is hopping mad because Johnny Phipps turned traitor and shacked up at the Laid Back Motel with Glenda.''

Good grief! thought Amanda. *What is Glenda trying to pull?* Maybe she was the vamp that Wife Number One and Two said she was. Amanda refused to let herself forget that Glenda had much to gain when Harv's estate was finalized.

Had Glenda lured Johnny into being an accomplice to set up Harv for that convenient farming accident? For certain, Johnny had no love for Harv. Why should he? Johnny's relationship with Laverne would have been less complicated with Harv out of the picture. Maybe Johnny had decided to use the same tactic on Laverne that Laverne had used on him. A little jealousy might have made the hot-tempered Laverne sit up and take notice of Johnny.

"Things are going great guns in preparation for the noodle supper and slave auction,'' Velma said as she yanked and tugged at Amanda's hair. "We've got eighteen men lined up for the auction. If each one brings a hundred dollars, plus the profit we raise from the noodle supper and cakewalk, we'll have a hefty sum of money to present to charity. I can't wait to see who buys Nicky.''

Well, it better not be one of Harv's harem, Amanda thought. *Thorn is not going to become a sex slave to some buxom bleached blonde!*

While the patrons and proprietor of Beauty Boutique launched into a lively discussion about who wanted to buy which man for the day, Amanda tried to put her investigative ducks in a row. She wasn't sure she could believe anything Wife Number One or Three told her. Their stories conflicted and the two women were playing tug-of-war with Johnny Phipps.

And Wife Number Two? Amanda wasn't sure about that woman, either. No telling where the woman was holed up. Rita hadn't registered at the Laid Back Motel—unless she had used an assumed name. And why would Rita feel the need to do that, unless she had something to hide—like guilt and involvement in the murder of her ex-husband.

And what about Corky Bishop, the desperate rancher who needed the payment from a new oil well site to keep his farm afloat? Could Corky be trusted to tell the truth?

The more Amanda thought about it, the more she thought it was unwise to cross anyone off the list of suspects. Corky Bishop had motive, opportunity, and a considerable amount of money to gain from Harvey's death.

Nor could she scratch off Dave Zinkerman's name. Harv owed Dave money, and Dave had conveniently left town with Amanda's secretary. Was that a coincidence or premeditated calculation? Had Dave buttered up Jenny during Amanda's Bahaman honeymoon, then struck Harv down the day Amanda returned to work?

If Dave committed the murder, was it a crime of passion fueled by anger? Or had he meticulously plotted to get even with Harv for refusing to pay the fourteen hundred dollars owed for hay? For certain, Dave was entitled to his money from the estate.

Amanda sincerely wished she knew exactly what had been going on in Harvey Renshaw's mind, what he wanted to discuss with her that fateful day—and never had the chance. What arrangements had he wanted to make with Amanda? What was going on in his life—from *his* perspective?

A dark, sinister sensation snaked down Amanda's spine, but she wasn't sure what prompted it. Maybe it was talk of Flower Child's fatal overdose that triggered the uneasy feeling. Maybe it was all the unanswered questions that were wreaking havoc with Amanda's natural tendency for logical organization.

"Surprise!" *Pop, crackle.*

Amanda was jostled from deep thoughts when Velma spun The Chair to face the mirror. Amanda bit back a howl of dismay when she saw her reflection. Long, uneven strands of hair—which didn't come close to matching her natural color—flopped over her shoulders and stuck out at peculiar angles from the sides of her head. Good Lord! She looked hideous! Maybe the actors and actresses in Hollywood had expert beauticians to alter their appearances for roles in movies, but Amanda was at the mercy of two amateurs—and it showed.

"You certainly look different," Millie Price said tactfully.

"Definitely different," Carla Short said hesitantly.

Velma combed her beefy fingers through Amanda's scraggly hair. "Nicky should approve of the length. He'll be pleased."

Pop, pop.

No, Thorn definitely would not be pleased with this disastrous 'do. Amanda could guarantee it.

"We'll make another appointment to trim up and blend in the extensions," Velma said. "Can't do it all in one day, hon. Got a perm scheduled in fifteen minutes. And Anita Blankenship is supposed to have a shampoo and cut at four-thirty."

Velma glanced around the shop. "Has anyone seen or heard from Anita? I heard she hasn't shown up for work this week. I wonder if she's going to keep her appointment."

No one had heard the lowdown on Anita. The woman seemed to have vanished into thin air.

Distracted by her reflection in the mirror, Amanda rose from The Chair. She paid handsomely for the cosmetic experiment, then strode outside where she could curse without being overheard. She didn't know which was worse—these scraggly, off-color hair extensions or the acidic dyes that Velma had dumped on Amanda's head previously.

It was too damn close to call.

Amanda drove away, reminding herself that the information gained for her investigations came with a price tag. As usual, Amanda and her head of hair paid dearly.

CHAPTER TEN

Driven by a need she couldn't pinpoint, Amanda headed for Harvey Renshaw's farm. She wanted to take another look around the house where Harv grew up and lived out the last two years of his military retirement. She wanted to study the collection of photos closely, to reexamine the house, hoping she would stumble onto a productive lead.

Amanda sincerely hoped Laverne was busy moving her belongings into the rental house and wouldn't be underfoot. Loud-mouthed Laverne would object to Amanda nosing around the farm.

Amanda breathed a sigh of relief when she veered into the driveway and saw that Laverne's gray Buick sedan was not on the premises. The Jeep and wheat truck were parked in the shed. The lawn hadn't been mowed in a week and the place looked neglected.

Glancing this way and that, Amanda climbed the steps to the porch. Since the door was locked, she removed the window screen and eased inside. She froze in her steps when she heard an unidentified noise.

"Laverne? Johnny? Anita? Is anybody home?"

Amanda strained her ears, but she was met with silence.

The moment Amanda entered the living room she planted herself in front of the bookcase that held numerous photos of Harvey and his bevy of bleached-blond beauties. Amanda recognized Laverne, Glenda, Rita, Anita, and Flower Child in her psychedelic clothes and a stripe of fluorescent pink hair extending from her hairline to the crown of her head.

In each photograph Harv had his arm around the woman beside him. There were pictures of Harv in civilian clothes and in military uniform. It looked as if Harv had worn his military haircut for years. In some photos he looked as if he had put on a few pounds, then taken them off. Sometimes he squinted into the bright light and sometimes he smiled. But his casual stance seemed the same in each photo—his left arm draped around the female.

Amanda squatted down to study the military citation on the bottom shelf, then stood up to scan the room carefully. The place was still a pit of microwave food wrappers and containers, wadded napkins and Styrofoam cups.

Pivoting, Amanda strode off to inspect Laverne and Johnny's downstairs bedroom. Talk about the proverbial pigsty! Clothes were draped on every stick of furniture. Hangers littered the floor, and the bed was unmade—there wasn't even a fitted sheet covering the mattress!

Amanda snorted in disgust. She was appalled at the way some folks chose to live.

If Laverne was in the process of moving, all she had gathered was clothes and shoes from the closet.

The thought put Amanda in motion. She tramped off to the kitchen to find the cabinet doors standing open and dishes missing. She appraised the room, then reversed direction to climb the stairs. She wanted to reinspect Harv's bedroom.

Amanda immediately set about scouring through the dresser drawers. She didn't know what she was looking for, she just hoped something interesting would catch her eye.

When she came across a drawerful of important-looking documents, she scooped them into her purse, wondering how she had overlooked them the first time she was here. Then she remembered B.J. had sent the signal that someone had turned in the driveway. Amanda had been forced to abandon her search immediately.

She found her footsteps taking her to the closet, then she frowned when she realized the oily boots she had noticed the first time she searched the house were missing. Something about those grimy work boots bothered her—and had since the first time she'd seen them.

Who had taken them? And why? Where was that tangled pile of clothes she had seen lying beside the boots?

Frustrated that a spark of realization didn't jump up and bite her, Amanda muttered, then wheeled around. She couldn't wander around here for very long. There was no telling when Laverne would return to gather another carload of belongings.

Swiftly Amanda replaced the window screen and returned to her truck. She stared at the tail end of the wheat truck Harv had been driving the morning he died—the truck LeRoy Ashton claimed he had seen Harv in, the truck Amanda had seen Johnny tooling around in when he followed Glenda to the private conference.

On impulse Amanda drove down to the shed to study the wheat truck and the Jeep parked beside it. She brushed her hand over the grill of the wheat truck and felt the greasy substance on her fingertips.

Was this the unidentified vehicle that left tracks at the crime scene? Had the driver washed hydraulic fluid from the truck hood and windshield but neglected to scrub the oily substance from the indentations on the grill?

Amanda glanced into the interior of the cab, noting the

key was in the ignition. Had Johnny Phipps left the key after he pretended to shadow Glenda to the rendezvous with Amanda . . . ?

A cracking sound roused Amanda from her thoughts. She had the uneasy sensation she was being watched. By whom? She didn't have the slightest idea. But this remote, vacated farm was no place to be attacked and whisked away. There were too many grain bins, dilapidated stock sheds, and piles of broken, outdated machinery, where a snoopy accountant, who was conducting an unofficial investigation, could be left for dead.

The thought prompted Amanda to hurry to her bucket-of-rust truck. She headed directly toward the crime scene, hoping the memory of what she had seen and heard that fateful morning, combined with the information that swirled around her brain, would provide a clue to break this complex case.

The first thing Amanda did after she climbed from her truck was inhale a deep breath of country air and clear her thoughts. She noticed the fluorescent stakes that indicated the location of the proposed well site had been pulled up. Amanda glanced north to see the colorful markers on Corky Bishop's property.

Amanda pivoted around, tucking that information away so she could concentrate on the crime scene. *Now then,* she told herself. *You arrived in the pasture that fateful morning to see the idling tractor and hungry cattle milling around the hay bale.*

Then what? Amanda frowned in concentration, trying to recall the image of that stormy, overcast morning as if it were a videotape rolling inside a VCR. Ah, yes, she remembered becoming impatient because Harv was nowhere to be found. She shooed off the cattle and circled the hay bale to see a pair of combat boots protruding from the bale. Then she noticed the hydraulic fluid, broken hose, and the clean area of grass that indicated the presence of a vehicle.

Was that vehicle Harv's wheat truck? If it was, did that

eliminate Corky Bishop, because he didn't have access to the vehicle parked in the shed? Or was the key always in the ignition? Could Corky have driven the truck to Harv's pasture to avoid suspicion from anyone who cruised past?

And what about Dave Zinkerman? If Dave had the audacity to hook up Harv's stock trailer without permission, he might have helped himself to the truck and driven to the pasture to confront Harv who refused to pay for the hay he had purchased. The hay bale Harv was feeding his cattle that morning undoubtedly belonged to Dave.

No, thought Amanda, she definitely couldn't scratch Dave or Corky from her list of suspects. Anyone could have confiscated the truck if Harv was in the habit of leaving the key in the ignition. And for sure, Laverne and Johnny wouldn't have paid much attention to what was going on outside . . . .

Unless Johnny Phipps was the one who took the truck and roared off to confront Harv in private.

"Damn," Amanda muttered. Every suspect she could name had reason to want Harv out of the way—permanently.

Amanda shifted her attention to the cattle herd that hovered near the creek that fed the farm pond. If she wasn't mistaken, the herd had been lingering around the creek last time she was here. Why hadn't the cattle waded into the farm pond to quench their thirst? And who was tending the herd now that Harv wasn't around to do it? Certainly not Johnny, Anita, or the three ex-wives who were hovering around Vamoose, waiting to see how much money they would inherit.

Amanda bounded into her truck and drove up the pond dam to check on the neglected herd. The pasture grass had been grubbed to the ground, indicating the cattle were scrounging to appease their hunger.

Amanda frowned when she spotted the dried hoofprints that led to the creek. *Why aren't the cattle drinking from this pond?*

And then she saw it—an object that reflected sunlight and glistened on the water's surface. A feeling of impending doom sank into the pit of Amanda's stomach as she stared at the pond. The object in question obviously made the herd feel so ill at ease that they avoided the area, opting to drink from the narrow creek.

Somberly Amanda tramped across the dam to reach the flat, red-clay bank on the west side of the pond. "Oh, damn . . ."

Either there was a miniature submarine, with its small periscope shining above the water's surface, or a vehicle was submerged—up to its aluminum radio antenna.

Amanda had the unmistakable feeling that it was a vehicle. She also had the unmistakable feeling she knew who owned it.

Whirling around, Amanda made a mad dash to her clunker truck, then made tracks across the pasture. The sound of bad mufflers serenaded her as she buried the needle of the speedometer in her frantic rush to find Thorn.

She and Thorn were not going to spend a leisurely evening at home, she predicted. This case—one that Thorn tried to shrug off as an accident—would soon be upgraded to a double homicide. Amanda had the inescapable feeling there was more than just a waterlogged vehicle at the bottom of this farm pond. She was pretty sure the driver had gone down with the car.

Nick slid from beneath the wheel of the squad car and flashed the speeding motorist his sternest expression as he approached. "You better ease up on the accelerator, sir. You were driving twenty miles over the speed limit in Vamoose. Step out of your car and hand over your driver's license."

The young man stood up, then reached for his wallet. Nick frowned when he checked the name on the license. Johnny Phipps.

"Where are you headed in such a rush?"

Johnny shrugged nonchalantly. "Nowhere special."

Nick glanced southward. "You're pointed toward Pronto. Where is Laverne?"

Johnny's gaze widened in response to the unexpected question. He shifted his weight from one grimy tennis shoe to the other. "Just give me the ticket, Chief, and I'll promise not to get heavy-footed again."

"You look a little nervous," Nick noted. "Why is that?"

"I'm not the least bit nervous," Johnny insisted as he shoved his hands into the front pockets of his jeans.

"I better have a look around your vehicle." Nick reached inside the open window to confiscate the key from the ignition.

"Geez, Chief, I admit I was speeding, but that's all," Johnny said.

Nick opened the trunk to find a pile of wrinkled clothes and a pair of boots.

"You're moving away from Renshaw Farm?"

"Yeah? So? Is that against the law?"

Nick dug around in the clothes to ensure there were no packets of drugs stashed in the pockets. Then he leveled a hard stare on the long-haired man who was dressed in frayed blue jeans and dingy T-shirt. "Did you and Laverne have a falling-out . . . ?"

His voice trailed off when he heard the roar of bad mufflers. Nick turned to see Hazard's jalopy truck breaking the city speed limit. When she screeched to a halt behind the squad car, Nick muttered under his breath. Hazard was making him look bad. He really wished she wouldn't do that.

"Oh, sure," Johnny smirked. "Stop me for doing twenty over the limit, but let Hazard off the hook because you're married to her. Now, that's fair."

"Clam up, Johnny. Hazard only speeds when there is an emergency."

"How do you know I wasn't having an emergency?" he retaliated.

Nick stared the scraggly-haired freeloader down. "You just

told me you were going nowhere special. Are you telling me that you lied?''

Before Johnny could reply, Hazard dashed forward. She glanced at Johnny's shiny Dodge Neon, then pinned the man with her scrutinizing gaze. ''Are you planning to spend the evening with Glenda?'' She shot a quick glance toward the open trunk, then zeroed in on Johnny. ''Moving in with Glenda at the Laid Back Motel in Pronto, I presume. Very interesting. So what have you done with Laverne?''

Johnny threw up both hands when Hazard came down on him like a ton of rock. ''Hey, back off, Haz—''

Hazard stalked forward. ''I have no intention of backing off, Phipps. And don't think for one minute that I don't know who was driving that wheat truck that trailed after this little Dodge Neon when Glenda and I drove out of town for a private conference. You and Glenda didn't fool me for a minute, but I'm sure she told you that already.''

Nick gaped at his wife. The first thing he noticed was the uneven, off-color strands of blond hair that dangled around her temples and brushed her shoulders. The second thing he noticed was her flushed cheeks and the outward manifestation of impatience that had her tapping her foot rapidly.

And how the hell did she know so much about Johnny's personal life? Nick was the one who had traced Laverne and Johnny's background—at Hazard's request—and Nick had yet to fill her in. And what was this business about Johnny shadowing Glenda to an out-of-the-way rendezvous with Hazard?

''I don't have the foggiest idea what you're talking about,'' Johnny said hotly.

''Oh, yes, you do,'' Hazard came right back. ''I followed Glenda after our conference. I saw her pull into the driveway at Renshaw Farm. You parked the wheat truck in the shed, then you climbed in the car with her. You want to explain why you were setting up that scam for my benefit?''

Johnny started getting twitchy, Nick noticed. The man

glanced everywhere, except at Hazard. "A guy has a right to hitch a ride with a babe when he feels like it."

"Answer the question, Romeo," Amanda snapped. "You agreed to help Glenda with her 'Poor Me' routine. Did you also think the arrangement would get Laverne to notice you?"

"Gee whiz, Hazard, where do you come up with all this stuff?" Nick asked in amazement.

"Later, Thorn." She didn't take her piercing gaze off Johnny for even a second. "Yes or no, Romeo?"

Johnny gritted his teeth. "Yeah, I've had my fill of Laverne flaunting herself in front of Harv. I decided two could play her game. So what's wrong with that?"

"Maybe you would have impressed Laverne by getting yourself a job instead of lounging around like her gigolo. Now tell me where Laverne is?"

"I don't know and I don't care!" Johnny all but shouted.

"And where is her car?" Hazard grilled him.

"Probably the same place she is," he said smartly.

"And where would that be, Phipps?" Nick demanded.

"I don't know. All I know is that I'm on my way to Pronto to meet Glenda." Johnny extended his hand—one that didn't have a single callus from a hard day's work on it. "Just gimme the speeding ticket so I can be on my way."

Nick wrote out the ticket, then returned Johnny's license.

"Don't think Thorn and I won't be keeping a close eye on you," Hazard put in. "And don't go sneaking into my office during the night again, or I'll press charges."

"Hey! I'll admit I followed Glenda like she told me to, but I didn't break into your office. This is the first I've even heard about it," Johnny insisted.

"Yeah, right." Hazard stared him down, long and hard. "You better hope your prints don't turn up in my office, pal. And don't leave the area, because Thorn will want to speak to you later."

"I will?" Nick asked.

"You will," Amanda confirmed.

Nick noted that Hazard had become an expert at intimidation after handling six unofficial investigations. She had Johnny squirming in his skin. The man couldn't return to his borrowed car and drive off fast enough.

"Obviously, you've had a busy day, Haz," Nick said.

"Definitely busy." Hazard lurched around and headed for her clunker truck. "Follow me, Thorn. This investigation has taken a turn for the worst."

"What does that mean?"

"Meet me at Harv's farm pond," she tossed over her shoulder. "I'll stop by Watts's tow truck service on my way out of town."

"What's going on, Hazard?"

Nick grumbled under his breath when Hazard didn't answer. She gunned the truck and made a U-turn on two wheels. Something was definitely bothering Hazard, and Nick wasn't going to find out what it was until he reached the farm pond.

Amanda clenched her fists around the steering wheel and drove north. Cecil and Cleatus Watts were right behind her with their tow truck. A sense of urgency gripped her as she drove to the crime scene. Unless she missed her guess—and what were the chances of that happening?—another corpse was about to turn up on the Renshaw property. And who had been watching Amanda while she prowled around Renshaw Farm earlier? Was Johnny spying on her? Had he parked Glenda's car out of sight, then tried to hightail it to Pronto, only to be pulled over by Thorn for speeding?

The way Amanda saw it, there were three people unaccounted for in this puzzling case. One of them was probably at the bottom of the farm pond. Amanda wasn't certain about the other two. There were still no leads that would help Amanda locate Harv's brother. Anita Blankenship hadn't been seen or heard from since Harv's death, and Laverne and her gray Buick hadn't been seen in town since the funeral.

Amanda forced herself to take another fortifying breath as she led the tow truck over the oil site access road and then veered toward the pond. Prepared for what she anticipated to be an unpleasant experience, she stepped down from her truck, then gave directions for the Watts brothers to ease down the pond bank.

"Hazard, what the hell is going on?" Thorn demanded impatiently.

Amanda gestured toward the antenna that was barely visible above the water's surface. "There is a vehicle submerged in the pond. I didn't notice it until this afternoon."

"Aw, damn," Thorn muttered as he strode toward the pond bank. He grabbed the free end of the tow chain and walked into the water. "Here, Hazard, take care of my pistol. I don't want it to get wet."

Thorn checked the safety, then tossed the pistol to Amanda. She tucked it in her pocket and watched Thorn wade into deep water. After he felt around for the bumper, he sank beneath the surface to hitch up the tow chain.

He resurfaced moments later and came ashore, dripping wet. "Haul it out, boys!" he called to the Watts brothers.

The chain creaked and groaned as the submerged car came slowly into view. Water gushed from the vehicle that was coated with a layer of red clay.

"It's not a gray Buick," Thorn noted.

"No, I didn't think it would be," Amanda murmured.

"Then who the hell does this car belong to?" Thorn asked.

"My guess is Anita Blankenship. She hasn't made contact with anyone since she tried to call me shortly after I found Harvey dead in the hay. I think Anita might have seen or heard something that put her in danger."

"Or maybe she was so overwrought that she decided to end it all," Thorn speculated. "Husbands, wives, and lovers have been known to bump off their mates then commit hara-kiri. It happens a lot, Hazard.''

"I don't think that's what happened in this case," Amanda said.

"Why not?"

"Just a hunch."

Thorn sighed audibly. "Okay, Haz. Two dead bodies have turned up in Vamoose in the course of one week. I . . . um . . . well . . . a . . . I think you might possibly be . . . right . . . in thinking Harv didn't die . . . um . . . accidentally.''

Despite the grim situation, Amanda smiled faintly. She knew Thorn hated it when she turned out to be right. Although Thorn hemmed and hawed awkwardly, he was man enough to admit he was wrong.

"Actually, there are three bodies," Amanda corrected. "Two years ago, Wife Number Four ended up in this same pond. I don't think it was an accident or coincidence.''

"Huh?" Thorn said, bug-eyed.

"You better make the ID, Thorn. I'm not sure I have the stomach to look inside this car.''

"Well, let me tell you, Hazard, this part of the job never gets easier," Thorn muttered as he turned on his heels and approached the vehicle.

Amanda waited anxiously while Thorn inspected the car— and its contents—at close range. Even the Watts brothers didn't venture close. Like Amanda, they preferred to wait at a distance.

Thorn opened the driver's door. Water gushed from the car. He poked his head inside to survey the situation. When Thorn turned toward Amanda, she noticed his expressionless face. That was his cop face, she reminded herself. When Thorn came upon a gruesome situation, he tried to distance himself emotionally and to proceed in a precise, professional manner. Amanda wasn't sure she could have held her composure as well as Thorn who, unfortunately, had lots of experience at this sort of thing.

"Hazard, get on the horn and call the medical examiner."

"Yes, sir." Amanda wheeled around and sprinted toward the squad car.

The greater the distance between Amanda and the water-logged victim the better. Thorn had given her an out. Like a squeamish coward she took it.

CHAPTER ELEVEN

Amanda plunked down in the La-Z-Boy recliner and absently petted the tomcat that hopped into her lap. Today had been hectic and she felt physically and emotionally exhausted. A dull headache thudded against her temples. Although she had covered a lot of territory in the investigation, she didn't feel she had made much headway.

Thorn ambled down the hall, fresh from the shower he'd taken to wash away red clay from the pond. Wearing nothing but jeans, he sank onto the sofa. Amanda tried to ignore the appeal of his broad chest and muscled shoulders. This was no time for distraction. Apparently, Thorn agreed, because he stared solemnly at her.

"I think we better swap information, Hazard," he said. "First of all, what's this about a third body?"

Amanda told Thorn what she had learned about Wife Number Four, who had been found floating in the same pond where Anita Blankenship turned up.

"You think this Flower Child person's death might be related to Anita and Harv's deaths?" Thorn asked.

Amanda nodded. The hair extensions curled around her shoulders like garden snakes. "According to my information, Flo died of an overdose, but I'm not sure it was self-injected."

"Any idea who might have wanted to get rid of her?"

Amanda shrugged. "It could have been Laverne. She didn't like competition, and she had some kind of fanatic fixation about winning Harv back. Or it could have been Glenda. She claims that she and Harvey never divorced. Wife Number Four could certainly have been a sore spot to her."

"But why didn't Glenda file charges against Harv years ago? She could have put him in jail."

Amanda snorted. "Think about it, Thorn. Would you want the father of your son in the slammer so the kid's schoolmates could harass him unmercifully?"

"Are you sure Harv is the father?"

"I saw the photo of the kid," Amanda told him. "Believe me, the family resemblance is easy to detect."

Thorn laid his head back against the sofa and propped his bare feet on the coffee table. He stared at the ceiling for a long, pensive moment. "Maybe Harv disposed of his fourth wife. From the sound of things Flo was a habitual user. It would have been easy for him to do the deed after he returned to Vamoose. None of Flower Child's family lived in the area to pose questions."

"Possibly," Amanda agreed. "The other three wives were conveniently left behind after Harvey made a military transfer. Flo may have followed Harv and he decided to get rid of her."

Amanda stroked the tomcat and frowned curiously. "I wonder where Harvey's brother is? He might be able to shed some light on that missing year between Harvey's retirement from the Air Force base in Georgia and his arrival in Vamoose. Unfortunately, all I know about Harold J. Renshaw is that he sold his half of the farm to Harv for one dollar. Now, why would he do that, and where the hell is he?''

"I didn't get much background on him," Thorn said. "For sure, there is nothing recent. His license was suspended for DWI when he was in his late teens, living in California. There was also a grand theft larceny related to another DWI arrest. But that's it. Harold's license expired about eight years ago and he never filed for a new one.''

"California," Amanda murmured. "That's where Flower Child came from. I wonder if there was a connection? Maybe Harold J. Renshaw lived in California and Harvey spent a year with his brother after he left Glenda in Georgia. Maybe that's where Harvey met Flower Child.''

Thorn sat up, his elbow draped over his bent knees. "Okay, Hazard, let's get back to standard operating procedure and go over the time frame. According to the medical examiner, Harvey died between nine and ten o'clock in the morning.''

"It had to be about nine-thirty," Amanda put in. "Harvey called me at nine-fifteen and I arrived at his farm about nine-forty-five. Wife Number Three claims she spoke with Harv at seven-forty-five. Glenda says Anita Blankenship was ready to leave for work, and Johnny and Laverne were drinking coffee with Harv. Anita didn't show up for work that day. She called me while I was out of the office early that afternoon.

"LeRoy Ashton, the oil field pumper, who just happens to be one of Laverne's old flames, told me Harv flagged him down at the oil site at eight-thirty.''

"Sounds like Harv had a busy morning.''

"Yeah," Amanda agreed. "Harv also had a confrontation with Corky Bishop before I arrived at the farm.''

Thorn frowned. "Corky? What's he got to do with this?''

"Harvey undercut Corky's asking price for the new well site," Amanda explained. "Now that Harv is gone, D and D Oil Drilling Company plans to renegotiate with Corky. He'll make several thousand dollars for providing water for drilling, for the lease of property, and royalties when the well comes in.''

''Interesting,'' Thorn murmured.

''Very. But Corky isn't the only one who profits. The ex-wives will come into money, especially Number Three. Her son's name is on the deed to the farm and the titles to the farm vehicles.''

''Maybe I should have a talk with the exes.''

''Good idea, Thorn. While you're at the Laid Back Motel interviewing Glenda and Johnny, check to see if a flashy yellow sports car is in the parking lot. It belongs to Rita, Wife Number Two. If she's around, you can question her, too. Better interrogate them first thing in the morning, though,'' she added. ''You are scheduled to become enslaved immediately after the chicken noodle supper served at the Methodist church tomorrow night.''

Nick groaned. ''Well, damn. I had planned to rev up my combine and the wheat truck on Saturday. The grain in the fields should be ready to harvest in a couple of weeks. Now I'll be spending my day off doing honey-do jobs.''

''For a good cause,'' Amanda reminded him, then frowned sternly. ''But do not let any of the divorcees and widows take advantage of you. I will not have my stud of a husband fooling around!''

Thorn broke into a roguish grin. ''Jealous, sugarplum?''

''You're darn tootin', Thorn. The only one around here who gets to put her hands on that magnificent body of yours is *me*.''

Thorn rose from the couch and swaggered over to scoop Amanda into his sinewy arms—She loved it when he did that.

''I think it's time to put this investigation to rest for the night,'' he whispered seductively.

Amanda wrapped her arms around his neck as he headed for the bedroom. ''Good idea, Thorn. I've been having trouble concentrating on the case since you walked out of the shower without your shirt.''

* * *

While Amanda was nursing her morning cup of coffee, a queasy stomach, and a dull headache, she retrieved the papers she had stashed in her purse while she was revisiting Renshaw Farm. It really bothered her that Harold J. Renshaw had not been notified about his brother's death. Where was the son who lived with his mother while Harvey grew up on the farm with his father?

And where was Laverne? Amanda wondered. She hoped the woman hadn't ended up in the same condition as Anita.

Amanda flipped through the stack of papers without her usual enthusiasm. Keeping up with business at the office and tracking down leads was wearing her out. She needed to solve this murder and give herself a day of rest.

A frown knitted her brow when she picked up an envelope with the return address of a California bank. Amanda opened the envelope to find a key similar to the one that had opened Harv's safety-deposit box at Vamoose Bank. *Now, what do you suppose Harv had stashed in the California bank? His will?* That could be why Amanda hadn't run across it.

Tucking the key in the pocket of her jeans, Amanda held up the next paper in the stack. A series of seven digit numbers had been hand-printed on college-rule notebook paper, then crossed out. Amanda had the suspicious feeling she was looking at savings or bank account numbers. She had worked with thousands of them in her professional experience.

Accounts from what? she wondered. *Certified deposits? Why were the numbers crossed out?*

"Damn it, Harv," she muttered. "I keep getting the feeling you were up to something sneaky."

Amanda recalled what Salty Marcum had said about Harvey being the type of individual who kept a racket going on the side while he was serving in the military. What side business had Harvey become involved in? Something dangerous, risky, illegal?

"Is that what got you killed, Harvey . . . ?"

Her voice trailed off when she noticed the official-looking letter from the U.S. Defense Department. Her eyes popped when she read the "I-regret-to-inform-you" letter that stated Harold J. Renshaw had died in action while serving his country during the Persian Gulf War. Three copies of the death certificate were stapled to the letter, and dog tags were taped to the bottom of the page.

Amanda slumped in her chair. Well, that explained why brother Harold J. hadn't renewed his driver's license; why no one had been able to notify him that Harvey had ended up dead in the hay.

Amanda's list of suspects was diminishing. She hoped Thorn had success grilling Wife Number Two, Three, Johnny Phipps, and Corky Bishop. Meanwhile, she was going to swing by her former rental house to see if Laverne was alive, well, and still in the area.

After swallowing down a couple of Tylenol, Amanda dressed, fed her pets, then strode to her truck. Bruno, the Border collie—who appointed himself as her bodyguard—hopped into the truck the instant Amanda opened the door.

"Do you feel like you've been missing out?" she asked the dog.

Bruno panted happily, then plunked down on the seat.

Amanda drove to the old farmstead where she'd lived since she first moved to Vamoose. When she saw Laverne's gray Buick and an oil field truck in the driveway, Amanda frowned.

From the look of things, Laverne had rebounded from her breakup with Johnny and landed in LeRoy Ashton's lap. Laverne, it seemed, was one of those women who simply could not function without a man in her life.

Was the same true of Glenda, Wife Number Three? Who had she been shacking up with after Harvey left the Air Force base in Georgia and spent a year in California with Flower Child and two years in Vamoose?

Leaving Bruno asleep on the seat of the truck, Amanda approached the house. Country-Western music blared through the open door. Amanda hammered her fist on the doorjamb, hoping to be heard over the fast-tempo tune.

No results.

She pounded both fists on the glass and yelled, "Hey! Is anybody in there?"

A few moments later a massive silhouette appeared in the hallway. Amanda found herself staring up at LeRoy Ashton. He frowned unsociably at her.

"What are you doing here, Hazard?"

"I used to live here," she said as she barged inside without invitation. "I just came by to make certain I didn't overlook any of my belongings. I have until this evening to remove my possessions. That was my agreement with my landlady."

"Laverne!" LeRoy bellowed over his buffalo-size shoulder. "We have company."

"We?" Amanda repeated. "Are you planning to live here, too? Be advised that my landlady does not approve of that sort of thing."

"As long as I pay rent, I reckon the landlady won't complain," LeRoy retorted.

LeRoy is paying the rent? Well, that explains why Laverne rekindled this affair. Laverne was obviously looking for a meal ticket, at least until she cashed in on the inheritance Harv left her.

Amanda wondered if Johnny Phipps was out of the picture for good. Must be. The man had taken off with all his worldly possessions in the trunk of Glenda's car. Johnny was in sad shape if all he had acquired, after thirty-some-odd years of existence, was a pile of wrinkled clothes. No doubt, it wouldn't be hard to talk that freeloader into a cut of the inheritance from Harvey's estate. Had Glenda made the kind of offer that prompted Johnny to join her cause?

Amanda scanned the living room, then frowned in dismay. Laverne's true calling in life was not in interior decoration. The woman had no sense of color or style. But Laverne did have a knack for swiping the furniture that had been in Harv's farmhouse yesterday afternoon, Amanda noted. No doubt, Laverne had taken advantage of Anita's absence and LeRoy's bulky size, and his oil well truck, to transport the unclaimed furniture to her new residence.

"Get out of here," Laverne snapped the instant she rounded the corner to see her unwanted visitor.

"Nice to see you again, too, Laverne," said Amanda cheerily. "As I just reminded LeRoy, I have until tonight to vacate this house. You jumped the gun by moving this stuff in already."

"There's nothing of yours left here," Laverne said rudely.

"I'll be the judge of that," Amanda replied as she stepped boldly around the hulk of man in front of her. "From all indication, Laverne, you have a tendency to take what you want, regardless of whether it rightfully belongs to you."

Laverne crossed her arms over her ample bosom, which was showcased by a skintight, low-neck cotton sweater. "What the hell does that mean?" she asked, thrusting out her square chin.

"Don't play the dumb blonde with me. You covet people and their possessions." She flashed Laverne a pointed glance on the way to the kitchen. "I'm sure that's only one of the Ten Commandments you've broken, but you'll have your chance to get that squared away on Judgment Day."

Laverne's makeup-caked face exploded with color. "I sure as hell do not have to stand here listening to your snotty insults!"

"Fine. If you would be more comfortable sitting down, then park yourself on Harv's sofa. Or was it Anita's? She certainly won't be coming around to claim it."

Laverne's gaze darted to LeRoy, then bounced back to Amanda. "And what is *that* supposed to mean?"

Amanda rummaged through the kitchen drawer to retrieve her spatula, pancake flipper, and manual can opener. "Thorn and I recovered Anita and her car from Harv's farm pond yesterday afternoon. Makes me wonder if you purchased those extra dresses you had in that garment bag for a second funeral."

At least Laverne had the grace to look surprised, though hardly saddened by the news. *Surprised, hmmm. As in "I didn't expect you to find the second body so quickly?"* Amanda wondered.

With a human gorilla like LeRoy to do Laverne's dirty work, she could accomplish all sorts of feats—like moving heavy furniture or removing witnesses who could point an accusing finger at her.

Amanda wished she could read minds, because she would dearly like to know what Laverne and LeRoy were thinking while they stared at one another.

Better get going while the getting is good, Amanda thought to herself. At this very moment Bonnie and Clyde might be plotting her demise. Bruno the bodyguard might not be able to spare her from disaster since he was shut in the truck. Thorn didn't have a clue where Amanda was. She and her clunker truck could be up to eyeballs and headlights in a muddy farm pond, and Thorn would be too late to save Amanda's bacon.

"Well, that's all that belongs to me," Amanda said as she moved swiftly toward the door.

She gulped apprehensively when LeRoy blocked her escape route.

"Me and Laverne didn't have nothing to do with whatever happened to Anita," LeRoy insisted.

"Okay," Amanda said carefully, then artfully sidestepped around the brawny brute and slipped out the door. "Thorn is waiting for me at the office. I better go."

It was a bald-faced lie, but Amanda felt the need to let

Laverne and LeRoy think Thorn would come looking for her if she didn't show up pronto.

During the drive to town Amanda asked herself if Laverne, Glenda, and Rita had prior knowledge of the amount of money and property they would inherit when Harv kicked the bucket. Had Harvey told his harem that he planned to provide for them? Was Anita to be left out completely? Not that it mattered now, Amanda thought glumly.

She still couldn't decide if Harv's death, and now Anita's, were crimes of impulsive passion or calculated greed. The circumstances surrounding Harv's death could have made it easy for someone to take advantage of his predictable daily routine. He was a rancher who fed hay to his cattle. He did it every day. So was this act premeditated or spontaneous?

And what the devil had Anita Blankenship seen or heard that landed her in the pond for her final swim? According to gossip at Velma's Beauty Boutique, Anita was crazy about Harv. She bought him gifts and catered to him. Could she possibly have struck out in anger after Glenda showed up? Had Anita been so overcome with anger and grief, after she disposed of Harv, that she drove into the pond to pay her comeuppance?

"What do you think, Bruno? Any theories?"

The dog pried open one eye, wagged his stub of a tail, then sprawled into a more comfortable position on the seat.

Grumbling at her inability to understand what brought Anita to her lowly end, Amanda veered into her office parking lot. She was going to sit herself down and compare bank account numbers from Vamoose Bank with the list of numbers she found on the paper in Harvey's dresser drawer. She also needed to study the phone bills she had confiscated earlier in the week. Who had Harv called recently? What had happened to the five grand he withdrew from his account?

"Don't get impatient with this case, Hazard," she softly told herself as she unlocked the office and let Bruno inside. Her spoken pep talk continued. "You'll find a correlation eventually. But whatever you do, don't overlook any minor details, because they might turn out to be important. Harvey and Anita's killer had to leave tracks or a paper trail. You'll find it . . . but you better hurry up before someone else turns up dead!''

CHAPTER TWELVE

Nick pulled his squad car into the parking spot near the office of the Laid Back Motel in Pronto. He didn't see any sign of the yellow sports car Hazard had asked him to check on, but he hoped to catch Glenda and Johnny before they sped off for the day. He had no trouble gaining cooperation from the employee at the registration desk. One look at his police uniform, his official badge, and his no-nonsense expression and he was directed to room 12.

Nick knocked briskly on the door.

"Yeah? Who is it?"

"Thorn, Chief of Police," he said in his most authoritative voice. "Open the door."

He leaned his ear against the crack between the door and doorjamb, listening to whispers and scurrying movements. Nick smiled. No doubt, he had interrupted an early-morning tryst.

Johnny appeared at the door in his faded blue jeans and a wrinkled T-shirt. Nick couldn't see Glenda because Johnny obstructed his view.

"I want to ask a few questions." Nick shouldered his way inside, noting tangled sheets, opened suitcases, and a closed bathroom door. "Glenda, I want you to participate in the questioning. Get out here now."

"I don't have any makeup on," she called back in her sticky-sweet voice.

"Doesn't matter. This interrogation doesn't require formal dress." Nick wasn't giving Wife Number Three the chance to pry open the bathroom window and dash off. Furthermore, Nick didn't overlook the possibility of a surprise attack. He kept the heel of his hand resting on the butt of his pistol.

"Hurry up, Glenda," Nick ordered brusquely. "If you aren't out here in two seconds, I'm coming in to get you and I'll come armed and ready to shoot."

The door burst open. Nick braced himself for possible attack, but none came. When he got a good look at Glenda's colorless face—a face devoid of eyebrows—he had to choke back a laugh. Glenda's questionable beauty was definitely the synthetic, artificial variety. The woman gave new meaning to "putting on a face." *Man, this woman could scare crows from a vegetable garden!*

"Sit down over here by Johnny," Nick instructed.

Dressed in a shorty nightshirt, the faceless blonde sat down on the edge of the bed.

"I recovered Anita Blankenship's body from the farm pond yesterday afternoon," Nick said bluntly. "Estimated time of death was the same day Harv was found crushed by a hay bale. According to my findings"—Actually, they were Hazard's findings but Nick left Hazard's name out of it, just to be on the safe side—"Glenda arrived at Renshaw Farm and met Anita on her way out the door." He stared intently at Johnny. "You were in the kitchen having coffee with Harvey and Laverne. Correct?"

Johnny nodded. His shaggy, uncombed hair drooped around

his thin shoulders. "That was the last time I saw Anita in person."

"Me too," Glenda put in quickly. "I swear, Chief, after Anita threw a fit, because I was at the door, she left the house and I haven't seen her since."

Nick focused his steely-eyed stare on Johnny. "Although Laverne sent you to the bedroom, you didn't stay there, did you?" It was just a guess, but if Nick had been in Johnny's sneakers he wouldn't have waited in the bedroom, twiddling his thumbs while his girlfriend had it out with Harv and another of his ex-wives.

Johnny compressed his lips, refusing to reply.

"Come on, pal. I can dust for prints in a matter of minutes to determine if you climbed out the window and circled around to the kitchen to eavesdrop. Then I'll be back here with a warrant for your arrest. Save me the time and yourself a stint in jail and answer the question."

Johnny's fist flexed and contracted in the bedspread. "Okay, I went around the house to eavesdrop," he admitted. "I heard what Laverne said about me, the manipulative bitch! I was nothing to her but a means to catch Harv's attention. She played up to him constantly because he had ready cash and government pensions. That's all she was interested in. Financial security. She used me and I didn't want to believe it until I heard the words from her own mouth."

"She was sleeping with Harv," Nick presumed.

Johnny cursed under his breath, then nodded. "Yeah. It got her a roof over her head, rent-free, but Harv refused to give Anita the boot. He said Anita was the best maid and housekeeper he ever had."

Nick glanced at Glenda, whose bleached hair stuck out from her head like porcupine quills. "I'm sure that comment didn't set well with you, either."

"No, it didn't. Harvey was in a foul mood. Everything he

said was a cruel contradiction to what he had said to me on the phone the previous night.''

"What did he say?" Nick questioned.

"He claimed his life was in shambles and that I was too good for the likes of him. He said I should catch the next flight to Georgia and forget I had ever met him. But that morning I realized he had played me for a fool a dozen times over. I was just another of the blondes in his life.''

"And you were so angry that you wanted to kill him for betraying you?"

"No!" Glenda's shrill voice ricocheted off the walls. "I just wanted to get even, to drive his harem of women away. He used all of us. Damn him and his split personality! He could be a charming Casanova when the mood suited him. And sometimes he could be obnoxious.

"He would return from one of his secretive training missions and it was as if I didn't know him. Fool that I was, I let him sweet-talk me into forgiving him for being cruel. My father was right. I should have kicked him out years ago and never given him a second thought.''

Whew! Talk about suppressed anger building like steam in a pressure cooker! Glenda was boiling. Nick noted that even Johnny was looking at the faceless blonde as if he had never seen her before.

Apparently, Glenda realized she had made a spectacle of herself, for she hunched her shoulders and dropped her head. "Then I met Johnny coming around the side of the house when I returned to my car," she continued softly. "He wasn't pretentious like Harvey and that mouthy witch I'd met.''

"You are referring to Laverne?" Nick clarified.

"None other," Glenda muttered. "I told Johnny that we were a matched pair of fools and that if we had any sense we would join forces against Harv and Laverne. Johnny was as hurt and frustrated as I was.''

Nick looked to Johnny for confirmation. The man nodded.

"Yeah, that's when I decided I wanted out of that bad relationship. I left with Glenda," Johnny added.

"To do what? Follow Harv to the pasture and confront him?"

"Certainly not!" Glenda interrupted indignantly. "I can vouch for Johnny and he can vouch for me."

How convenient, thought Nick.

"We had nothing to do with Harv's accident, and I never saw Anita after that, either," Glenda said hurriedly.

"Did *you*?" Nick asked Johnny a second time.

Johnny shifted uneasily on the bed.

"Tell me the truth," Nick demanded.

"Yeah, I saw her driving around the section while I was standing outside the kitchen window. Or at least I assume she was the one driving her car. Can't say for sure, but the driver kept circling the section as if keeping surveillance."

So it's possible Hazard is right, Nick thought. Anita might have seen something while she was cruising the country roads, waiting to speak privately with Harvey. And then again, Anita could have put Harvey out of her misery, and then done herself in. Nick wasn't ready to let go of that theory just yet.

"According to my information, Johnny followed Glenda to a private meeting with Hazard," Nick continued. "Were you trying to throw suspicion on Laverne by doing that, Johnny?"

"I'm not sure Laverne didn't deserve to have suspicion thrown on her, Chief," Johnny said, and scowled. "She can be a real spitfire when she's mad, and she was damned sure mad at Harvey after he called her a conniving slut, told her she was off his payroll. He told her to get out of the house for good."

"Can you verify that, Glenda?" Nick questioned.

She nodded. "I was in the house when Harv told Laverne to take a hike."

"Was that before or after Harv told *you* to take one?"

"Before. Laverne threw herself at him and pounded him on the shoulders. Harv wrenched her arm up her back and shoved her into the bathroom to cool off. Then he came back to tell me he was tired of pretense. He said he'd had his fill of dim-witted blondes.''

''Now, I'm going to ask you one more time, Johnny,'' Nick said firmly. ''Did you sneak into Hazard's office to search for the deeds and will, because Glenda asked you to do it?''

''No!'' Johnny howled. ''I swear it, Chief. It wasn't me or Glenda.''

Nick pivoted toward the door. ''Don't leave the area,'' he ordered. ''I may have more questions later.''

''But I have a son in Georgia,'' Glenda reminded him. ''I can't stay here indefinitely.''

''Sorry for the inconvenience, but you'll have to make arrangements for your son,'' Nick said before he left.

The instant Nick sank onto the seat of his black-and-white he reported to the dispatcher. ''Tell Deputy Sykes to remain on patrol until further notice, Janie-Ethel. I have another stop to make before I return to the police beat.''

''Sure thing, Chief. Deputy Sykes has you covered.''

Nick made the trip from Pronto to Vamoose with lights flashing. He needed to get to the bottom of this double homi-cide—or homicide–suicide—as quickly as possible. If he had to spend the following day enslaved, then he needed to gather facts. If he didn't come up with satisfactory answers, Hazard would spend her day off digging for more information. Nick didn't want Hazard digging too deeply when he wasn't available for backup. The woman could get herself into trouble when she got carried away with a strong lead.

Nick hung a right and sped over the gravel road, leaving the city limits behind. He was curious to learn what Corky Bishop had been doing while Harv was smothering under a ton of hay.

Nick lifted his foot off the accelerator when he saw Corky Bishop's battered farm truck in the pasture. Corky's string-bean frame was silhouetted against the glaring morning sunlight. Nick frowned when he noticed the fluorescent stakes for the proposed well site.

A semi-truck, filled with gravel, sailed over the hill, stirring up a cloud of dust. Apparently, Corky had signed the contract with the drilling company, and work had begun immediately on the new access road.

Now that Harvey was gone, Corky's bank account was enjoying an influx of money. Nick knew times were hard on the farm. He battled increased expenses and marginal profits himself. Corporate farms were taking their toll on family farms.

The times, they were a-changin', Nick reminded himself. Luckily, he had a steady paycheck to see him through the lean times. Corky Bishop didn't. Nick wondered if desperation had caused Corky to do something drastic in order to keep his farm from going under.

Corky shifted uneasily when Nick pulled up in the squad car. "Hi, Chief, what brings you out this way?"

Nick slid off the seat, then stared solemnly at Corky. "I think you know why I'm here." He gestured toward the fluorescent stakes, then at the approaching gravel truck. "If not for Harvey's death you wouldn't have this contract with D and D Drilling Company. We both know that."

"I suspect I have your new wife to thank for this visit," Corky grumbled.

"No, I think we can safely say that your conflict with Harv brought me out here. Now that Anita Blankenship's body has been recovered, more questions have risen."

Corky stepped back, wringing his hands. "And you think I did it?"

"Did you?" Nick asked him point-blank.

"Of course not!" he all but yelled.

"Good. Now suppose you tell me where you were Monday afternoon and who can verify your alibi."

The color seeped from Corky's ruddy features. He looked

like a deer caught in high-beam headlights. "I was at the farm, mowing the grass."

"Was anyone with you?"

"No."

"Did anyone drive past your house who can substantiate your claim?"

"No."

Nick shifted mental gears quickly. "What time did you see LeRoy Ashton and Harvey together at the second well site on Renshaw Farm?"

"What?" Corky shook himself, as if to jump-start his stalled thoughts. "Early. I was feeding range cubes to my cattle."

"So you waited until LeRoy left and Harv returned on his tractor to confront him."

Nick could tell that Corky was mentally watching where he stepped, for fear of tripping on an unseen land mine. "Yeah, that's right."

"According to my information, you and Harv had words, none of them pleasant. Is that correct?"

"I never had pleasant words with Renshaw. He was an asshole."

"While you were doing farm chores, did you see a compact, plum-colored Chevy cruising around the section?"

Corky nodded. "That must have been Anita, right? I saw the car cruise around three times."

"While you were speaking to Harvey?"

Corky nodded again. "Yeah. Harv scowled and muttered under his breath when the car went by. I couldn't understand what he said," he added in anticipation of the next question.

"Did you see Harv's wheat truck approach during your conversation with Harv?"

Corky frowned pensively. "Now that you mention it, I do recall seeing a farm vehicle coming from the south as I drove away."

"But you weren't the one driving it." Nick gauged Corky's reaction carefully.

"Hell, no. Why would I be?"

"Because you wouldn't arouse much suspicion if you drove up in Harv's truck, after parking your pickup behind his shed."

"Now hold on, Chief!" Corky squawked. "I told you I was in my pickup. I saw the wheat truck cruising up the hill. How could I be two places at once?"

Since Nick had Corky rattled, he fired another question. "Precisely what time did you drive over to Harv's pasture to confront him about undercutting your negotiations with D and D Drilling Company?"

"Nine-fifteen, I'd say," Corky replied hurriedly.

The roar of falling gravel interrupted their conversation. The semi-truck dumped its load on the graded path that led to the fluorescent stakes.

Nick frowned, waiting for the racket to subside. If memory served him correctly, Hazard had told him that she received a phone call from Harv at nine-fifteen.

"You're sure about the time?"

"Yeah, it was nine-fifteen," Corky insisted. "Come to think of it, I heard the disc jockey on the Country-Western radio station announcing the time before he played his next song."

"What song did he play?"

"I don't remember."

"You remember the time but not the song?" Nick asked dubiously. It sounded like selective memory to Nick.

Corky jerked up his head. "I wasn't paying attention because I was thinking about what I intended to say to Harv."

Nick studied Corky intently. He couldn't tell whether or not the man was lying. The farmer was becoming hostile, feeling threatened. Continuing this line of interrogation was pointless, Nick decided.

"One last question," Nick said. "Do you know if Harvey carried a cell phone with him?"

The question caught Corky completely off guard. "What does that have to do with anything?"

"Just answer the question."

"I don't have the slightest idea whether Harv had a cell phone."

Nick pivoted on his heels and strode to his car. It suddenly became very important for him to know if Harv carried a cell phone. He got in the squad car and drove south, then impulsively whipped into Harvey's pasture when he saw the hay bale sitting on the far side of the pond. Who had fed cattle after he and Hazard discovered Anita's car in this pond yesterday afternoon?

Nick stared across the pasture, noting the indentation left in the grass. Whoever had delivered the hay had driven across the wheat field to the pasture rather than using the gravel road. Why was that? Did the driver want to avoid being seen?

Nick put the car in reverse and wheeled around. He wanted to check Harv's tractor for a cell phone. It was becoming increasingly clear there was a discrepancy in Corky's story. Harv could not possibly have called Hazard at approximately the same time he spoke to Corky, unless he was talking on a mobile phone while Corky approached.

Somebody was lying, and Nick didn't think it was Hazard.

Nick veered into the driveway at Renshaw Farm and headed toward the John Deere tractor that was parked north of the machinery shed. He hopped onto the step and opened the glass door of the tractor cab. Hurriedly he searched around the seat, hoping to find a cell phone that might have tumbled to the floor or got wedged between the hydraulic levers and seat.

His search turned up nothing but the wrapper from a Dolly Madison snack-size fruit pie—cherry flavored. Nick climbed down from the tractor and placed his hand on the engine. The metal was still warm. Yep, someone had definitely fed a hay bale with this tractor—recently.

But who? Nick had no idea.

Returning to his car, Nick drove to the farmhouse, then

knocked on the door. The door was locked. Nick scowled. He was going to have to resort to Hazard's tactic of climbing through the window. He hated it when he had to stretch the rules to accommodate the need for quick information. He made a pact with himself not to tell Hazard what he had done. She would never let him hear the end of it.

Nick made a swift search for a cell phone. Again, he turned up nothing.

An unidentified creak put Nick on immediate alert. He snatched up his pistol and moved cautiously toward the sound. Nick stared curiously at the back door, where Johnny Phipps claimed to have exited so he could eavesdrop on the conversation in the kitchen that fateful morning.

Damn, he must be paranoid after he unlawfully entered the house. Of course, things like that didn't faze Hazard when she was in her investigative mode. She thumbed her nose at regulations.

Spinning around, Nick wandered into the living room to peruse the bookcase that was filled with the photos Hazard had mentioned. She was absolutely right, thought Nick. Harvey Renshaw had a trophy case of blondes, all of whom looked alike. The man definitely suffered from the Harem Complex.

Nick glanced around the room to locate the phone. He dialed Hazard's office number.

"Hazard Accounting."

"Haz, Thorn here. You said you had Harvey's phone bill, right?"

"Yes," she replied.

"Take a quick look to see if there is a separate billing for a cell phone."

"Hold on a sec."

Nick waited.

"No, I don't see one," she said a minute later. "Why are you asking?"

"Because I just spoke to Corky and he claims he confronted Harvey in the pasture around nine-fifteen."

"That can't be right. *I* talked to Harvey about nine-fifteen."

"You're certain of the time?" Nick asked.

"What do you think, Thorn?"

"I think you *think* numerically. I figured you knew what you were talking about."

"That's one of the nicest things you've ever said to me," she said with a hitch in her voice.

"No, it isn't. I said some pretty swell stuff last night ... late last night," he murmured.

"Meet me at the house for lunch at high noon and I'll let you say them all over again," she purred into the phone.

Nick beamed in anticipation. He could spare time for a nooner. "I'm there, doll face."

Nick replaced the phone and strode out the door. No way was he going to be late for a steamy tryst with his gorgeous wife. Besides, he had to recap his interviews with Glenda, Johnny, and Corky. Hazard would want to know exactly who said what about this case.

CHAPTER THIRTEEN

The queasy stomach and dull headache that greeted Amanda that morning were long gone after her midday tryst with Thorn. She had the feeling her allergies were acting up when the mold count rose. Either that or a lingering flu bug had caused the unpleasant sensations. Fortunately, by one o'clock Amanda was feeling like her old self and had shifted into high gear.

After Thorn left the house, Amanda concentrated on mixing the ingredients for two chocolate cakes. Velma had called earlier, requesting that Amanda bake two cakes for the cakewalk that was being held after the chicken noodle supper. On her way home for lunch Amanda had stopped at the mom-and-pop grocery store to pick up cake mixes and canned icing.

Since Amanda had alphabetically organized Thorn's kitchen it didn't take long to put her hands on the needed utensils and mixing bowl. She popped four layer-cake pans in the oven and set the timer. She was in the process of tidying up her culinary mess when the phone rang. Amanda removed her hands from the dishwater, dried them off, then scooped up the phone.

"Hazard's . . . um . . . Thorn's residence." It was going to take awhile to get used to her new name, Amanda realized.

"Is Nicky there?"

Amanda tensed. She recognized the voice. "Hello, Mom Thorn."

"Oh, it's you," Mom said, deflated. "Is Nicky there?"

Mom made it clear that she preferred to avoid conversation with Amanda. "Sorry, Thorn's back on patrol duty. I'm baking cakes for the noodle dinner." *Maybe that would impress Mom.*

"Really? Since when did you learn to cook? I thought you were the queen of take-out."

And then again, maybe not.

Amanda clenched her hand around the phone, pretending it was Mom's neck. "Do you want me to take a message for Thorn?"

"No, I just called to chitchat."

With Thorn, but not with me.

Mom had just hung up when the phone shrilled again.

"Thorn's place."

"Hi, doll."

Amanda rolled her eyes. A call from Mom *and* Mother? Wasn't this Amanda's lucky day!

"Hello, Mother. What's new in the city?"

"I'm still at an impasse with your infuriating sister-in-law," Mother muttered. "I want to see my grandchildren and I want to see them NOW!"

Amanda jerked the phone away from her head before Mother blew out an eardrum. "Then give Regina some sort of peace offering," she suggested. "It's Friday night. Tell Regina that you're treating her to a night on the town and that you'll baby-sit."

"You want me to *bribe* her?" Mother yowled.

"Have you come up with a better solution?" Amanda countered.

"Well, no, but since Regina won't take my calls I doubt that will work. You'll have to call her to set up the arrangements."

"Fine," said Amanda. "I'll tell Regina that she and my darling brother are going to Giovanni's Restaurant and then out dancing and the expense will be on *you*."

"Giovanni's?" Mother crowed. "Good heavens, doll, that's the most exclusive restaurant in the city! It will cost me a hundred dollars for dinner and dancing."

"Bribery doesn't come cheap, Mother. Pay or pass. Which is it going to be?"

"Oh, all right," Mother said, and scowled. "I'll pay."

"And you'll keep the kids overnight so your daughter-in-law and son can spend some well-deserved time away from the kids . . . . Let's say at one of the nicest hotels in the city."

"That will be another hundred, at the very least!" Mother hooted.

"Make up your mind," Amanda said impatiently. "If I'm going to the bargaining table for you I intend to go loaded for bear. I want to have the kind of tempting offer that Regina can't refuse, even if she is pissed off at you."

"Do not use that kind of language, doll," Mother chastised. "I raised you better than that."

"Yes or no, Mother."

"Fine, make the offer. I'll drive by the bank and withdraw my life savings to sweeten this bribery pot."

Mother and Daddy's life savings wouldn't be dented, Amanda reminded herself. She should know, because she figured Mother and Daddy's state and federal income taxes—for free.

Smiling triumphantly, Amanda said, "I'll get on the horn and call Regina. I'll let you know how the bribery tactic went over."

When Mother hung up, Amanda phoned Regina. As expected, an all-expense-paid evening on the town at an exclusive restaurant and luxury hotel softened Regina up. All systems were go. Amanda called Mother and left a message on her answering machine, stating the arrival time of her grandchildren would be six o'clock.

"Now," Amanda said to herself, "if only this dead-in-the-hay case could be resolved that easily."

Plunking down at the kitchen table, Amanda contemplated the information Thorn had given her at noon. Thorn didn't think Johnny Phipps was the one who broke into her office. The prints Thorn had lifted from the door and file cabinet didn't match. The more Amanda thought about it, the more she had to agree that Johnny didn't have all that much to gain, and neither did Glenda. Amanda had the feeling she knew who was responsible for the break-in, and she would confront her prime suspect this evening at the noodle supper/slave auction. It would be a safe place for the confrontation—lots of people around as witnesses, in case things got nasty.

When a fleeting thought struck her, Amanda reached for the phone and dialed her old number. Laverne answered on the second ring.

"This is Amanda Hazard-Thorn."

"Now what?" Laverne said rudely.

"Since you are the one who handled Harv's final arrangements you should have received several copies of the death certificate," Amanda said in a businesslike tone. "I will need at least two official copies. I have to attach one to the estate tax forms."

Laverne snorted. "And you want *me* to deliver them to *you*? Who the hell do you think you are? The Queen of Vamoose?"

"No, I'm Harvey's accountant. Do you want *me* to see that *you* get your cut of the inheritance?" Amanda fired back.

"Of course I do."

"And what do you think you're getting from the estate, Laverne?"

The question hung in the air and Amanda smiled craftily. She could almost hear the cogs of Laverne's peroxide-rusted brain clicking, wondering how she should respond without incriminating herself.

"I don't know," Laverne said finally. "What am I inheriting?"

"I guess you'll have to wait and see, just like everybody else." Amanda glanced at the oven timer to check on the cakes. "Bring the certificates to my office in an hour," she instructed.

"Can't make it. I'm busy," Laverne said snippily. "I'll bring them in the morning."

"I won't be there in the morning and I need them this afternoon so I can complete the tax reports."

There was a long, irritated pause.

"Oh, all right, Hazard. If you're going to get pushy about it, I'll be there in one damned hour!"

Amanda hung up, then staggered on her feet. *Whew!* Where had this light-headed feeling come from? Was Thorn poisoning her kibble? Of course not. Maybe her own cooking was making her queasy and dizzy.

Amanda propped herself against the table and fanned herself vigorously. She was too young to be having menopausal power surges. Maybe what she fixed for lunch hadn't agreed with her. According to the medical reports she had seen on the news, mild cases of food poisoning were more commonly responsible for queasy stomachs than flu bugs. Maybe the left over chicken teriyaki was the culprit.

Amanda definitely needed a day off. She had been meeting herself coming and going all week. Exhaustion must have caught up with her, she diagnosed. After the hectic dead-in-the-driver's-seat investigation, the last-minute wedding arrangements, the honeymoon and a fast and furious week of catching up at the office—plus a new investigation—Amanda's energy tank was running on fumes. Her resistance was way down. She really could use a nap, since she couldn't spare an entire day of rest.

She glanced at the oven timer again. She had fifteen minutes to rest before the cakes were ready to come out.

Fifteen minutes is better than nothing, Hazard. Take it.

Amanda wobbled to the sofa and collapsed.

She didn't know how long the timer had been buzzing when she finally woke up, but the smoke alarm was blaring and a cloud of gray smoke rolled from the oven.

"Well, damn!" Amanda removed the cremated cakes, then flung open the windows. She would have to stop by the mom-and-pop grocery in Vamoose and pick up frozen cakes for the noodle supper.

So much for her culinary attempt. For a woman who could balance accounts and solve crimes, why was she so lousy at cooking?

Oh, well, Amanda thought as she headed for her office. *We all have our own special talents. Mine just doesn't happen to be the creation of exceptional cuisine.*

"You're home early," Amanda said when Thorn ambled through the door. She glanced at her watch. "Does this mean Vamoose is without police protection?"

Thorn unbuckled his pistol holster and draped it over the back of the sofa. "Deputy Sykes is taking my shift until five o'clock. The new part-time cop from the county sheriff's department will be on duty during the chicken noodle supper."

He sprawled in the recliner. "I decided to treat myself to an hour of R and R before the church dinner." Thorn glanced up at Amanda. "Any new developments on your end of this investigation?"

Amanda shrugged. "Nothing much, I'm afraid. I got the death certificate for the estate tax forms from Laverne. She, of course, wanted to know exactly how much inheritance she would receive and when to expect the check. Nothing greedy or impatient about that bimbo."

"Has Rita, Wife Number Two, called to ask when she'll receive her cut of the money?" Thorn questioned.

Amanda frowned. "I haven't seen or heard from Rita today. I wonder where she is. Not the same place as Anita, I hope."

She sank down on the arm of the recliner. "This business about Harv meeting with Corky, while Harv was talking on the phone with me, is starting to bug me. Why would Corky lie about it?"

Thorn draped his arm around Amanda's hips. "Damned if I know. If Harv didn't have a cell phone, there was no way he could have driven to the house to make that call and then returned in time to confront Corky. The trip from the pasture to the house, and back again, would take at least fifteen minutes, even if he was driving his John Deere tractor in road gear. And who the hell fed hay to the Renshaw cattle herd this morning?"

"Whoever it was should have done the chore two days ago. The pasture grass is down to its roots, and the cattle have been scrounging for food."

Thorn sank a little deeper in the chair, his eyelids at half-mast. "It's been a busy month, Hazard. I don't want to be a dud, but I really could use forty winks. I'll probably have to work my butt off tomorrow while I'm enslaved."

Amanda patted his arm affectionately. "Just lie back and relax, handsome. I'll do some paperwork while you're napping."

She tiptoed to the kitchen, wondering why she bothered being quiet. Thorn was asleep the instant he closed his eyes. The poor dear man had been as busy as she had.

Spreading the estate tax forms on the table, Amanda filled in the information quickly and efficiently. The real estate appraiser had finished his report and dropped it by her office shortly before Laverne arrived. Amanda had the forms in proper order in a matter of minutes. She glanced at the death certificate to ensure Laverne had given her an official copy, then paper-clipped it to the tax forms.

Setting the file aside, Amanda studied Harvey's phone bill. She frowned when she noticed several long-distance calls to Georgia, Texas, California . . . .

Amanda wondered who Harvey had called in California. The bank perhaps? Or was there an ex-girlfriend, or prospective girlfriends, out there somewhere? With Harv's track record Amanda wouldn't be surprised if there were several on the West Coast, and a couple more waiting in the wings.

When Amanda heard the TV flick on, she knew Thorn had roused from his nap. She smiled to herself. She liked this warm, fuzzy feeling of contentment. Only these sporadic sensations of dizziness and nausea spoiled her mood.

Amanda instinctively sensed that information about this case was beginning to gel in her mind. There were a couple of tidbits of facts that refused to settle neatly into place when she reconstructed the incidents that took place the day Harvey ended up squished in the hay. One puzzling piece of information was Corky's insistence that he was with Harv at the same time Amanda was talking to the victim on the phone. Another tidbit that bothered her was: Who was driving Harv's wheat truck that had hydraulic fluid oozing from the grill and front bumper?

As soon as Amanda figured that out, she would know who bumped off Harvey, then silenced Anita—who obviously saw more than she was supposed to that fateful morning.

"Haz! What do you say to a shower before we go to the noodle dinner to pick up my slave collar," Thorn called from the living room.

Amanda smiled in gleeful anticipation. Piecing this complex puzzle together could wait until tomorrow, she told herself. Besides, she could sleep on all the information, and hopefully, she would have a clearer view of where this case was headed. Thorn would be enslaved for the day, so she could concentrate intently on solving this case. But for now, she had a muscular male chest to lather up.

"Last one in the shower is a rotten egg!" she called as she hotfooted it to the bathroom.

The Methodist church was packed, Amanda noted as she carried in her store-bought cakes. The serving line stretched from the front door, through the foyer, into the reception hall. Practically every Vamoosian was on hand to lap up the heaping servings of chicken noodles, green beans, a variety of Jell-O salads, and homemade hot rolls.

Amanda put her cakes in the kitchen, then stopped to tickle little Sissy's chin. The newest Hix arrival wasn't even a week old and already her parents were dining out, showing off the new baby.

The little girl looked like her toddling brother—chubby cheeks and hair so blond that it blended in with the pale skin on their heads, making them look bald. While Amanda oohed and aahed over little Sissy, Bubba Jr. leaned out from his father's bulky arms to hug Amanda's neck.

"No, B.J.," Bubba told his son.

B.J. squawked and leaned forward again, his pudgy arms outstretched. Clearly, the little tyke had not adjusted to having his baby sister receive all the attention.

"Come here, kiddo." Amanda took Beeje and propped him on her hip. "You haven't had a chance to see Thorn lately. How about if you have supper with us."

"Are you sure?" Sis Hix asked. "B.J. gets kinda messy when he eats."

Amanda was well aware of that. She had confiscated the mustard and catsup from the boy while they were having lunch at the Last Chance Cafe.

"No problem," Amanda replied. "I'll bring Beeje back before the slave auction begins."

With B.J. flapping his arms and chattering unintelligibly, Amanda returned to her place in line beside Thorn.

"Hey, squirt, what have you been up to?" Thorn asked B.J. The boy yammered in a language no one but his parents could understand.

"He's feeling slighted because his new sister is stealing his thunder," Amanda murmured confidentially.

Thorn scooped up B.J. and planted the kid on his broad shoulders. "How's the view up there, kiddo?"

B.J. yammered some more, content with his bird's-eye view of the crowd.

Amanda glanced behind her. "I see Laverne and LeRoy are in attendance. I hope a fight doesn't break out when Laverne notices that Johnny and Glenda are at the front of the line."

"If a fight does break out you'll be within hearing distance, hoping somebody gets careless and flings a comment that will give you a lead in this case," Thorn said, then smirked. "Admit it, Haz, you live for this stuff."

Amanda flashed him a saucy smile. "I have to have something to do in between double-occupancy showers, don't I?"

The grin that spread across Thorn's face was priceless. Amanda was learning how to shut Thorn up and effectively distract him from razzing her about her investigative compulsions.

"Tomorrow night we are going to sit ourselves down and go over the facts of this case," Thorn murmured in her ear, assuring her that her tactic of distraction wasn't one hundred percent effective. "Once we figure out whodunit, I'm going to devote my spare time to enjoying all the fringe benefits of married life."

"Except for spending time putting your combine and wheat truck in proper working order for harvest," Amanda reminded him.

"Yeah, except for that," Thorn grunted. "Thanks for spoiling my fantasy and reminding me that my Saturday has been shot to hell because of this charity benefit."

"Don't swear in church, Thorn, especially with Beeje in

hearing range," Amanda cautioned. "The kid picks up on naughty words and repeats them like a jabbering parrot. It's the only thing he says that I understand perfectly."

Turning, Amanda surveyed the crowd of Vamoosians who sat around the folding tables, gobbling up chicken noodles. Velma, her sister, and her niece were gossiping between bites. They waved the moment they spotted Amanda and Thorn. Amanda waved back, then glanced left to see Rita Renshaw sitting beside the Watts brothers and their cousin, Sparky Watts. All three men were ogling Rita, whose painted-on blouse emphasized her oversize chest.

Men, thought Amanda. *They can never overcome their lusty instincts.*

Well, at least Rita was alive and well, Amanda mused. For the past few days she'd wondered if Harv's second wife had ended up like his recent girlfriend.

Amanda noticed that Glenda and Johnny were cozying up at the head of one table, but they looked uneasy when they spotted Amanda and Thorn. Their uneasiness intensified when Laverne and LeRoy stepped around the corner to pick up their plates and silverware.

Amanda supposed she should have told the harem of women who would inherit what, but she was reluctant to divulge the information before she figured out who did Harvey in. If she was to remain in suspense, then so could her prime suspects.

Leading the way around the reception hall, Amanda hunted for empty seats. She watched Laverne and Glenda glare daggers at each other, while Johnny and LeRoy visually pitched hatchets. Rita watched with a smirk and her usual air of aloofness. That smug expression—as if Rita knew something the rest of the world didn't—bothered Amanda. What was Rita up to?

"No, Beeje, you have to eat with your fork, not your fingers,"

Amanda instructed when the toddler made a grab for his food. "You have to mind your manners in public."

From that moment on, Amanda didn't have time to study her suspects. She had her hands full teaching B.J. acceptable table manners.

"Corky just arrived," Thorn reported.

Amanda glanced up. "Where?"

"Row four, south end of the table."

Amanda watched the lean-framed farmer slouch in his chair. For a man who had recently come into several thousand dollars, he didn't look all that cheerful. Instead, Corky looked as if he wished he were invisible. Was his guilty conscience bothering him?

After Amanda swallowed down her meal in record time, she hoisted B.J. from his chair.

"Where are you going?" Thorn demanded. "Don't start trouble."

"Little ol' me?" she drawled, then batted her eyes.

"Yeah, you, little Bo Peep," he said suspiciously. "Now, precisely where are you going?"

"I'm only going to the rest room to wash B.J.'s hands and face. He's wearing more food than he consumed."

"And then you are coming right back."

"Geez, Thorn, you're getting awfully possessive after only three weeks of wedlock, aren't you?"

"No, I simply know how you operate." Thorn scooped up a quarter pound of butter and smeared it on his hot roll. "Don't start anything I can't finish, because I plan to go back for seconds. I really would like to eat in peace."

Amanda sniffed as she turned away. "Don't tick me off, Thorn, or you can kiss all the double-occupancy showers in your future good-bye."

Quick as a wink, Amanda washed B.J.'s hands and face in the lavatory, then wiped off his grimy shirt with a paper towel.

"P-pee!" B.J. said.

"Good boy." Amanda patted him on the head, then directed him to the toilet. "Have right at it, kiddo."

After another round of hand scrubbing, Amanda hoisted the little fellow onto her hip and headed toward the table where Laverne and LeRoy were putting away an amazing amount of food.

She looked down at their heaping plates. "Did someone forget to tell you that this is an all-you-can-*eat* supper, not all-you-can-*carry*?"

Laverne glanced up, then muttered a few foul words under her breath. "What does it take to get rid of you, Hazard? You're worse than a chronic rash. Why don't you go pester Rita and Glenda. I don't want them to feel slighted."

"Since they aren't the ones who broke into my office, I don't have a bone to pick with them," Amanda retorted.

Laverne's square chin went airborne. "Don't spoil my appetite with false accusations."

"Laverne wouldn't do that," LeRoy said in her defense.

Amanda scoffed at the gorilla-size oil pumper. "Are you kidding? Of course she would do it. She is champing at the bit to know how many greenbacks she'll get to fondle."

Laverne's face exploded with color. "You can't prove shit, Hazard."

Amanda didn't waste her breath telling Laverne not to curse in the church. It wouldn't faze this coarse, hard-edged woman.

"You don't think I can prove it? Well, you're wrong. Thorn lifted prints from the doorknob and the side of the file cabinet. He plans to take your prints after supper to make the comparison." Since Thorn was watching her intently, Amanda made a big production of waving to him. "I know you did it, Laverne, you may as well own up to it and save yourself the embarrassment of being printed in the parking lot, while the whole town watches."

For the first time Laverne actually looked worried. The tough-gal facade slid off her makeup-caked face. "All right, damn it, I admit I got overanxious and I was pissed at you, so I broke into your office to check Harvey's file. But there wasn't any information in the file. I didn't intend to leave the place in a mess, but Deputy Sykes drove by and I panicked.''

Laverne stared across the room at Johnny. ''But I didn't bump off Harvey. You should ask *him* where he was when Harv kicked the bucket.''

''I already did,'' Amanda replied. ''Funny thing, he says he didn't do it, either. He thinks maybe you did it.''

Laverne let loose with one of her unladylike snorts. ''He would say something spiteful like that since I tossed him out on his ear.''

''That isn't the way Johnny tells it,'' Amanda inserted.

''Well, I wouldn't bet my inheritance on anything he says. He is unreliable.''

Amanda wanted to grill Laverne further, but B.J. got extremely squirmy. He was ready to get down and run a few laps around the reception hall. Amanda decided to let Beeje exercise before she took him back to his parents. After all, what was the benefit of being an honorary aunt if you couldn't dump the little tyke off on his parents at your convenience?

''Okay, Beeje, you can walk around the room, but you have to hold my hand,'' Amanda insisted as she set the toddler on his feet.

CHAPTER FOURTEEN

Amanda took the long way around the reception hall so B.J. could burn off some of his youthful energy. She passed the table where County Commissioner Sam Harjo was sitting.

"Hello, gorgeous," Sam murmured.

Amanda smiled in greeting. Sam, the younger version of Clint Eastwood during his spaghetti Westerns, winked at her.

"Long time, no see," Sam said.

"How are you, Harjo?"

"Depressed, now that you're married to the Lone Ranger instead of me."

Amanda ignored that. "The Bahaman honeymoon was enjoyable."

"I'm sure it was. Wish I could have been there with you."

Amanda ignored that, too. "I'm baby-sitting B.J." She gestured to the little tyke who was crawling under the table. "He is having trouble coping because his new baby sister is stealing his limelight."

Sam grinned wryly. "I know how he feels. Somebody stole

my baby and my limelight." He glanced over Amanda's shoulder. "Hello, Lone Ranger. I figured you would gallop over here the second Hazard stopped to chat with an old friend."

Amanda rolled her eyes when Thorn and Harjo stared each other down like gunfighters at twenty paces. "I'm really getting tired of this machismo nonsense that you two have going. We are not going to have one of these little scenes each time we meet."

Amanda stared at Thorn, then at Harjo. "You two shake hands and stop this silliness. That's an order."

Harjo peered at Amanda for a long considering moment. "Are you happy? Truly happy with this heap big chief?"

"Deliriously happy," Thorn answered for Amanda.

"I didn't ask you, Lone Ranger. I asked *her*," Harjo said.

"Yes, I'm happy," Amanda declared. "And Harjo, I count you as one of my dearest, most trusted friends. Now can we call a truce, once and for all?"

"Don't expect me to kiss and make up," Harjo grunted.

"Definitely no kissing," Thorn snorted.

"Fine. No kissing. Just shake hands and make up," Amanda demanded impatiently.

Reluctantly Tom Selleck's look-alike and Clint Eastwood's clone shook hands.

"Now, then, Harjo, you are invited over to our house tonight after the chicken noodle supper and auction winds down. We'll have cake and coffee and you can help Thorn rearrange the living room furniture."

Thorn's brows shot up like exclamation marks. "What's the matter with the way I arranged the furniture?"

"I want to turn the living room around so the TV is on the wall where we walk in the front door," Amanda explained. "It will make better use of room space."

"I have had the furniture arranged the same way for seven years," Thorn grumbled. "It works for me."

"Well, it doesn't work for *we*," Amanda replied, then glanced at Harjo. "You will be there tonight, won't you?"

"Sure, why not? A peace-treaty supper and furniture moving sounds like great fun," he enthused—to irritate Thorn, Amanda speculated.

"Good. We will rejoin you after the slave auction." Amanda grabbed Beeje by the seat of his pants and pulled him from beneath the table. "I'm taking this little tyke back to his parents. I'm sure two intelligent, mature men like yourselves can carry on a civil conversation without me serving as your mediator."

To Amanda's relief, Thorn and Harjo did engage in conversation—as if they actually enjoyed each other's company. Amanda knew for a fact that they did. She was anxious for them to put this ridiculous male rivalry behind them and reestablish their friendship.

Bubba Hix uplifted his arms when Amanda returned with B.J.

"No!" Beeje clamped himself to Amanda like clinging ivy.

"Come on, Son. 'Manda let you run around all over the place. It's time for you to sit down with us."

"No!"

Amanda noted that "no" was one of the words B.J. had learned to say quite clearly. She reached up to pry the little tyke's hands loose, then deposited him in his father's lap. "When I come by your house to see how much your little sister has grown, you and I will go to the park," she told the disappointed boy. "In the meantime, you need to help your mom and dad take care of your new sister. They'll need all sorts of help fetching diapers and putting Sissy to sleep. She is very lucky to have a brother like you, Beeje. You have an important job, you know."

Beeje looked down at his sleeping sister, then back at Amanda. He jabbered unintelligibly.

"Remember, I'll be at your house the first of next week."

"Thanks, 'Manda," Sis murmured confidentially. "Bubba Jr. thinks you are wonderful."

Amanda combed her fingers through B.J.'s hair, then winked fondly at him. "I happen to think he's pretty swell, too. We've had some interesting adventures, haven't we, kiddo?"

Amanda circled the reception hall. Since she wanted to give Thorn and Harjo plenty of time to chitchat, she visited with dozens of her clients and stopped to say hello to Pops and Salty Marcum. Then she made another swing past the suspects who were in attendance. After a half hour Amanda wandered back to her seat and took a load off.

"I'm proud of you, Hazard," Nick said when she returned to her seat beside him. "You didn't start a food fight when you bore down on Laverne earlier this evening."

"Hey, I can mind my manners when I have to. And I am proud of you and Harjo. Now everyone in Vamoose realizes there are no hard feelings between the two of you after I married you instead of him."

If Nick didn't admire and respect Sam Harjo so much he wouldn't see the county commish as such a worthy rival. It was going to take time and a conscious effort to forget about Harjo's romantic interest in Hazard.

Nick suspected it was going to take a considerable amount of time for Harjo to forget about it, too.

Nick decided he didn't want to discuss the topic of Harjo further, so he said, "Did you learn anything interesting from Laverne?"

"Sure did. Laverne admitted to breaking into my office to find out how much she was going to inherit. Unfortunately for her, I had the documents at the house and she still doesn't have a clue as to how much money she is going to get."

When Nick tried to stand up, intent on reading Laverne the riot act for breaking into the office, Hazard jerked him down.

"Cool it, Thorn. I'm not pressing charges against Laverne. She was in a state of stress at the time. Johnny had bailed out and Harv was gone. Laverne was scrambling to find a male replacement, because she doesn't feel complete without a man underfoot."

"Her state of stress might have spilled over onto retaliation against Harvey," Nick pointed out.

"I don't think so."

"Why not?"

"Just another hunch."

Nick sighed. He was doomed to a life of dealing with Hazard's hunches.

"May I have your attention!" Velma Hertzog bugled above the murmur of conversation.

Dressed in purple, looking like a giant plum, Velma pounded her gavel on the table. "I would like our slaves to gather at the food table so we can begin the bidding."

Grumbling, Thorn got to his feet. "Next time Vamoose raises money for charity, remind me to write out a check and bypass participating in these kinds of activities," he said. "And one more thing, Haz, don't you dare buy Sam Harjo as your slave!"

Having delivered his ultimatum, he filed into line with the other slaves who were headed toward the auction block.

Amanda sat back to enjoy the auction. Buzz Sawyer, the local carpenter, received impressive bidding. Several widows and divorcees were anxious to have him at their beck and call. When all was said and done, Buzz sold for $110. He was to be Christina Horiwitz's slave for a day.

Glory Frye paid dearly for Phillip Fawcett's plumbing skills, Amanda noted. The timid plumber flushed when Glory got so excited that she hugged the stuffing out of him.

Velma Hertzog turned the gavel over to her sister so she

could bid on Sparky Watts. Velma bumped up the bidding by twenty-dollar increments and wrote out a $140 check for her slave. According to Velma, the Beauty Boutique would soon have two ceiling fans and several more electrical outlets to accommodate the wattage needed for all her curling irons and hair dryers.

When Sam Harjo came onto the auction block, Thorn stared Amanda down. Vamoose's single women got into a lively bidding war over the handsome commish. He racked up $130 for charity.

Amanda considered bidding on Thorn, but he went exceptionally high. Lucille Pomegranate paid $150 for Thorn to mow and weed-eat her lawn, trim overgrown shrubs, replace rotting boards on her deck, and . . . . Amanda frowned, disconcerted, when Lucy rushed up to plant a smacking kiss right on Thorn's lips. The divorcee seemed entirely too eager to claim her slave!

And Thorn was worried about Harjo coming on too strong? He was a meek lamb compared to Lucy the Wolf!

Nobody messed with Hazard's man. Amanda vowed to sic the IRS on that well-built brunette if she got up-close and personal with Thorn in private!

Amanda clamped down on her possessive tendencies and watched Thaddeus Thatcher, then the Watts brothers, take their places on the auction block. Several women in town were anxious to have their vehicles repaired by these skilled automotive specialists.

By the time the last man was sold into slavery the Methodist Women's Society had raised over two thousand dollars, not counting the profit from supper. The cakewalk earned another eight hundred dollars. But to Amanda's dismay, she had to buy back her store-bought cakes.

She was the only one who even bid on the darn things!

* * *

"There has been a change of plans," Amanda announced as she breezed from the church with Thorn and Harjo at her heels.

"Now what?" Thorn grumbled.

Amanda kept her gaze trained on the buxom blonde who was sauntering toward her yellow sports car. "We have to make a detour before I serve cake and coffee." She glanced over her shoulder. "Harjo, you can ride along with us, then we'll swing back here to pick up your truck."

"Hazard, what are you up to?" Thorn demanded as he slid behind the wheel of his 4X4 pickup.

Amanda scooted to the center of the seat so Harjo could ride shotgun. "Follow that yellow car, Thorn. I want to know where Rita Renshaw is holing up. If she isn't staying at the Laid Back Motel, and she isn't living out of her little sports car, then she has to be bedding down somewhere else for the night. I want to know where, and I want to know with whom."

Harjo chuckled as Thorn cruised down the street, keeping a discreet distance from the yellow sports car. "I presume we are tailing one of your suspects in the Renshaw–Blankenship case. Is this what you two do for fun?"

"It's what Hazard does for fun," Thorn muttered. "See what I have to put up with while Hazard is obsessed with an investigation?"

"Don't knock it, Lone Ranger, she has been right several times," Harjo commented.

Thorn shot him a dark look. "You don't have to remind me. She does it constantly."

"Turn into the parking lot, Thorn," Hazard ordered when Rita zipped into the handicapped space near the front door of the Hitching Post Tavern.

"I ought to give her a citation for taking that space," Thorn grumbled. "I hate it when unauthorized vehicles do that."

"Calm down, Thorn. You'll have to overlook Rita's parking

infraction this time. I don't want to make her suspicious right now. There are more important matters to investigate.''

Hazard half turned to focus her full attention on Harjo. ''Since you are the eligible bachelor here, you are the most likely candidate to keep surveillance on Rita.''

''Me?'' The commish gaped at her. ''You want me to pick Rita up?''

''Of course not,'' Amanda said. ''I just want you to swagger into the bar and find out who Rita latches on to.''

''And what are you two going to be doing while I'm shadowing Rita?'' Harjo wanted to know. ''You aren't going to leave me stranded here, are you?''

''Certainly not. I invited you for cake and coffee, didn't I? I happen to be a woman of my word.''

''Not to worry, Commish,'' Thorn said as he slid his arm around Amanda's shoulders. ''We'll be sitting out here necking while Hazard has you on this unofficial stakeout.''

Harjo muttered under his breath, then shouldered his way from the truck. When he disappeared inside the bar, Thorn stared curiously at Amanda.

''Just what is it you suspect Rita has going on?''

Amanda shrugged as she lounged leisurely on the seat. ''I don't have a clue. That's why we are following her. She has been mysteriously absent since I interviewed her in the Last Chance Cafe. Rita doesn't have family in this area, so that rules out visiting relatives. After seeing Rita sharing a table with the Watts brothers and their cousin at the noodle supper, I was wondering if Rita is in the habit of running as fast and loose as Harvey did. I also want to make certain that Rita hasn't seduced some man—who thinks with the head located below his belt buckle—into disposing of Harvey for her.''

''Holy smokes! You think she hired an assassin?''

''I don't know Rita well enough to know what she is capable of doing,'' Amanda replied. ''That's what we're here to find out.''

Ten minutes later Harjo exited from the tavern, wearing a sour frown.

"Well?" Amanda asked the instant Harjo opened the pickup door.

"Thanks a helluva lot, Hazard," he muttered as he flounced on the seat. "Rita hit on *me*."

"Not surprising. You're a very attractive man," she replied matter-of-factly.

"Thanks. When I showed no interest in going back to my place for some bedroom gymnastics, Rita sashayed up to the bar to hold court. Cleatus and Cecil Watts were there panting over her, but she singled out Pete Tyson from Adios."

"Who?" Amanda and Thorn asked in unison.

"He's a trucker who has a mobile home on the lake," Harjo explained. "From the scuttlebutt I picked up from the bartender, Rita has been a regular visitor this week. The bartender claims she leaves with somebody different every night. She's already developed quite a reputation with the bar crowd."

"A slut on the prowl," Amanda muttered in disgust. "Rita and Laverne must have a common flaw. Neither one of them seems capable of functioning without a man underfoot."

"If Rita is playing her version of musical chairs, then she must be biding her time until you have Harvey's estate settled," Thorn presumed.

"Maybe." Amanda watched Rita and the trucker, who was wearing boots, jeans, and a ten-gallon cowboy hat, exit the tavern. "But I'm not going to scratch Rita off the suspect list, just because she has set a pattern of passing favors around the clientele at the bar. She might have another hidden agenda for hanging around Vamoose."

When Rita and her date for the evening cruised from the parking lot, Thorn glanced at Amanda. "Can we go home now?"

Amanda nodded. The uneven hair extensions jiggled on her

shoulders. "Good idea, Thorn. I know you're anxious to arrange the living room furniture."

Thorn's sarcastic snort indicated he was nothing of the kind.

"Harjo, since you spend a great deal of time traveling around the county, checking on road conditions, have you seen much activity at Renshaw Farm?"

"I noticed an oil truck and faded gray car in the driveway a time or two this past week," he reported.

"That would be Laverne and LeRoy moving her belongings into the house I used to rent," Amanda informed him.

Harjo frowned pensively. "When I was northeast of town this morning I saw someone driving Harvey's tractor down the path beside the wheat field."

Thorn perked up immediately. "Was a hay bale perched on the prongs of the front-end loader?"

Harjo nodded.

"Who was driving the tractor?" Thorn asked.

"Sorry, I didn't really give it much thought at the time. I figured one of Harv's neighbors had taken it upon himself to feed the cattle since Harvey wasn't around to do it. I was preoccupied with checking the damaged bridge west of Renshaw Farm. It needs repairs and I put in a call to one of my road crews to give the job number-one priority. If that bridge caves in while a truck, carrying a semi-load of cattle to the stockyards, is on top of it, the Commissioner's Office will have dozens of complaints."

Thorn pulled into the church parking lot so Harjo could retrieve his truck. When Harjo strode away, Thorn glanced at Hazard in amusement.

"You are one sneaky broad, Hazard," he told her.

"What an awful thing to say," Amanda said, feigning indignation.

Checking both directions, Thorn turned from the parking lot into the street, then drove toward home. "I wondered why you decided to invite Harjo over for a visit tonight."

"I told you, I wanted you two to renew your friendship while you were rearranging the furniture."

"No, those were your logical excuses," he contended. "You really wanted to grill Harjo about the Renshaw case, because you know he spends considerable amounts of time driving around the countryside, making certain the roads in his district are up to speed."

"Okay, so I consider him an asset to this investigation," Amanda admitted. "I knew better than to approach him in private, because you get all jealous and huffy. But I was curious to know if Harjo might have seen something suspicious going on and simply wasn't aware of the ramifications involved in this case."

"The mysterious tractor-driver, for instance?" Thorn asked.

Amanda smiled. "Precisely, Sherlock. But did it seem odd to you that Harjo didn't mention seeing an extra vehicle in the driveway when he saw Harvey's tractor and the unknown driver cruising down the path beside the wheat field?"

Thorn frowned ponderously. "Maybe Harjo didn't think about mentioning an extra vehicle."

"*If* there was one parked in plain sight," Amanda contended. "Now, if you were being a good neighbor who showed up to tend neglected cattle, would you hide your vehicle so passersby like Commissioner Harjo wouldn't see it?"

"No, probably not," Thorn replied.

"One more thing," Amanda added. "The second time I inspected Harvey's home I thought I heard noises. I had the uneasy feeling someone was watching me."

"I experienced the same sensation," Thorn put in.

Amanda's gaze swung to Thorn. "You did? Were you in the house?"

Thorn squirmed on the seat, but he kept his eyes on the road, avoiding Amanda's direct stare. "I was at the farm this morning. That was when I noticed the tractor had been driven recently."

Amanda watched Thorn astutely. He seemed ill at ease for

no reason she could account for. "Thorn . . .?" She flashed him a suspicious glance. "Is there something you aren't telling me?"

"Ah, here we are!" Thorn said with more enthusiasm than necessary. "Home again, home again, jiggity-jig. Why don't you set the coffee maker to perking and cut the cake while Harjo and I move furniture."

Amanda watched Thorn scoot off the truck seat and hurry along the sidewalk to unlock the door. *What is that all about?* she wondered as she followed him to the house.

CHAPTER FIFTEEN

Nick breathed a huge sigh of relief as he unlocked the front door. Hazard hadn't pressed the issue of his visit to Renshaw Farm. He didn't want to have to confess that he had been inside the house—using her unlawful-entry technique.

When Harjo arrived, Nick made a big production of welcoming the commish—anything to keep Hazard from circling back to the subject of visiting Harvey's home.

"Now then," Hazard said as she glanced thoughtfully around the living room. "I think the sofa would look best on the west wall. Put these two end tables"—She gestured to the oak tables she had brought from her rented farmhouse—"on either side of the sofa. Put my La-Z-Boy recliner in the southwest corner, and Thorn's chair and ottoman in the northwest corner. That should balance the room."

When Hazard wheeled around and strode into the kitchen to make coffee, Nick grabbed one end of the couch. Harjo positioned himself at the other end. Within ten minutes Nick and Harjo had the living room arranged according to Hazard's specifications. It took a few more minutes to move the TV and cable cord to the opposite end of the room.

Hazard stepped around the corner, studied the room critically, then shook her head. "This isn't going to work. Thorn's chair will look better sitting in the southwest corner."

Nick frowned as he surveyed his chair. "What difference does it make which chair sits where? Both of them provide an unhindered view of the television."

"Yes, but the colors in your chair clash with the sofa. My chair color blends in much better. Furthermore, your chair and ottoman make this side of the room look too heavy."

When Hazard turned around and walked off, Nick rolled his eyes in exasperation. "Clashing colors and heavy walls," he grumbled.

"Do you think she's going to change her mind after we switch the chairs?" Harjo asked.

"You can bank on it, Harjo." Nick hoisted up the ottoman, then set it aside. "Ready?"

Simultaneously Nick and the commish hoisted up the chair and repositioned it. When the chairs had been switched, Nick called to Hazard.

She appraised the room again, then shook her head.

Nick realized that the shake of her head meant she still wasn't satisfied with the furniture arrangement.

"The end tables beside the chairs need to be switched, too," she insisted. "As for that piece of junk—"

"Junk?" Nick hooted when Hazard pointed to the antique smoking stand that sat beside his chair. "That happens to be an heirloom. It belonged to my great-grandfather."

"Maybe so, but it doesn't fit in with the rest of the furniture. Stands out like a sore thumb. Find somewhere else to put it, Thorn."

"Like where?" he said in a challenging tone.

Hazard smiled sweetly. "Like in the barn. It should fit perfectly."

When Hazard was out of earshot, Nick muttered, "Suddenly all my stuff isn't good enough."

Harjo snickered at Nick's sour expression. "Ah, the joys of married life. Apparently, a man is the king of his castle until the queen shows up."

"Yeah, to hear Hazard talk, you'd think I didn't have any taste for furniture arrangement until she walked in and took over."

Harjo smiled wistfully. "But now that she's here, I'm sure there are more important benefits to married life besides furniture compromises."

For once, Nick didn't gloat over the fact that Hazard had married him rather than Harjo. In fact, Nick kinda felt sorry for the commish . . . .

Nick jerked upright when he stumbled over that sympathetic feeling for his former rival. *Hazard really and truly is one sneaky broad.*

She had strategically invited Harjo over to the house in hopes of strengthening the bond of friendship that had been severed because of this male rivalry. Harjo couldn't help the way he felt about Hazard. Nick, in good conscience, couldn't hold that against Harjo, because Nick felt the same way about Hazard himself—despite her insistence on switching his furniture arrangement.

"Thanks for helping me move this stuff, Commish," Nick said appreciatively.

"No problem, Lone Ranger." Harjo gave him a genuine smile.

"I would like you to become a regular visitor here, Harjo. I want you to feel free to stop by any time."

"I'd like that," Harjo murmured. "Thanks."

"Yo! The coffee is ready and the cake is served," Hazard called from the kitchen.

Nick and Harjo took their places at the table. Nick could sense that Hazard wasn't finished with her sneaky-broad tactics.

He knew she was up to something when she turned her dazzling smile on Harjo.

"This Renshaw case still has me stumped," she said as she dumped cream and sugar into her coffee. "Did you encounter Harvey often, while tending your commissioner duties?"

"Harvey was an odd character," Harjo replied. "Sometimes I would see him several times in the course of a few days, coming and going from his farm and driving around town. Then a month would pass and I would rarely cross paths with him."

"Could be that he was busy with farming chores during part of that time," Nick put in. "Farming seems to go in flurries. Too many things to do and not enough time to do them. When the lull hits, you sit back and catch your breath, because you've put in so many double days."

"Maybe." Harjo shrugged a broad shoulder, then took a bite of chocolate cake. "But that's not exactly what I meant. I'd see Harv tooling around in his Jeep, then an hour later he would be zipping down the road in his wheat truck. And then I would see him whizzing off with Anita Blankenship, or in Laverne's car. For a *retired* military man he seemed pretty busy."

"Can you blame him for not staying home much?" Nick smirked. "Harv had a live-in girlfriend and an ex-wife and her boyfriend underfoot. I can't imagine that his home life was all that relaxing."

"Did you happen to see Anita Blankenship cruising around the section several times Monday morning or afternoon?" Hazard asked Harjo.

Harjo nodded. "Now that you mention it, I do remember seeing her wearing a path on the gravel roads. I had one of the graders working the ditch near the bridge we need to repair. Anita went past my road crew two or three times."

Hazard perked up like a bloodhound on the scent. "Did you notice if she stopped to talk to anyone?"

"Yeah, Harvey was in the wheat truck. She stopped to talk with him that morning. Then later—"

"How much later?" Hazard interrupted.

Harjo shrugged. "Around noon, I'd say. I was taking off for lunch. She had stopped on the oil site access road beside the tractor. There was someone in the car with her, but I couldn't tell who. I wasn't paying all that much attention, because I hadn't heard about Harvey's death at the time, so I wasn't expecting anything suspicious to be going on."

Hazard peered curiously at Nick. "Did you take Harv's tractor back to the house after you investigated the scene?"

"Yeah, I parked it beside the machinery shed, and the medical examiner gave me a ride back to my squad car."

"That's odd," Hazard mused aloud. "Who do you suppose Anita encountered? That noontime conversation must have prompted her to contact me at the office."

"Another question unanswered," Nick murmured.

Harjo finished his cake, then stood up. "I better get home. If I'm going to be a slave for the day I'll need my rest." He grinned at Hazard. "I wonder if part of my job description includes moving furniture. Thanks to you, I'm practiced up and I'll be able to tell at a glance if one side of a room is heavy and furniture clashes."

"Glad you came by, Harjo. We appreciate the help," Hazard said as she followed him to the door.

Harjo pivoted, glancing first at Hazard, then at Nick. "I'm glad I came by, too. Maybe you two can come to my place next week and Hazard can color-coordinate and *un*clash my living room furniture. I could throw some hamburgers on the grill."

"Sounds good," Hazard said. "Thorn and I would love to come, and we would be happy to return the favor, wouldn't we, Thorn?"

"Sure thing, Commish."

When Harjo left, Nick stared inquisitively at Hazard. "Who do you suppose Anita met in the pasture that fateful day?"

"The same person who did-in Anita and Harvey and has been feeding hay to the cattle, is my guess." Hazard sighed tiredly. "I'm going to have to mull over the information Harjo gave us tomorrow. I'm really worn-out, Thorn. I feel as if someone installed a spigot to drain all my energy. Are you ready for bed?"

Nick smiled rakishly. He was always ready for bed—if Hazard was sharing it with him.

"Wipe that look off your face, Thorn," Hazard ordered. "Nothing is going to happen tonight."

He slid his arm around her waist to usher her to the bedroom, then he moved his hand onto intimate territory. He kissed that ultrasensitive spot at the base of her neck and heard Hazard moan.

Nick was quite pleased to note that Hazard wasn't quite as exhausted as she first thought she was.

Nick frowned when he noticed Hazard was eating saltines for breakfast. "Something wrong with the eggs I fried for you?"

Hazard shrugged, then looked up. Her face was as white as baking soda. "I must be suffering from a flu bug or something. My stomach has been doing back handsprings since I got up this morning. Or maybe the chicken noodles didn't agree with me. And here I thought only my own cooking bothered me."

"Maybe your allergies are acting up," Nick said.

"Could be," she murmured. "My head is a little stuffy, too. Maybe that's what's making me dizzy."

"Do you want me to refill the prescription Dr. Simms gave you last month? I can pick it up on my way home."

"I'll take care of it," Hazard insisted. "Eat your breakfast. You have a hard day of labor ahead of you."

Nick stared at Hazard's peaked face while he consumed three over-easy eggs, sausage, biscuits, and coffee. "I think you should kick back and relax today. You don't look so hot, Haz."

"Thanks," she grumbled. "You do know how to make a girl feel better."

"Just don't go rushing off to follow a lead, okay? I won't be available, in case you get into trouble."

"Sure thing, whatever you say," she mumbled as she propped her head on her hand and choked down another saltine cracker.

"Promise?" Nick persisted.

She glared at him. "What do you want? My statement written in blood?"

"I'm not leaving until I hear you say that you won't do anything rash without consulting me first. I want you to take it easy today."

"Okay, okay! Are you satisfied?"

Nick polished off his breakfast, then hurried outside to gather his tools and load up his gas-powered weed eater and hedge trimmer. He was feeling reasonably confident that Hazard wouldn't charge off to harass the suspects in the hay case. She could barely hold up her head. If Nick was lucky, Hazard would spend the day lounging around the house, catching up on sleep and doing the laundry that was bulging from the clothes hamper. He wouldn't have to wonder where she was and what she was up to.

"Thorn!"

Nick closed the tailgate on his truck, then turned to see Hazard leaning heavily against the doorjamb. "Yeah?"

"If you let that oversexed divorcee put her hands on you, I'll cut them off with a chain saw."

Nick grinned, exceptionally pleased. "I see you're a little possessive, too."

"It seems I'm a lot possessive," she said, flashing him a stern glance. "You tell Lucy to cool her heels, or whatever part of her anatomy has the hots for you. That one hundred fifty bucks she paid does not include doing the horizontal hoochie-koochie with you.''

''Yes, ma'am,'' Nick drawled. ''I'll tell her.''

'' 'Bye, Thorn.''

''Go to bed, Hazard.''

''I will, but you damned well better not!''

Wow! What a grouch, Nick thought as he drove away. Although Hazard was usually a cheerful morning person, the flu—or allergies—had a fierce and mighty hold on her disposition. Nick sincerely hoped the symptoms of grouchiness waned by the time he returned home. He much preferred Hazard's sassy, upbeat temperament to the irritable shrew who sat across the table from him during breakfast.

By midmorning Amanda felt like showering and facing the day. The sky was overcast and a stiff wind blew from the southwest, sending the pollen and mold count into the high category.

Thorn was right, Amanda decided as she dried off from her shower. She should refill the prescription for the allergy medication Dr. Simms had prescribed the previous month. Now, where had she put that prescription bottle and the printout of side effects caused by the medication?

Because of the hurried move from her rented farm to Thorn's homestead the empty bottle could have ended up anywhere. Munching on soda crackers, Amanda began her search for the missing bottle.

The prescription bottle was not in the kitchen where she arranged the aspirin, Benadryl, Pepto-Bismol, and Tylenol in alphabetical order. Nor was it in the junk drawer where Thorn stashed everything from ice picks to scissors in random disorder.

Squeezing the moisture from her hair extensions with a towel,

Amanda strode down the hall to the bathroom. She checked the medicine cabinet, finding Thorn's outdated prescription for an antibiotic. Amanda tossed the empty bottle in the trash.

Maybe Thorn had crammed the allergy medication bottle in the new bathroom, which was located off the spacious master bedroom he had built while she was investigating the dead-in-the-driver's-seat case.

It wasn't there, either.

Grumbling, Amanda searched the dresser drawers and finally found the empty container and printout of precautions under her underwear—*Not* the place *she* would have put it!

Amanda read the precautions, then gulped. *Oops. Looks like I should have read about the side effects before I took the entire bottle of tablets. Well, it's too late to stew about that now.*

Amanda tucked the prescription bottle in the bathroom where it belonged, then ambled down the hall. She was going to browse through Harvey Renshaw's bank statements, phone bills, and farming receipts one more time, hoping for an inspirational lead that would help her crack this case. She was determined to see a closure to these two unexplained deaths. Then she was going to focus her energy into putting her new home in efficient working order and rearrange the rest of the furniture in the house. With Harjo's help, this homestead could rise to her high expectations.

Amanda gathered up every scrap of information she had collected from the safety-deposit box and from Harvey's home. She spread the papers on the kitchen table and began her methodical study of every bank statement Harv had received the past year.

Her eyes widened when she realized that Harv had been withdrawing large amounts of cash each month. It looked as if he deposited his military retirement pension, then took a third of it in cash within the next week to ten days—but not at the time of the deposit.

Why had he done that? To prevent Laverne from fleecing

him? But if Harv was concerned about his first wife getting her sticky fingers on his money, why had he rented Amanda's farm home for Laverne and Johnny? And where had Harv kept the cash withdrawals? Surely, he hadn't wired the money to the California bank for safekeeping. Was he afraid Wife Number Three was going to take him to court, because he had not divorced her before he married Wife Number Four?

Amanda reexamined the bank statements, searching for checks written to Glenda for child support. There weren't any. But then, she reminded herself, if Harvey hadn't divorced Glenda, no lawyer would have been after him to pay child support. Who was helping to support Glenda and her son? Was it Glenda's father? The retired military soldier who was glad Harvey was out of his daughter's and grandson's life?

Her hand stalled above a deposit slip that was among the canceled checks. It was from Bishop Farm—to the tune of seven hundred dollars. What was that about? Amanda wondered.

Hurriedly she sifted through the canceled checks to find two other deposit slips that indicated Corky Bishop had paid Harvey several hundred dollars.

Amanda picked up the phone, called information, then dialed Corky Bishop's number.

"Hello?"

"Corky, this is Hazard. I need to ask you some questions."

"I've already answered dozens of questions. I'm a busy man. I have fences to repair, a combine to overhaul before harvest. Thorn was just here yesterday, you know."

"This will only take a minute," Amanda assured him.

"Fine, that's how much time I've got to spare. I was on my way out the door when you called."

"Are you sure you drove over to Harvey's pasture at nine-fifteen Monday morning?"

"Yes, I already told Thorn that."

"Why were you paying Harvey money?" she asked abruptly.

There was a noticeable pause.

"Look, Corky, we can do this the easy way or the hard way. If you don't want to deal with me, then we can make it official by having Thorn bring you to headquarters for questioning about Harvey's death. When he calls you in, it won't matter how busy you think you are, because he will hold you indefinitely for questioning and you'll be—"

"Okay, Hazard. I get the point. But the checks I wrote to Harvey don't have anything to do with this case."

"Then why were you paying Harvey?" Amanda demanded.

"Because he sold me three pieces of farm machinery. A disc, a field cultivator, and a six-bottom plow. He knew damn well that I was counting on the money for the new oil well site to pay for that machinery, and he still undercut me. I told you he was an asshole."

Amanda frowned. "Why was Harvey selling his machinery? He was planning to work the ground and plant wheat, wasn't he? How was he supposed to do that without equipment?"

"He rented his farm ground to me."

"What?" Amanda howled. "Why didn't you say something about it before now? You didn't even like the man. Why would you rent his farmland after what he did to you?"

"Geez, Hazard, who said you had to like a man to buy his machinery and rent his farmland? Harvey's place is right across the road from my farm. Convenience is important, you know. If I had a machinery breakdown in the field, I wouldn't have to drive ten miles both ways to gather the tools to make the repairs."

Well, that made sense, thought Amanda. But it still didn't explain why Harv sold his machinery and rented his farmland. It sounded as if Harvey was retiring from farming. What about his cattle? What had he planned to do with his herd?

"Were you going to buy Harvey's cows and calves?" she asked.

"No, Dave Zinkerman planned to buy them, but that was

before Harv stiffed him on the hay. I don't know if the deal fell through or not.''

Dave Zinkerman? Amanda's secretary's new boyfriend who had conveniently left town the same afternoon as the double homicide?

"What do you know about Dave Zinkerman?" she questioned.

"I thought you said this would only take a minute," Corky complained.

"Last question. Where were you Monday afternoon when—?"

"Buzz. Time's up, Hazard. I gotta go. I'm burning daylight."
Click, hum . . . .

Amanda cursed at the phone, since Corky wasn't on the line for her to take out her frustrations. She needed more answers, but Corky cut her off. Well, she would just have to kick around the countryside to see what turned up.

After rearranging the bank statements and bills in neat stacks, Amanda's gaze came to rest on the "I-regret-to-inform-you" letter that indicated Harold J. Renshaw had died during Desert Storm. She tucked the death certificate beneath it, because there were no helpful leads in the information. Harold J. was long gone. And now, so was his brother, leaving all sorts of questions unanswered.

Amanda grabbed her purse and headed for the door. She carried along a package of saltine crackers and 7UP, in case that queasy feeling returned. She climbed into her clunker truck. When Bruno insisted on tagging along, Amanda patted the seat. The Border collie loaded up eagerly.

Amanda drove straight to Renshaw Farm. To her surprise, the stock trailer and wheat truck were nowhere to be seen. Amanda zoomed from the driveway and raced up the gravel road to Harv's pasture. To her astonishment, there wasn't a single cow, calf, or bull grazing in the pasture. Someone had stolen Harvey's herd while he wasn't around to protest!

Dave Zinkerman . . . .

Eyes narrowed, teeth clenched, hands clamped on the steering wheel, Amanda reversed direction and headed south. Dave had obviously returned from his tryst with Amanda's secretary and had swiped Harv's cattle. The man definitely had a lot of explaining to do!

CHAPTER SIXTEEN

"Oh, Nicky, the lawn looks wonderful!" Lucy Pomegranate exclaimed as she stepped onto the front porch, wearing skintight cotton-knit shorts and a midriff blouse that clung to her ample bosom.

Nick wiped the sweat from his brow and set aside the gaspowered weed eater. He glanced in Lucy's direction for no more than a millisecond. Hazard would have a conniption if she knew Lucy was dressed like a second-rate harlot, and he had gawked at this display of considerable assets.

"Thanks, Lucy, I'm doing my best," Nick said as he stared at the overgrown shrubs that were next on his agenda.

To his dismay, Lucy didn't disappear into the house. The busty brunette slinked down the steps and made her drumroll walk across the freshly mowed lawn. She was carrying two glasses of iced tea.

"Break time, sugar."

Reluctantly Nick accepted the glass, then drained it dry. "I didn't know slaves were allowed to take breaks. But that really hit the spot.'' He thrust the empty glass at her. "I better get back to work. There's lots to do.''

"No, no, sugar. You deserve more than a thirty-second break,'' she purred. "I've got lunch ready.''

"Lunch?'' Nick said, staring at the air over her head, refusing to let his gaze drop to her showcased chest.

"Well sure, sugar. You think I'd let my expensive slave starve? No way, I plan to take very good care of you,'' she said, then winked.

No way was Nick going to do lunch *inside* the house with Lucy, especially not when the neighbors had been in and out of their houses all morning, keeping an eye on the goings-on in Lucy's front yard. Hazard would know the moment Nick walked into the house and exactly what time he came back. Hazard's network of spies was everywhere!

"Why don't you bring lunch to the porch and we'll have a picnic,'' Nick suggested.

"Eat outside in this wind?'' Lucy sniffed. "No, *slave*, I insist that we eat in the house. I already set the table.''

Resigned to catching hell for dining privately with Lucy, Nick followed her up the steps and into the house.

"Besides, sugar, I have a few things for you to do in here,'' she murmured.

"I'll go wash up—''

Nick stiffened when Lucy slid her arms around his waist and sidled close. "Whoa, Lucy, this isn't part of my job description.''

She batted her eyes at him and smiled seductively. "I prefer to make up the rules as we go along, stud.''

Nick could almost hear Hazard screeching in outrage. He felt guilty and he wasn't doing a damn thing wrong!

Determined, Nick clamped his hands on Lucy's bare arms and forced them to her sides. "I'm flattered, but I am very *married*.''

"So? I was married once upon a time. But I can tell you for

a fact that nothing lasts forever. I spent a lot of money just for the chance to let you know that you can stop by here anytime you're on your police beat and I'll have tea, and *me*, waiting for you.''

Nick blinked in disbelief. He was being propositioned when he had only been married for three weeks?

"Don't look so dumbfounded, sugar," Lucy said as she walked her fire-engine-red acrylic-tipped fingers up his chest. "I've been your secret admirer for years. Just between you and me, I don't think Hazard is the kind of woman who could satisfy a stud like you."

"You would be surprised about Hazard." Nick wheeled around and practically ran down the hall to wash his hands. He locked the bathroom door—just in case.

Damn it, why hadn't one of the elderly widows bought him off the auction block? But no, he couldn't be that lucky. He'd gotten snatched up by a young, oversexed divorcee who had other things on her mind beside having Nick do her yard work. Hell!

"Are you hiding from me, Nicky?" Lucy called from the other side of the locked door.

"Yes," he said honestly, then unlocked the door.

Showdown time, Nick decided, *there and then.*

He put on his cop face. His arm shot forward. "Go sit down at the table, Ms. Pomegranate."

Lucy stuck out her glossy bottom lip, turned around, and sashayed down the hall, providing Nick with an unhindered view of her gliding hips.

She sat down and leaned forward so that her bosom was propped on the edge of the table like a lunch entree.

"Cut that out," Nick ordered brusquely.

"Cut what out?" she asked in feigned innocence.

"That thing you're doing with your chest. Now let's get one thing straight, right now, right here. I am a happily married man. I am not about to screw up the good deal I've got going.

I was shanghaied into slavery by Velma Hertzog, and I agreed to go through with this because the charity benefit serves good community causes. It also helps out those who need a handyman to catch up on work that needs to be done around the house.

"But I have no intention whatsoever of jeopardizing my relationship with Hazard."

"You think I'm setting you up? You think I'd tell her?"

Nick gnashed his teeth. "*I* would know, and I would feel as if I was betraying a trust. Your nosy neighbors are probably speculating about what we are doing in here right now. I do not want to invite trouble."

Lucy slumped in her chair, staring bewilderedly at him. "You're serious, aren't you?"

"Hell, yes, I'm serious!"

"Well, then, you're one of a kind, sugar," she said. "Harvey Renshaw didn't care that he had an ex-wife and a girlfriend living under the same roof with him. It sure as hell didn't stop him."

Nick's midnight-black eyes nearly popped from their sockets. *Harvey came by here to trip the light fantastic with Lucy? She wasn't even blonde . . . .*

Nick suddenly remembered that Lucy had been a platinum blonde until recently. "You and Harvey?" he bleated.

She nodded. "He was a regular Don Juan, I can tell you for sure. But he quit coming around after I colored my hair brown. I thought about going blond again, but he . . . well . . . " Her voice trailed off and she shrugged.

"He what?" Nick persisted.

"He died. So what was the point?"

"So you decided to hit on me?"

"That's one way of putting it," said Lucy, grinning saucily.

"Did Anita or Laverne know about you and Harvey?" he asked.

"Anita did. We saw her drive by late one afternoon when she was supposed to be at work."

Nick shook his head in wonder. *How could Harv fool around with so many women at once? The man must have had an insatiable appetite.*

Maybe Nick's first hunch about Anita Blankenship was right on target. Maybe she'd had her fill of Harvey's philandering and lashed out in anger. Afterward, when she realized what she had done, guilt and grief tormented her and she drove into the pond to end her misery.

Nick took a chair at the far end of the table. "After lunch I'm going to clip the shrubs, then repair the two rotted boards on your back deck," he said in a no-nonsense tone. "That should take a little over an hour. While I'm working outside, you can make a list of house repairs and I'll do as many of them as time allows before I go home to my wife."

Lucy stared at him for a pensive moment. "I don't know if Hazard deserves you, sugar, but she is damn lucky to have someone as loyal and devoted as you. My ex-husband never turned down an offer, I can tell you for sure."

"Then he was ten kinds of fool, Lucy," Nick told her as he picked up his fork. "Find somebody who deserves *you* and don't settle for meaningless flings."

Lucy chuckled. "Just what I need, a lecture from the chief of police. Okay, sugar, I'll let you eat and get back to work. But, hey, you can't blame a woman for trying. You're the best-looking hunk in town. I always did think so."

Nick didn't reply. He ate the tasty meat loaf, baked potato, and broccoli swimming in cheese sauce. *Damn, it's too bad Hazard can't cook like this.*

But then, Nick quickly reminded himself, *Cooking is about the only thing that Hazard doesn't do well.* He could survive on her tasteless meals. *So Hazard isn't Julia Child. Nobody's perfect.*

* * *

Amanda pulled into Dave Zinkerman's farm, noting the rows of round hay bales that lined the wooden corral. She glanced toward the pasture, wondering how many of the grazing cattle were fresh off Renshaw Farm. A couple of dozen, at the very least, she speculated. Either that or Dave had bypassed the possibility of being caught rustling and hauled the cattle to the stockyards immediately. That would certainly alleviate his money shortage, wouldn't it?

When she climbed from the truck, Bruno tried to hop out, but Amanda closed the door. "You have to stay here, boy."

The dog looked at her pitifully, then settled down on the seat.

Amanda glanced at the two-story Victorian-style house that boasted a fresh coat of pastel-blue paint and glossy-white shutters, then she strode up the limestone sidewalk. Amanda pounded on the door, then waited an impatient moment. She raised her hand to knock on wood again, but the door swung open.

Dave Zinkerman's eyes narrowed warily. "What do you want, Hazard? We just got back in town last night. Sure didn't take you long to show up."

Amanda didn't pussyfoot around. She wanted answers and she wanted this case wrapped up ASAP. "Why didn't you tell me you were going to buy Harvey Renshaw's cattle herd?"

"You didn't ask."

Amanda shouldered past Dave, noting the string of clothing that lay like bread crumbs, leading down the hallway and into the bedroom.

"Jenny? Are you here? It's Amanda!" she called out.

"Leave her out of this," Dave hissed behind her. "She's already worried that she's fallen from your good graces because of our week-long getaway. She stewed about it the whole damn time we were gone."

Amanda glanced over her shoulder at Jenny's good-looking boyfriend. Well, the man had made one point in his favor, she decided. He was being protective of Jenny. It was probably a novel experience for Jenny, since the other men in her life were full-fledged losers.

"Jenny, come out here," Amanda hollered.

The bedroom door opened just enough for Jenny to poke out her disheveled head. "Boss?" she said apprehensively.

"Where was Dave last night and early this morning?" Amanda asked without preamble. "I want the absolute, swear-on-a-Bible truth, Jen, and I want it right now."

The color returned to Jenny's face in an immediate rush. "He was with me, boss."

"The entire time?" Amanda grilled her secretary relentlessly. "He hasn't left your side for more than one hour at any given moment?"

Jenny shook her head. "No, we've been right here, together constantly. My parents aren't expecting us back until this evening so we . . . um . . . decided to enjoy our . . . er . . . allocated time together, even though we ran out of cash to spend on another day at the resort. That is the absolute, swear-on-a-Bible truth, so help me, God!"

Amanda spun around to confront the smug-looking Dave. "You damn well better be treating her like royalty," she said for his ears only.

"I have treated her like a princess, only this prince is running on a low-range budget at the moment."

"The range of your budget could have taken a mighty leap if you hooked up Harvey's stock trailer, loaded his cattle, and sold them in your name at the stockyards."

Dave's eyes popped, his jaw scraped his chest. "You think I rustled Renshaw's cattle? You think I took Jenny with me to do that?"

"You better not have, because I don't want her to be an accomplice to anything illegal," Amanda insisted. "Harvey's cattle were in his pasture yesterday afternoon and they are gone this morning. Most of the town was at the noodle dinner/slave auction last night, so it would be easy to make the heist. It seems to me that stealing cattle would be a quick and easy way for you to recover the money Harvey owed you for hay—and then some. But obviously, you were here with Jenny, so my suspicions are ill-founded. I guess I owe you an apology.''

Dave stood there, his unshaven jaw still scraping his chest.

Jenny was still craning her neck around the partially opened door, staring owl-eyed at Amanda.

"Okay, so I screwed up!" Amanda muttered to Dave. "Nobody is perfect.''

"Boss?''

Amanda lurched around to see Jenny step into the hall, dressed in one of Dave's oversize T-shirts.

"I want you to be the first to know that Dave and I got married. We have been on our honeymoon, but we wanted to keep things simple and quiet.''

"Married?'' Amanda wheezed.

Jenny nodded.

Amanda lurched back around to gape at Dave.

"Married,'' he confirmed, then lifted his left hand to display the gold band encircling his ring finger. "And by the way, I think you should give Jen a raise. She is dedicated to you. I am not going to be very happy if she continues to work for peanuts, since she has been taking those accounting classes at night to improve her skills. I would like to quit my job as security guard on the graveyard shift so we can spend more time together. Timmy needs a father figure who spends quality and quantity time with him.''

Amanda blinked in amazement. Jenny had found a reliable, responsible, devoted man to be her husband and a conscientious father to Timmy? *Hallelujah! It was about time!*

"Now, about that raise,'' Dave prompted.

"Done,'' Amanda said without hesitation.

"Good." Dave opened the door. "I don't want to sound rude, but if you'll excuse us, Hazard, we are still on our honeymoon. I would like to spend every spare minute enjoying my wife's company."

"I have one more question for Jenny," Amanda insisted. She glanced back at her secretary. "Do you recall what time Anita Blankenship tried to contact me Monday?"

Jenny frowned pensively. "It must have been about eleven-forty-five," she said. "I stacked all your messages on the desk so you could return your calls in the order they came in. That's the way you have instructed me to do it."

Amanda recalled what Harjo had said about seeing Anita in the pasture somewhere around noon. Anita had placed the call immediately before she made the drastic mistake of confronting whoever had bumped off Harvey. Had Anita decided to bribe the killer? Why else would she have risked danger? It must have been someone she knew, Amanda concluded, or Anita wouldn't have taken the risk.

"See you bright and early Monday morning, boss," Jenny prompted, when Amanda continued to stand there mulling over her speculations. "Thanks for the raise. I really appreciate it."

Dazed, Amanda walked outside. She thought she might have found Harvey and Anita's murderer—a man who had both motive and opportunity, a man who left town until the smoke had cleared. Instead she had crashed a honeymoon and accused her secretary's new husband of cattle rustling. But Dave obviously had more important things on his mind than revenge and money.

"Damn it, if Dave didn't do it, then who killed Harv and Anita?" She glanced down at Bruno, who contributed nothing to the conversation.

Thorn's theory of Anita striking out in revenge no longer seemed probable. Amanda didn't think Anita had attacked Harvey in a fit of rage and jealousy, then hung around a couple of hours before taking her own life.

Maybe Amanda had misjudged Laverne. Wife Number One could have broken into the accounting office, too anxious to wait out legal proceedings to discover what she inherited— *after* she bumped off Harvey. Laverne was certainly capable of fits of temper. According to Thorn, Johnny Phipps had called her a spitfire. Johnny would know, since he had been living with Laverne for several months.

Maybe Harvey's harsh words and degrading comments had lit a fire under Laverne . . . .

But who had the premeditated forethought to grab Harv's oily boots from the closet and wear them to the pasture . . . ?

Where did that thought come from?

Amanda stopped in her tracks when the question continued to buzz through her brain. *Bingo!* That was the clue that she hadn't been able to puzzle out.

This could not possibly have been a crime of impulsive passion. Someone had deliberately swiped Harvey's work boots and clothes and used his wheat truck to drive to the pasture. The killer had wanted to pose as Harvey.

Corky Bishop claimed he had seen a wheat truck topping the hill while he was confronting Harvey. Sam Harjo claimed he had seen Anita speaking with someone who was driving the wheat truck. Could that someone have dressed himself, or herself, in Harv's clothes to ward off suspicion, making it seem that Harvey was in two places at once?

And who really called Amanda on the phone that fateful morning? It had definitely been a man, a man who knew about Harvey's business dealings. That was Harvey's voice she heard . . . wasn't it?

Or had she *assumed* it was Harvey, because the man on the other end of the phone said so? True, Amanda only spoke to Harvey twice a year and she wasn't all that familiar with his voice. She could have been fooled.

Confused, Amanda started her jalopy truck and drove off.

She had a quick errand to run in Pronto before she returned to Vamoose.

Her mind whirled like the spin cycle of a washing machine. That pile of dirty clothes she saw lying on the closet floor in Harvey's room could have been used as a disguise by the killer, along with the boots.

Nothing like hiding clues in plain sight, she thought to herself. If that was the killer's MO, then what other clues had Amanda overlooked that could lead her to the person who had stolen the cattle? Dave Zinkerman was the only suspect who hadn't attended the noodle supper, but he had a concrete alibi. Had one of the other suspects sneaked out during the slave auction, and Amanda had failed to notice?

Glancing at the dashboard, Amanda realized her fuel tank was sucking fumes. She headed for Thatcher's Oil and Gas, hoping her gas-guzzling truck wouldn't leave her stranded by the roadside.

CHAPTER SEVENTEEN

Amanda barely made it to the service station. The truck quit her when she pulled in the driveway. She coasted to the pumps.

Bruno barked when Bubba Hix lumbered outside. "Down, boy, he's a friend," Amanda said. The dog plunked down on the seat.

"Hi, 'Manda. Want me to fill 'er up?"

Amanda nodded. The hair extensions flip-flopped on her shoulders. "I guess you're holding down the fort while Thaddeus is seeing to his slave duties."

Bubba nodded as he crammed the nozzle into the fuel tank. "Yep. Rose Posey bought Thaddeus so he could overhaul her car engine for her. He's up to his elbows in crank shafts. Sure was a good dinner last night, wasn't it, 'Manda?"

"Best chicken noodle supper I've had since I can't remember when," Amanda agreed.

"The chief stopped in a while ago," Bubba said conversationally. "He ran out of gas while he was mowing Lucy's lawn."

"Oh, really?" Amanda had intended to drive straight home, sit herself down, and figure out who had dressed as Harvey to bump him off. But since she was in town, she decided to cruise past Lucy's house. She had an investment to protect, after all. And Thorn had damn well better be outside trimming shrubs, or he was a dead man!

"Sure can't thank you enough for baby-sitting B.J. while I took Sis to the hospital to deliver little Sissy," Bubba said, then smiled gratefully. "Beeje kept jabbering about stealing from the bank and robbing a farm." Bubba chuckled in amusement. "That boy has developed quite an imagination."

"Quite," Amanda agreed. She extended a twenty-dollar bill. "Will that cover the gas?"

"Sorry, 'Manda, but you're four bucks short. This old truck has a big tank."

"And fuel is high," she added as she reached into her billfold for more cash. "Give that new baby a hug for me, Bubba."

"Will do."

Amanda shoved off, determined to check on Thorn.

Her gaze narrowed suspiciously when she noticed the weed eater propped against a tree, and Thorn nowhere in sight. Amanda glanced at her watch. It was twelve-fifteen. She hadn't thought to ask what Thorn was doing about lunch. She was going to find out how and where he was taking his noon break.

Quick as a wink, Amanda was standing on the porch, rapping at the door. She swore profusely when Lucy answered, wearing a getup that emphasized every curve and swell—natural or otherwise—she possessed.

"I would like to speak to Thorn," she demanded in a no-nonsense tone.

"Sure, come in."

Amanda skidded to a halt when she saw Thorn sitting at a table overloaded with food. *Good grief! Sexy clothes and a meal fit for a king? Lucy was really laying it on thick, wasn't she?*

Thorn smiled at her. "Hi, Hazard. You must be feeling better. You definitely look better than you did this morning."

"I'm just swell. Could I speak privately with you?"

Lucy sauntered over to take her seat and finish her meal. "You're excused, slave. You've had three helpings. That should be enough to hold you until time for supper."

Amanda lifted an eyebrow. Thorn never took three helpings of the meals she served.

"I'm glad you came by," Thorn said as he ushered Amanda onto the back deck.

"So am I. I think I need to lay down the law to Ms. P."

"I already did. Told her I've got the woman I want."

"You did?"

"Yep, flat-out. After that incident at my bachelor party I wasn't going to take any chances of a misunderstanding between us. But get this, Haz, I found out that Lucy was fooling around with Harvey Renshaw."

"What? He had a girlfriend and ex-wife to fool around with, and he hit on Lucy?"

"That's exactly what *I* said, but Lucy confirmed it. She said Anita knew about the affair. Harvey was really pressing his luck, wasn't he?"

"But Lucy is a brunette," Amanda pointed out.

"She is now," Thorn clarified. "But Lucy claims she and Harvey had a thing going before she turned her blond hair brown."

"How could Harvey possibly have time for so many women? Maybe I should check his prescriptions to see if he was taking Viagra."

"Beats me how Harv could have kept up such an active sex life." Thorn grinned rakishly. "As for me, I'm more than satisfied with one woman. That woman is you, Hazard." He leaned closer. "No offense, but I wish you would do something about your hair. You look like a mangy sheepdog with those off-color extensions."

Amanda was so busy digesting the information Thorn imparted that she didn't have time to be offended by his comment. "I just came from Dave Zinkerman's farm. Harvey's cattle are missing from the pasture, and I thought maybe Dave decided to make a little profit now that he is married and has a wife and son to support."

"Married? To whom? When did this happen?" Thorn asked, startled.

"He married Jenny this week."

"Jenny Long?" Thorn chirped.

"None other," Amanda affirmed. "They tied the knot before they spent the week at a state resort. My theory that Dave stole the cattle doesn't hold water, because Jenny swears she and Dave had been inseparable since they returned to his farmhouse yesterday evening. So who the hell rustled Harvey's herd, do you suppose?"

"There is one quick way to find out. Call the stockyards in the city and ask for the names of sellers who delivered livestock last night or early this morning. Whoever swiped the herd wouldn't want to risk having us notice the cattle were gone and give us time to track him down before he collected the money.

"Whoever rustled the cattle must be the same person who used Harvey's tractor to feed a hay bale yesterday," Thorn said thoughtfully.

"Whoever it was must be the same person who bumped off Harv and Anita and is familiar with farming operations."

"Yeah, someone like Corky Bishop," Thorn mused aloud. "No wonder there was a discrepancy in his story about his nine-fifteen meeting with Harvey."

Thorn stared somberly at Amanda. "When I get home this evening, you and I are going to pay Corky a visit. He has the know-how, motive, and opportunity to commit murder."

"He could have been the one who was wearing Harvey's clothes, boots, and driving his wheat truck."

"Huh?" Thorn stared at her, uncomprehending.

"He could have driven to the house, unnoticed, because Johnny and Laverne went different directions after the confrontation in the kitchen that morning. Corky claimed to have seen the wheat truck coming over the hill, but no one can substantiate that claim. *He* could have been the one in the truck."

"How did you come up with that?" Thorn asked.

"Never mind. I'll tell you about it later. What time can I expect you this evening?"

Thorn gestured toward the rotten boards on the deck. "I have to replace these, hook up a new garbage disposal, and stick a new shower head in the bathroom. I hope to be finished by five." He glanced quizzically at her. "Did you stop by to refill that allergy medication?"

"No." Amanda glanced across the recently mowed back yard. "I—" She hesitated, then said, "I'll tell you about that later, too."

"Tell me about what?" Thorn asked as he followed her through the kitchen door.

"Nothing, Thorn. I don't want to detain you from your slave chores." Amanda tossed Lucy a meaningful glance. "Don't wear him out. He has responsibilities at home . . . if you know what I mean."

Lucy lifted her tea glass in a toast. "You have quite a man, Hazard."

"I'm well aware of that. Maybe you should put on something warmer than those skimpy shorts and blouse, Lucy. The weather forecast is calling for very little sunshine and cooler temperatures this afternoon."

Having made her point, Amanda got in her truck, gave Bruno a pat on the head for waiting patiently, then left. She noticed several neighbors milling around their yards. Amanda smiled to herself. Thorn couldn't screw up, even if he wanted to. The neighborhood watch was keeping a cautious eye on him for her.

* * *

Amanda drove home, mentally clicking through her list of suspects. She decided to cross Dave Zinkerman off her list, because his behavior indicated his time and energy had been focused on beginning his married life with Jenny. Amanda hoped she wasn't making a mistake by giving Dave the benefit of the doubt. But for now, he was off the investigative hook.

Although Thorn's money was on Corky Bishop, who definitely had opportunity since he was in the area, Amanda wasn't sure he was responsible. But if nothing else, Amanda hoped to gain a clearer picture of the time frame they were working with when they interrogated Corky again.

Corky's insistence that he was confronting Harvey at the same time she talked to him on the phone still had her stumped. She couldn't possibly have been wrong about the time, could she?

Or had she been fooled by the voice on the phone?

Amanda frowned pensively. Johnny Phipps was familiar with Harvey's house and his habits. That was a given. Johnny had reason to want Harvey out of the way. And, of course, Johnny knew how to drive the standard shift on the wheat truck, because Amanda had seen him driving it before, and after, her conference with Glenda . . .

Whoa, back up the buggy, Hazard. You are assuming a man pulled on Harvey's boots, and maybe those grimy clothes lying on the closet floor, then drove off in the wheat truck to flatten Harvey with a hay bale.

That brought Amanda back to the two women present at the house at eight o'clock Monday morning. Laverne and Glenda had their feelings trounced on by their ex-husband. One or the other woman might have schemed to keep her identity hidden by dressing as Harvey.

But who was the man on the phone, and who rustled Harvey's cattle?

"Well, damn!" Amanda said, and scowled. "If I don't shift into high gear in this case it might become one of the county's unsolved mysteries. Too many suspects with too much to gain and no concrete evidence that suggests which one of them might have cut the hydraulic hose—"

Cut or yanked on the hose? Amanda asked herself. *Where is that faulty hose Thorn replaced so he could move the hay bale off Harvey?* Suddenly Amanda felt the need to inspect that hose—up close.

Amanda veered onto the gravel road that led home. *Maybe Thorn tossed the hose in the trash barrel.* As soon as she reached the house she would call him and find out.

It was a good excuse to ensure Lucy wasn't backing Thorn into a corner to seduce him.

When Amanda hung a right into the driveway, the other two dogs were barking to beat the band. "Rats, I forgot to feed you this morning, didn't I? Sorry about that, boys."

Amanda watched Bruno bound from the truck to greet his canine buddies, then she tramped down to the barn to scoop up dog food. Since Thorn was occupied for the day, Amanda tossed a bucket of pellets and a block of alfalfa hay to the sheep. She noticed one of the ewes had wandered off by herself and was lying in the corner of the pen, refusing to answer the call for feed. Amanda climbed over the wooden fence to check on the downed ewe.

Two newborn lambs lay behind the ewe that was still sprawled on her side, bleating and straining. "Triplets?" Amanda questioned. "Gee whiz, aren't you the good sport!"

Amanda waited until the third undersize lamb lay in the grass and "baaed" for breath. Twins would be time-consuming, but triplets? Sure as the world, she and Thorn would have to give supplemental bottles of milk to the three new additions to the flock.

Ah, life on the farm, Amanda mused as she turned away. To think she had spent so many years cramped up in the city. She wasn't sure she could tolerate living in town after spending time in these wide-open spaces of Vamoose County. This was where she was meant to be.

Amanda had just set one foot on the porch when a troubled thought came out of nowhere.

Out of nowhere? No, that wasn't precisely correct. Watching the triplet lambs being born had inspired the thought that swirled through her mind.

Damn, her curiosity obviously had abandoned her in mid-investigation. She had stared at Renshaw's death certificates at least three times and she had overlooked very important data. She remembered registering the information on the estate tax forms, but she had neglected to lay the death certificates side by side.

Amanda had an unshakable feeling that she was not going to be surprised when she compared the documents. She kept sensing that Harvey was making arrangements that indicated drastic changes in his present lifestyle. But who had stepped in and foiled his mysterious plans?

With grim resignation Amanda sorted through the papers on the table to retrieve Harold J. Renshaw and Harvey W. Renshaw's death certificates. She laid them side by side to compare the information. Sure enough, there was no younger or older brother. The Renshaw offspring had been twins!

Four ex-wives, countless girlfriends. Dozens of photos of Renshaw with various women. But who was to say that Harvey was the man in every picture?

Amanda checked the date of death on Harold J. Renshaw's certificate. Her shoulders slumped. For a moment she had thought she might be onto something, but Harold had been gone more than seven years.

She stared pensively at the military dog tags. All evidence indicated Harold J. Renshaw had preceded his twin brother in death. So what was the California connection that sent Harvey to the West Coast for a year after he left Wife Number Three in Georgia and married Flower Child, who ended up in the farm pond shortly after her arrival in Vamoose?

A feeling of unease settled over Amanda as she glanced down at the stack of papers on the table. The documents were not where she had left them. The bank statements were mixed up with the car titles and insurance policy. The estate tax forms were by her left elbow, not by her right elbow where she placed them before she left the house.

"Uh-oh," Amanda wheezed.

She remembered the dogs barking when she arrived. "Double uh-oh," she said to herself.

Bounding from her chair, Amanda sped toward the front door.

"Sit down, Hazard, you aren't going anywhere."

The gruff voice came from the shadows of the hall. Amanda glanced over her quaking shoulder. The first thing she saw was Thorn's shotgun aimed at her back.

The second thing she noticed was that Harold J. Renshaw was holding the lethal weapon.

"Obviously, the Persian Gulf War wasn't as deadly as the dog tags and death certificate led me to believe," Amanda said with more bravado than she felt.

Renshaw smiled craftily. "I said, sit down, Hazard. Do it!"

Since it sounded like an order, backed up by a loaded shotgun, Amanda sat down. "You are Harold, the identical twin, I presume."

CHAPTER EIGHTEEN

Renshaw advanced from the shadows, holding the weapon like a man who definitely knew how to use it. "You presume wrong, Hazard."

She blinked, surprised. "Harvey? You bumped off your own brother and let everyone think it was *you*?"

"It was an accident."

Amanda didn't believe it for a minute. Too many things pointed to premeditated murder. That list of bank accounts that had been crossed out had aroused Amanda's suspicions. The boots and clothes in Harvey's closet had drawn her curiosity. The monthly withdrawals from Vamoose Bank indicated a scheme in the making. The sudden cattle sale was another red flag of warning.

Harvey halted in military fashion at the head of the table. "I take it you aren't buying the claim of an unexpected accident."

"Not hardly."

He shrugged a muscled shoulder. "Well, it doesn't matter now. Calling you up and asking you to meet me in the pasture served its purpose. Knowing your reputation, I knew I could count on you to start digging and keep everyone in such turmoil that I could complete the arrangements without unnecessary hassle.''

Amanda glanced at the antique clock on the wall. *Damn, Thorn won't be home for at least two more hours.* Amanda wasn't sure she could stall that long.

"I presume you are referring to this morning's cattle sale. Or did you haul the herd to the city last night? Last night is my guess. Most everyone was in town for the church dinner.''

"You noticed the cattle were gone? My, you have been a busy little beaver, haven't you?''

"No stone unturned, as they say," she replied flippantly.

Harvey clucked his tongue at her sassy retort. "Good thing you weren't in the military service. You would have been demoted for insolence.''

"Not to worry, I found my true calling.''

Before he decided to blow Amanda out of her chair, she rushed on. "I am assuming your twin brother didn't die in action during the Gulf War.''

"Obviously not." Harvey pulled a face. "He was a lousy soldier, but he knew how to make extra bucks by providing drugs and hooch for his buddies. Right before his superior officers were ready to come down on him, Harold took a convenient out. He switched dog tags with one of the soldiers in his squadron that he came across in the desert. Then Harold checked out of the war and flew home.''

"Sounds like a clever opportunist," Amanda commented.

"Exceptionally clever." Harvey's expression altered. "He kept showing up to have flings with my ex-wives. He got his kicks out of fooling everyone into thinking he was me.''

Amanda remembered what Rita and Glenda had said about Harvey seeming different when he made return visits. The face and body may have been the same, but the personalities were different. Yet, after several months of separation, the ex-wives were unaware they had encountered Harvey's twin brother.

"I can see that having an uncontrollable double would be a problem," Amanda commented, then shot another discreet glance at the clock. Shoot, she had only killed ten minutes. "I assume Flower Child was Harold J.'s wife rather than yours. Bigamy didn't fit your MO. So, which one of you sent Flo for a one-way midnight swim? You or your bro?"

"Harold did it. He had to," Harvey said. "Flo saw the two of us together when she showed up from California unexpectedly. Harold planned to use my practice of leaving the women in his past when he came to Oklahoma. He tried to convince Flo that she was hallucinating on the drugs he provided for her, but she swore she would tattle about what she knew if we didn't give her a cut of the drug-trafficking profits."

"That reminds me, why did you buy half the farm from your brother for a buck? Did Harold need fast money and you didn't want to pay the full price of document stamps on the sale of the property?"

"Very good, Hazard. That's why you have been in charge of the accounting. You're the only one in the county with a quick mind."

Not quick enough, thought Amanda. She had been beating her head against the proverbial brick wall for a week. Only today had she circled back to facts she had overlooked in her haste to fill out the estate tax forms.

"So, Harold J. has been in and out of Vamoose for two years. I'm surprised the two of you didn't slip up occasionally by being in two different places at once—say on the phone and in a confrontation with Corky Bishop?"

Harvey's face puckered in a scowl. "He was getting too cocky and daring for my tastes. He wasn't reliable, either."

"I'm sure you weren't pleased when Harold J. struck up an affair with Lucy Pomegranate," Amanda speculated.

"That was a stupid thing to do. He was already banging

Laverne and she didn't know the difference. He would sneak into the bedroom and wake her up while Johnny slept, then lure her into the spare bedroom. Then when I told him his foolishness was too risky, he promised to pay Laverne's rent if she moved into your farmhouse.''

"What about Rita and Glenda?''

Harvey smiled wryly. "They never knew the difference, either. When Harold flew off to pick up drugs he would stop to visit them in Texas and Georgia, then make the drug drops at the Air Force bases.''

It was becoming increasingly clear to Amanda that Harold J. had been a racketeer who came and went from the family farm, dealing his drugs, working under an assumed name when it was convenient, borrowing Harvey's name when it was to his benefit. For Harvey, it was like having an alter ego running around out of control. No doubt, Harvey decided there was only one way to stop his double.

"I assume Harold J. was in the habit of running fast and loose while he was in California, living with his mother,'' Amanda said.

"A regular hell-raiser, his mother was.'' Harvey let loose with a distasteful snort. "Lousy influence on a kid. A toss of the coin decided which twin would stay on the farm and which one would follow the *Grapes of Wrath* route and end up with a prostitute for a mother.''

Amanda frowned at the bitter note in Harvey's voice. Clearly, Harvey had no respect for his mother, who abandoned him and his father. She found herself listening intently to what he said, but also the way he said it.

"Harold didn't have much of a chance as a kid, but the Air Force tried to make a respectable man of him. Sometimes a kid just can't overcome his lowly raising,'' Harvey continued. "Fact is, our mother didn't have the sense God gave a goose, and parental guidance wasn't her thing. She was too busy indulging herself in personal pleasure to waste time raising a kid.''

Yep, Amanda confirmed. Harvey strongly disliked the West Coast connection of his family tree.

''This is just a wild guess, but did your mother happen to be a bleached-blonde?''

Harvey blinked. ''Yeah, she was. Why would you want to know that?''

Amanda shrugged noncommittally. She had the unshakable feeling that all the women Harvey left behind symbolized what he considered to be his mother's betrayal. This, she decided, was the triggering mechanism for the Renshaw Harem Complex.

She checked the clock again. Thirty minutes down, an hour and a half to go.

Harvey gestured the spitting end of the shotgun at the maroon folder. ''I noticed you have the estate tax forms in perfect order. Knew I could count on you to distribute the inheritance to the exes.''

''Considering the scheme you and Harold J. had going with drug trafficking, you could have been more generous,'' Amanda said, and smirked. ''But I'm sure you wanted to ensure you had a tidy nest egg stashed away for yourself. Those account numbers in the California bank were closed. That's why you scratched them off the list. I assume you stashed cashier's checks in your safety-deposit box.''

Amanda obviously said the wrong thing, because Harvey snapped up the shotgun and glowered at her. ''Everything was moving along as planned until you sneaked into the house to swipe the key to my safety-deposit box. Now where is it, Hazard? If I could have found it, while you were running around like a chicken with its head cut off this afternoon, you wouldn't find yourself in such an unfortunate predicament now.''

If she hadn't found the key, Harvey would never have approached her, and she wouldn't be sitting on needles and pins, wondering if Thorn would return to save her from what looked to be catastrophic disaster.

"Safety-deposit key?" she said in feigned ignorance.

"Don't play stupid with me, Hazard. You may be a blonde, and by the way, those hair extensions look ridiculous on you, but you have more brains than all those bimbos I married put together. Now, where is that damn key!" he shouted.

The dogs on the porch barked their heads off. Amanda glanced at the door, wishing Bruno, her bodyguard, was inside the house. But Thorn had insisted that Bruno live outside when they moved to his farm. Amanda should have put her foot down on that issue. If she had, Harvey would never have sneaked up on her.

"Don't even think about it," Harvey warned when he noticed the direction she was staring. "I'm an exceptional marksman. Those dogs don't stand a chance against this shotgun, and neither do you. I've come too far, made too many arrangements, to have some smart-ass female accountant screw this up."

Well, that pretty much stated what Harvey Renshaw thought of the women in the world. But Amanda already knew he regarded women as second-class citizens who were to be used and discarded like an old shirt. She wondered if he was taking out his anger against his mother's abandonment, and her age-old profession, and on all the women who came and went from his life. Probably.

"You still haven't told me how Anita ended up in the pond. My curiosity is k—" Amanda slammed her mouth shut. "Killing" was not a good word to toss at a man holding a lethal weapon.

But then, it was apparent that Amanda wasn't supposed to live to convey the tale of twins exchanging places for their fiendish amusement and convenience, now was she? With Harvey's military connections in the States, and his experiences with his tours of duty abroad, there was no telling where he and his stash of cash would relocate to enjoy a new life of leisure.

No one would be the wiser about Harvey's secret life if Amanda was out of the way. The inheritance would pay off the ex-wives, who had been duped repeatedly. The farm would go to Harvey's son. Meanwhile, Harvey would be sprawled on some tropical island beach, soaking up sun rays, drinking piña coladas and spending his money freely.

Or maybe, being the arrogant, self-absorbed man Harvey was, he planned to spare Amanda so she could inform the women in his life that they had been screwed over—literally. He might delight in having them wonder where he was, what he was doing . . . and who he was doing it with.

Amanda wasn't sure which of her theories on Harvey's plans was accurate. She sincerely hoped it was the latter, that he *wanted* her to live to tell his cunning story.

"Poor Anita."

Amanda couldn't honestly say that she detected even a hint of remorse in Harvey's voice. She figured he was only turning a phrase.

"Anita certainly has my sympathy," Amanda put in. "She was exceptionally devoted to you," Amanda wanted to add: "Better than a cocky, conceited, murdering jerk like you deserved." She decided it wasn't advisable to antagonize a man with a shotgun trained at her chest.

"I put a stash of cash in Anita's purse that morning, because I hadn't taken time to make compensations for her," Harvey explained. "But my brother went through her purse after he suffocated her and took the money."

"Suffocated her?" Amanda echoed.

Harvey nodded curtly. "Anita got all upset when Glenda showed up that morning. Harold saw her circling the section and flagged her down while he was in the wheat truck, then he went back to the house to get the tractor and feed hay for me. He had already driven the car into the pond before I showed up in the wheat truck.''

Chalk up two murders for Harold—Anita and Flower Child had died at his hands—if Harvey was to be believed. Amanda got the feeling Harvey didn't care about Anita, because there was no sentiment in his voice. He had used her as he had used the other women in his life. But Harold's lethal act of violence had given Harvey one more reason to want his troublemaking brother out of the way. Harvey had plotted and schemed to end the complications of dealing with his hellion of a twin.

"So you cut the hydraulic hose and let the hay bale drop on Harold J.''

"I yanked it loose," he corrected. "From there, everything went according to my plans. You were there to get everyone riled up and distracted. But you asked for trouble when you broke into the house to snatch the safety-deposit key before I could retrieve it. Not smart, Hazard. You should have left well enough alone. Now I have no choice but to silence you.''

Well, so much for wishful thinking. Harvey had dispelled her theory of letting her live to tell his clever story.

"Now, where the hell is that key?" Harvey growled at her.

Amanda's mind was buzzing ninety miles a minute, trying to figure out how to distract Harvey and give herself a sporting chance of escaping. The key was her ace in the hole.

When inspiration struck, she began digging in the pockets of her jeans. "I stuck the key in my pants pocket while I was at your place," she insisted. "Oh, wait a minute! These are the wrong jeans. They must be in the pocket of the Levi's I threw in the dirty-clothes hamper. I'll get it.''

Unfortunately, Harvey refused to let her out of his sight. He shackled her arm the instant she stood up.

"Don't try any funny business, Hazard," he warned gruffly.

To emphasize his comment, he rammed the shotgun barrel in her spine. "March, Hazard.''

Being an ex-soldier, Harvey might mean that literally. She

decided not to take any chances, so she paced down the hall in rhythmic steps. She focused absolute concentration on the partially opened door to the master bedroom. This was her one and only opportunity to catch Harvey off guard, she decided.

Amanda reached out as casually as she knew how, as if to open the door. And then, with an explosive burst of speed, she shot sideways, simultaneously slamming the door in Harvey's face. He roared like an enraged lion. Amanda barely had time to turn the lock before Harvey slammed his body against the door.

Her heart pounding like a piston, she raced toward the bathroom to put another locked door between them. Hands shaking, she jerked open the window. She stepped onto the toilet seat and rammed her head against the window screen in her haste to escape. As she fell out the window she heard Harvey crashing through the bedroom door. He cursed like a madman when he encountered the second locked door.

Amanda knew he had completely lost his temper, and patience, when she heard the shotgun blast splintering the wood of the bathroom door.

Thorn would not be pleased, Amanda thought as she took off across the lawn at a dead run. He had barely finished the carpentry work on the new master bedroom and bath addition before their wedding. Now he would have to make repairs.

Huffing and puffing for breath, Amanda darted into the old wooden barn and scrambled up the ladder to the loft. She hoped and prayed Harvey would take the time to check the pockets of the jeans in the laundry hamper. That would buy precious time to collect her wits and plot her next move.

Of course, the key wasn't in the laundry hamper. It was in the pocket of the jeans she was presently wearing. She hadn't had time to do laundry all week.

And the only way Harvey was going to get his greedy hands on that safety-deposit key and all the money he had stashed away was over her dead body . . . .

Amanda grimaced. She should have selected another cliché. That one struck a little too close to home!

Nervously Amanda waited for the sound of Harvey barreling from the house to locate her. When the dogs put up a ruckus Amanda knew Harvey was outside. She heard several yelps and a whine, and she bristled angrily. No doubt, Harvey had used the butt end of the shotgun to discourage the dogs from attacking him. She would see to it that he stood trial for double murders and animal cruelty . . . if she lived to file charges.

"Damn you, Hazard!" Harvey bellowed. "I'm not leaving without that key!"

Amanda dug into her pocket for the key, then set it atop the 2X12 joist in the loft. If Harvey managed to take her out, he was not going to have access to his stash of cash.

A shotgun blast sent a spray of buckshot thudding into the stack of alfalfa hay bales that Thorn kept on hand for his flock of sheep. Amanda nearly jumped out of her skin when the sound came from close range.

"I know you're in here, Hazard," Harvey snarled menacingly. "This Border collie is standing here, staring up at the loft. Is that where you are?"

"Oh, shit," Amanda whispered. Her faithful bodyguard had sniffed her out. Bruno had an endearing habit of wanting to be wherever she was. If only Bruno had cut and run after Harvey shotgun-whipped him.

Amanda hit the panic button when she heard Harvey's boots thump on the rungs of the ladder. She was running out of time, and Thorn wasn't due home for another hour!

Frantic, Amanda glanced around the loft, searching for something—anything—that would serve as a weapon of defense. If she didn't latch onto something—fast—Harvey would silence her permanently. The man had plotted to kill his own brother, so he wouldn't think twice about blowing his accountant to smithereens!

CHAPTER NINETEEN

Nick wormed and squirmed beneath the sink in Lucy's kitchen, cursing the new garbage disposal that refused to glide neatly into the cramped spaces.

"Lucy, are you in here?" Nick asked as he wedged his head under the sink-trap pipe.

"Yeah, sugar, whatcha want?"

"I need the water pump pliers."

"What's that?"

"The yellow-handled tool," he said, then scooted sideways to worm his left arm through the opening in the cabinet doors.

When a feminine hand clamped around his thigh, he jerked. His head slammed against the sink-trap pipe.

"Here you go, sugar."

The wrench came into view, but the feminine hand remained on his upper thigh. "Lucy," he said warningly.

"Geez, Nicky, you're no fun at all," Lucy pouted. "Here you are, sprawled faceup, from the broad chest down, under my sink, looking every bit the hunk you are. What's a girl to do?"

"You heard what Hazard said. She doesn't like that sort of stuff. Neither do I."

The feminine hand withdrew reluctantly. Nick concentrated on jockeying the garbage disposal until it was situated in its bracket. Using the pliers, he tightened the gasket leading to the drain.

"Done," he announced. "Move back. I'm wiggling out of here."

Nick shouldered his way from under the sink cabinet to find Lucy standing over him. When he looked up, he was treated to a view of long legs in short shorts and a full bosom in a form fitting blouse. *Damn, this woman just wouldn't quit!*

"Well, that takes care of your honey-do list. I'm on my way home."

Lucy smiled sensuously at him. "Hazard isn't expecting you for another thirty minutes."

Nick propped himself up on his elbows. "I'm going home to my wife. We have already had this discussion. Now please move so I can get up."

Lucy's face puckered in an exaggerated pout. "Fine, I gave it one last shot. But you really do have a will of iron, don't you, Nicky?"

"Morals and scruples and ethics," he added as he rolled to his knees, then climbed to his feet.

He gathered up his tools and headed for the door. He was never so glad to be headed home in his life!

"Nicky?"

He glanced over his shoulder to see Lucy propped seductively against the doorjamb, her arms folded beneath her chest. "Yeah, Lucy, what is it?"

"Tell Hazard I said that she is one exceptionally lucky woman. I guess this crush I've had on you for years will remain just that, a crush."

Nick managed a faint smile, but he was careful not to encourage Lucy in the least. "Good-bye, Lucy."

" 'Bye, sugar."

Nick strode outside to his truck, then breathed a huge sigh of relief. This was definitely his last slave charity. Next year, when the slave auction rolled around, he was sitting it out!

After a full day of frustration he was finally headed home to Hazard. Nick smiled in expectation. She would be at home, cooking up one of her nauseating meals, and he would praise her efforts until hell wouldn't have it, even if he had to choke down the slop. Then he and Hazard would question Corky, return home, and spend a quiet evening nestled up in spoon fashion on the couch, watching TV. And later . . .

Nick grinned devilishly. Later, he was going to make positively certain Hazard knew he appreciated everything about her. It was going to be a relaxing, splendidly romantic evening.

Nick drove off, with erotic fantasies dancing in his head.

Amanda spotted the broken handle of a pitchfork among the scattered straw in the barn loft.

Clomp, clank, clomp, clank.

Harvey was making his way up the ladder. If Amanda didn't move quickly to attack his blind side, she would have to deal with the spitting end of the shotgun!

Hardly daring to breathe, for fear Harvey would hear her terrified snatches of breath, Amanda inched toward the opening in the floor of the loft. She had to knock the shotgun from his hands, then she had to shove Harvey off balance. It would take some doing, because he outweighed her by seventy pounds.

She waited tensely for him to poke his head through the opening. Instead, the shotgun barrel swerved around like a cannon attached to an army tank.

Survival instincts came to life. Amanda whacked at the shotgun with her wooden handle. When Harvey pulled the trigger, the blast left her ears ringing. The gun kicked against Harvey's shoulder, forcing him to steady himself on the ladder.

Amanda pounced. She clobbered him on the head with the broken handle, and simultaneously struck out with her foot to divert the shotgun barrel away from her.

"HELP!!!" she screamed at the top of her lungs.

Harvey spouted several crude oaths, which would have offended Mother's ears.

The trio of dogs barked their heads off from the ground below.

"Bruno!" Amanda called frantically. "Here, boy!"

The protective Border collie leaped up at Harvey. Amanda heard the rending of cloth that indicated Bruno had bit into Harvey's pants leg. Harvey howled in outrage, and Amanda suspected the dog had also clamped his sharp teeth in Harvey's flesh.

"I'll kill that sonuvabitch!" Harvey hissed as he jerked the shotgun down to take his measure on the dog that was hanging on his leg.

"No!" Amanda tried out one of the karate moves she had seen Steven Seagal perform in his adventure movies. Her boot heel thumped against the side of Harvey's head, making his neck whiplash.

The maneuver worked so effectively that Amanda repeated it.

Harvey's furious curses threatened her to eternal damnation, but Amanda kept hammering at him with her boot heel and her wooden handle until he fell off balance. His howling screech ended with a thud and another foul oath.

Amanda heard the sound of another cartridge being shoved into the chamber of the shotgun. She knew Harvey had run clean out of patience. He intended to blow her out of the loft.

She lurched around and darted off the instant before buckshot sprayed through the opening in the floor of the loft.

Hands trembling, she unlatched the upper door of the barn and looked down. If she took a flying leap, she might get lucky enough to land on one of the three round hay bales that Thorn had lined up behind the barn.

Another shotgun blast exploded beneath her. Amanda heard the dogs yelping and scrambling for safety. If there was one thing dogs didn't like, it was a weapon discharging too close to their sensitive ears. Even hunting dogs had to be trained to stand their ground.

There wasn't a bird dog among the canine trio. They cut and ran.

Amanda inhaled a fortifying breath, then jumped from the second-story opening of the barn. She landed on her knees on the middle hay bale, then slithered to the ground. Harvey blew another hole in the floor of the loft, unaware that Amanda had escaped.

"Damn it, Hazard! You're really starting to piss me off! Come down from there!"

Amanda scrambled around the side of the barn, unsure where to hide. The distance between her and her clunker truck was too far to risk. The cattle shed provided no protection whatsoever. She couldn't bring herself to hide in the hay, since that was what started this complicated case. It would be too ironic if *she* ended up dead in the hay, too.

Amanda stared at the cattle shed, then at Thorn's workshop, then at the house. If she could skulk from one locale to the next—without Harvey spotting her—she could reach the phone and call for help. No matter what else happened, she wanted someone to know that Harvey Renshaw wasn't as dead as he wanted everyone to think he was.

The instant the next shotgun blast exploded inside the barn, Amanda raced to the tin-covered cattle shed and plastered herself in the shadows of the inner wall. She sucked in another breath, checked to see if the coast was clear, then darted to the workshop.

Buckshot pattered against the tin on the outside of the workshop.

Rats! Harvey had spotted her. There was only one exit from Thorn's workshop. She was trapped!

Praying for divine intervention, Amanda squatted down on her haunches beside the door. Harvey stalked toward her, his mouth curved in undisguised triumph.

"Gotcha! You might as well come out, Hazard. There is nowhere else to run."

Give up? Amanda Hazard! Like hell I would!

Amanda pivoted around. Her frantic gaze landed on Thorn's riding lawn mower. She plunked down on the seat and started the engine. She reached down to hoist up the cement block that Thorn kept nearby so he could prop open the door when he needed ventilation in the workshop. The block would keep enough weight on the seat of the lawn mower so the automatic shutoff wouldn't go into effect when Amanda hopped off the seat while the mower was in gear. That safety feature was fine and dandy for standard mowing, but it was a pain in the butt for this situation.

Sitting on the concrete block, Amanda shoved the mower into gear. The lawn mower lumbered through the exit, and Amanda hopped off, crawling on her hands and knees, using the mower as her shield.

Her ingenuity obviously caught Harvey by surprise, because it took him a moment to snap the shotgun into firing position. He drew down on the lawn mower that plowed toward him . . . but the sound of an approaching vehicle racing over the gravel road caught his attention.

"Thank you, God!" Amanda whispered when she recognized Thorn's black 4X4 pickup truck.

All Nick's fanciful thoughts of sexual ecstasy went up in smoke when he turned into the driveway. He could see Hazard's shapely butt behind the lawn mower that had a cement block in the driver's seat.

Fear jolted through him when he saw the shotgun—held by a man Nick didn't recognize from the rear view—pointed at Hazard. Nick gunned the truck and roared toward the armed assailant. When the man whirled around, Nick wasn't sure he could trust his eyes.

Harvey Renshaw? It couldn't be! Nick had positively ID'd the body that he removed from beneath the round hay bale. The medical examiner had pronounced Harvey Renshaw dead at the scene. *What in the hell was going on?*

When the shotgun—his own shotgun, damn it!—blasted his windshield, Nick threw himself onto the seat. Shards of safety glass sprayed over him, but he didn't take his foot off the accelerator. He was going to run down Harvey before he turned his firepower on Hazard.

Nick's timely arrival provided Hazard with the chance to hightail it around the side of the workshop. *Good, Nick noted, she was safe—for the moment.*

Harvey dived to the ground and rolled sideways as Nick's truck raced forward. Nick slammed on the brakes, threw the gear shift into park, then plunged out the passenger door.

"Look out, Thorn!" Hazard yelled frantically.

Harvey pulled the trigger, but there was no blast, only a click.

Praise the Lord, Harvey was out of shells!

Nick bounded to his feet, then hopped into the truck bed so he could leap at Harvey, who had scrambled to his feet to beat a hasty retreat. Nick made a classic, textbook-style, diving tackle. Harvey fell facedown in the gravel, cursed loudly, then twisted around to raise the shotgun like a club.

Nick grimaced as the butt end of the shotgun slammed against his shoulder. He flung up his arm to deflect the second blow that was aimed at his head.

Hazard appeared out of nowhere, a shovel clamped in her fists. Cursing mightily, she took a swing at Harvey's skull. The shovel clanked against Harvey's head, momentarily dazing him, allowing Nick to confiscate the shotgun.

Hazard, however, wasn't satisfied with leaving a knot on Harvey's noggin. She clobbered him twice more for good measure.

When she raised her makeshift weapon the fourth time, Harvey wrapped both arms around his head. "Get her away from me!"

Harvey had wasted his breath. Hazard let him have it—and how!

Harvey slumped, unconscious, in the gravel. Hazard dropped the shovel and leaped into Nick's arms.

"Oh, Thorn! I didn't think you would ever come home!"

To Nick's surprise, Hazard burst into tears, then lapsed into a series of loud wails, hiccups, and snorts that bordered on hysteria. He held her shuddering body in one arm, while she soaked the front of his T-shirt, but he never took his eyes off Harvey.

The moment Harvey roused to consciousness, Nick gave Hazard an abrupt shake. "Snap out of it. You can finish blubbering later. Get the spare set of handcuffs out of my truck . . . and stop that lawn mower before it plows into the side of the barn!"

Hazard didn't seem to know which order to follow first. Watery-eyed, chest heaving, she looked this way and that, then darted over to shut off the lawn mower. She arrived only seconds before the mower put a dent in the barn. Whipping around, she charged toward the truck to retrieve the handcuffs.

"Here, Thorn."

"Thanks." Nick squatted down to snap the cuffs in place. "Now, go call Deputy Sykes. He's ten-ten."

"He's what?"

"Out of service at home. Tell him I have a Code thirty, with a ten-fifteen, and I need a ten-sixteen. Got it?"

On legs that wobbled, Hazard headed toward the house, chanting, "Code thirty, ten-fifteen, ten-sixteen."

When Harvey opened his eyes, Nick was in his face, teeth bared. "I thought you were dead, you son of a bitch!"

"I got better," Harvey smarted off. "Where is that wild woman? You aren't going to let her hit me again, are you?"

"I will if she feels like it. And don't *ever* think about harming my wife again, Renshaw!"

Suppressed rage, combined with heart-stopping fear, erupted with volcanic intensity. Nick was so furious that he was shaking. Even though this was Hazard's seventh near brush with calamity, Nick couldn't handle it any better now than he had the first time she had scared the living hell out of him. Nick wanted to take his frustration out on the man responsible for this trembling fear.

Although Nick was itching to slam Harvey's head into the gravel, and bury a fist in his smart mouth, he didn't want a countersuit for unnecessary roughness. Hazard got to vent her fury, but Nick had to sit and smolder. It was one of the aggravating drawbacks of being a cop.

"I assume you had an identical twin," Nick growled. "Why did you kill him?"

"I demand to see a lawyer," Harvey growled

"I thought you didn't like lawyers. Now answer the question."

"I don't have to!"

"Don't worry about it, Thorn. I've got all the answers you want."

Nick glanced over his shoulder to see Hazard, her face white as caulking, staring at him.

"Harvey told me the whole story. Put me on the witness stand and I will make certain he gets the death sentence. And make sure you add animal cruelty to murder in the first and assault with a deadly weapon."

When Bruno limped toward Hazard, she squatted down to

comfort her injured bodyguard. "You helped save my life, Bruno. No matter what Thorn says, you have earned your place in our house."

Hazard glanced at Nick, daring him to argue with her. Nick didn't say a word. He had been married for three weeks and he had learned when to keep his trap shut.

This, he decided, was one of those times.

"Harold J. Renshaw faked his death during Desert Storm," Hazard informed Nick as she stroked Bruno's head. "He was trafficking drugs to Air Force bases, using Harvey's ID to get him where he needed to go. The Renshaw twins were stashing money in accounts in a California bank, then Harvey decided to copy Harold's clever vanishing act, so he could be rid of his troublesome twin.

"I suspect Harvey made a trip to California to have cashier's checks drafted from his accounts, then he put them in a safety-deposit box. I just happened to have found the key that Harvey was so determined to take away from me today."

"Go on," Nick prompted.

"It was Harold J. who did away with Flower Child when she realized the Renshaws were twins. It was also Harold J. who killed Anita. Harvey pulled the hydraulic hose off the tractor so the hay bale would drop on Harold. I think the twins were planning to leave Vamoose, but Harvey decided he wanted to go it alone so he wouldn't have to split the cash with his brother and deal with the kind of complications Harold J. brought with him when he came to Vamoose.

"That's it in a nutshell, Thorn. I'll give you the details later, but right now, I'm starting to feel sick . . . ."

Hazard took off for the house in a dead run.

Nick hauled Harvey to his feet and secured him to the bumper of his truck with a rope. Nick walked over to start the lawn mower and returned it to the workshop. To relieve some of his frustration, he paced back and forth a dozen times in the shop, spewing curse words.

The sound of blaring sirens heralded Deputy Sykes's arrival. Having gained some semblance of control, Nick walked outside.

Wide-eyed, Benny Sykes leaped from the squad car and gaped at Harvey. His astounded gaze swung to Nick. "I thought he was dead!"

"That's what Harvey wanted everybody to think before he flew off to begin his new life, with a briefcase full of drug money to support him."

Dumbfounded, Benny stared at Harvey. "But who was dead in the hay?"

"Harvey's identical twin, Harold."

"Identical twin?" Benny chirped. "I never knew he had one."

"The family split up forty years ago. Harold has been presumed dead since the Gulf War." Nick glowered at Harvey. "It's a helluva note when a man's brother sacrifices him for a stash of cash and a new lease on life."

"That is sick," Benny said in disgust.

"You said it," Nick seconded. He hitched his thumb toward Harvey. "Better hit him with the Miranda. Then get him out of my sight before I forget I'm a cop and beat the hell out of him for going after Hazard with a shotgun."

"After Hazard with a shotgun?" Benny parroted. "Is she okay?"

"Badly shaken," Nick reported. "I'll check on her and get her statement. I'll be down at the station in a half hour."

"Right, Chief. We'll be waiting for you."

Nick watched Deputy Sykes whisk Harvey off in the squad car, then he turned toward the house. Nick told himself that it wasn't Hazard's fault that Harvey had come gunning for her. He told himself she was so rattled that she had become nauseous. He told himself she needed compassion, not a lecture.

But damn it to hell! Nick had been terrified when he saw Harvey Renshaw taking aim at Hazard, who was trying to hide behind a lawn mower, for crying out loud! If Harvey had taken a shot at the fuel tank, he would have blown Hazard to kingdom come.

The very thought sent a chilling sensation down Nick's spine. He had come frighteningly close to losing Hazard today. *Damn it, this had to stop.* That woman was going to drive him to an early grave if she didn't quit chasing down murderers, single-handedly, and leaving herself in the lurch.

Grimly Nick entered the house. "Hazard?"

"I'm in the bathtub," she called back to him.

Nick muttered a colorful curse when he saw the splintered bedroom door. He swore profusely when he saw the holes blasted in the new bathroom door.

"My God, Hazard! Things were worse than I thought!"

Nick skidded to a halt when he saw Hazard's peaked face above a tub full of fragrant bubbles. Her faithful bodyguard, Bruno, lay beside the bathtub.

"Are you going to yell at me like you usually do when a case blows up in my face?" she asked.

He wanted to, he really did. But he decided not to, because Hazard looked wrung-out. Judging from the condition of the new doors he had installed last month, she had been chased through the house and around the barnyard.

"Well? Are you?" she asked when he lingered so long in thought.

"No, Hazard, not this time." He knelt by the tub to pull a piece of straw from her shaggy hair extensions. "Where did this come from?"

"I had to make a flying leap from the opening of the barn loft to your row of hay bales."

"You what?" Nick wheezed.

Hazard smiled weakly. "I've had a rough afternoon, Thorn, but there is something I need to tell you."

"I know you are anxious to give me your statement about the attack and fill me in on the information you have on the murders."

"That's not what I—"

"Short and precise, Haz," Nick interrupted as his gaze wandered over the shifting bubbles that granted him an intimate view of her gorgeous body. "I told Deputy Sykes that I would meet him at the station so we could process the paperwork for Harvey's arrest. Can I bring you anything while I'm in town?"

"Pick up some burgers and fries from the Last Chance Cafe," she requested. "I don't feel like cooking tonight."

"Done, now fill me in on the details of this case."

Hazard repeated everything Harvey had told her, then she gave her account of the run for her life. Nick came to his feet, then turned away. He didn't want to think about how many times Hazard had dodged bullets in the past two hours. If she were a cat she would have used up all nine lives in this case. If she became involved in future investigations, she would definitely be living on borrowed time!

Nick retrieved the safety-deposit key that was exactly where Hazard said it would be, then drove into Vamoose to throw the book at Harvey Renshaw. No way in hell was the man going to beat this murder rap, Nick promised himself. By the time he tacked on assault with a deadly weapon, resisting arrest, and animal cruelty, Harvey was going to wish his twin brother was alive to help him serve out his sentence!

CHAPTER TWENTY

Fifteen minutes after Thorn left the house, Amanda jerked straight up in the bathtub, splashing water and bath bubbles on the tiled floor and soaking Bruno. "Holy cow!" she yelped when a troubled thought struck her. Bits and pieces of conversation buzzed through her brain like a swarm of wasps. An image flashed in her mind's eye. The information Harjo had given her sent up red flags.

Amanda climbed from the tub and grabbed a towel. She padded into the bedroom to pick up the phone and made a quick call to police headquarters. She had the unmistakable feeling that this case—one she thought was wrapped up—wasn't. She wanted to put Thorn on immediate alert. She knew he had the connections to double-check the suspicions that descended on her while she was lounging in the tub. Having made the call, Amanda collapsed on the king-size bed to rest.

Unfortunately, the phone rang nonstop for the next forty-five minutes. Friends and acquaintances called to sympathize with Amanda's harrowing experiences of being chased around the farm by a maniac with a shotgun. Velma Hertzog chomped her gum and demanded all the details so she could spread the story around the beauty shop. Gertrude Thatcher offered to cook supper and bring it out that evening. The list went on and on.

After taking the consecutive calls Amanda sank onto the La-Z-Boy recliner to relax, the faithful Bruno sprawled at her side. Amanda had tended the cut on Bruno's head and cooed over him until he nearly wagged off his stubbed tail.

Amanda checked her watch, wondering when Thorn would return. He had been so intent on hearing her statement for the police report that he hadn't allowed her to tell him the news that she had kept to herself all day.

The roar of an automotive engine indicated Thorn had arrived. Bruno bounded up and raced to the door. He backed off when he caught Thorn's scent.

"Dinner has arrived," Thorn said as he came through the door, carrying a greasy brown paper sack in his hand. "Everyone in Vamoose sends his and her condolences for the rotten day you've had."

"Apparently so," Amanda said. "The phone has been ringing off the hook . . . . Ohmigosh!" She jerked upright in the chair. "Your mom called a couple of days ago and I forgot to tell you that she wants you to call her back."

"Great," Thorn grumbled. "Your forgetfulness, despite the fact that you had a gazillion things on your mind, will give her one more excuse as to why we aren't meant for each other."

"I have been exceptionally busy," Amanda agreed. "This was the most perplexing case I have come across to date. Too many unknown factors in the equation. By the time I weighed all the variables I had concluded that it was *Harold J. Renshaw* who had returned from the dead to dispose of *Harvey*." She stared curiously at Thorn. "By the way, were you able to confirm my suspicions?"

Thorn nodded. "Turns out . . . you were right on target, Haz." The admission was obviously difficult for him, because he had to clear his throat before he continued. "Just as you suggested, I called the medical examiner and asked him to check the dental records for Harvey Renshaw. And guess what?"

So she was right, she presumed. "It turned out that it was *Harvey* who was actually dead in the hay, not Harold J."

"You got it, Haz. Harold must have assumed his brother's identity so many times through the years that he decided to play out the role to the end. I guess Harold's inflated ego refused to allow him to admit that he was the one who made the oversight by leaving the safety-deposit key where you could confiscate it."

Amanda nodded pensively. "That's what sent up the first alarm in my mind. I couldn't understand why Harvey would leave the key with Harold J.'s death certificate and the official letter from the War Department. I would have expected it to be with Harvey's important documents."

Thorn blinked. "That's what made you think that Harold was still playing the role of Harvey when he came gunning for you? *That's it?*"

"No, there were other things that didn't fit with what I knew about this case," Amanda told him. "I think Harold J. was making withdrawals from Harvey's bank account each month after the military retirement pensions were deposited. It seemed odd to me that Harvey made the deposits, then waited a week to ten days to write a check for large amounts of cash. Harold was swindling his brother, and I wouldn't be surprised if Harvey finally realized what was going on and confronted his sneaky twin. In fact, I'm willing to bet that was why Harold J. decided to leave Harvey dead in the hay, instead of both of them vanishing into thin air with the stockpiles of money.

"Neither one of them was able to stay in one place very long, you know. Harvey had been here over two years and I suspect he was getting restless. That's why he sold his farm machinery to Corky Bishop and made preliminary arrangements for Corky to rent the farm ground."

Thorn gaped at her, trying to keep up with her rapid-fire comments.

"And while I was being held at gunpoint, Harold J. told me about his irresponsible, self-absorbed mother. It sounded to me as if he was speaking from firsthand experience, not hearsay. Harold's real feelings kept coming to the surface, even though he was pretending to be Harvey."

Thorn's mouth dropped open, but he didn't interrupt while Amanda was on a roll.

"There was also a discrepancy in his story that didn't coincide with what Harjo told us," Amanda continued. "Harold J. claimed Anita's car was driven into the pond before the dead-in-the-hay incident, but Harjo saw Anita in her car talking to someone around noon. I think Anita must have showed up unexpectedly and caught Harold J. by surprise, two hours after his identical twin was squashed in the hay. Harold J. must have disposed of Anita shortly after Harjo left the area to have lunch. I had already double-checked with Jenny to pinpoint the exact time Anita called my office. It was before noon that Anita tried to contact me. She must have made the lethal mistake of confronting Harvey's dangerous twin by herself."

"I have to hand it to you, Haz, you kept digging until you solved this case. I never would have thought to check the dental records when I tossed Harvey . . . er . . . Harold in the slammer. But after you called, I decided to do a little digging on my own. I checked Harold's arms, and sure enough, I found evidence of needle marks. He may have been using part of his brother's money to support his own drug habit." Thorn sighed tiredly. "This has been a long day and I'm beat. But I better take time out to call Mom, or we will both be in the doghouse."

"Thorn, there is one more thing."

"Can't it wait, Haz? I've had it."

"Okay, but maybe if you tell Mom you're going to be a daddy she won't be quite as irritated with us."

Thorn halted in midstep. His back went rigid and he stood

utterly still. Amanda wished he hadn't been walking away so she could have seen the look on his face when she gave him the news. When he turned around, she was granted a view of the startled expression that was frozen on his ruggedly handsome features.

"You wanna run that past me one more time?" he croaked, frog-eyed.

Amanda squirmed beneath his unwavering stare. "You aren't upset about this, are you? I know we haven't been married very long, but our biological time clocks are ticking and—"

"You dived through the bathroom window and ran around the farm as fast as your legs would carry you *in your condition*? You leaped through the second-story opening in the barn loft and landed on hay bales *in your condition*?" He erupted like Old Faithful.

"What did you want me to do? Hang around the loft while Harvey—Harold J. blasted holes in the flooring, hoping I was standing above the spot he shot at? Geez, Thorn, it wasn't like I had several options available."

"Good God!" Thorn's legs folded like a tent and he hit his knees. He gaped at her in distress. "If Harold had silenced you permanently I would never have known. Good God . . . !"

"Thorn, get a grip on yourself," Amanda said curtly. "If you are going to fall apart when you receive the news, I shudder to think how you will react when it's time to deliver this baby. You are going to remain cool and calm, like you do when you're handling police work, aren't you? You aren't going to have a panic attack like Bubba Hix did, are you?"

"How . . . ?" was all he could get out as he wobbled unsteadily to his feet and staggered across the living room. "When . . . ?"

"How?" Amanda snorted sarcastically. "Really, Thorn, you know how things like this happen. When? Last month, when I filled the allergy prescription." Amanda pulled the pharmacy printout from her pocket and handed it to him. "I didn't read the fine print on precaution number four. It's the one about drug interactions. According to this printout, allergy medications often decrease the effectiveness of birth control pills."

"I'm going to be a daddy?" Thorn said to the room at large.

"Apparently so. I picked up a home pregnancy test in Pronto, shortly after I spoke with Jenny and Dave Zinkerman. I didn't want to take the risk of buying the stuff in Vamoose. Velma Hertzog would have picked up the news and spread it around town before you got home and I had the chance to tell you in person."

"The headaches, the nausea," Thorn mused aloud. "The grouchiness."

"Hey! I'm not the least bit grouchy," Amanda said, highly offended.

Like a man rousing from a trance, Thorn rushed toward her. "Can I get you anything, Haz? Are you feeling okay now? Do you want a cola? Soda crackers? Are you craving ice cream and pickles already?"

Amanda glanced around his shoulder to see the greasy sack on the table. "How about serving up the hamburgers from the diner."

Thorn whipped around and scurried off.

"One thing, Hazard," he said over his shoulder.

"What's that, Thorn?"

He handed her a burger, fries, and a napkin. "This is the end of your gumshoe career. I am not wavering on that issue." He stared her down. "I mean it this time, Haz. You have scared the pants off me seven times when you've gotten caught up in the backlash of an investigation gone sour."

"I see." Amanda chewed on her fries. "So you intend to give up your police beat, too. Right?"

He stared blankly at her. "Well, no. What does that have to do with your being in the family way?"

"*We* are in the family way, with responsibilities of child rearing ahead of us," she corrected. "Kindly explain to me why man and wife, sharing an equal matrimonial partnership, should expect one spouse to cool her investigative heels while the other spouse isn't cooling his?"

While Thorn was trying to figure out how to respond to her logical question—without getting himself in scalding water—Amanda bit into her cheeseburger.

"What are the chances of me winning this argument?" he asked after a moment.

"One in a million," Amanda told him flat out.

"I was afraid of that." Thorn chewed on his cheeseburger, then swallowed. "Okay, maybe another murder case won't turn up in the next seven and a half months."

"Probably not. What are the chances of that happening?" Amanda replied.

"So maybe—"

"Eat your supper, then call Mom," Amanda cut in. "Then I'll call Mother and we can both call it a night." She flashed him one of those suggestive glances that usually got him all steamed up.

Sure as shootin', it worked every time.

Thorn returned her grin. "I'll be looking forward to calling it a night. No matter how tired I am, I always save a little back. In fact, I think we should call it a night before we call Mom and Mother."

Amanda watched Thorn gobble his meal. Then he scooped her up and carried her to the master bedroom in a melodramatic fashion that would have done Rhett Butler proud.

Instinct told Amanda that she was going to have a teensy-weensy problem getting Thorn to behave normally for the next seven and a half months. Already, he was being unnecessarily protective and possessive, anxious to cater to her slightest whim.

Hopefully, when the shock of learning he was going to be

a father wore off, he would be his old self again. If not, Amanda would have to spend her spare time training Thorn to behave in a reasonable manner and stop treating her like an invalid. She was not—*not, repeat with emphasis!*—going to spend a half year housebound. It simply wasn't her style.

Dear Readers,

I hope you enjoyed accompanying me through my latest investigation of *Dead in the Hay*. The next book in the Amanda Hazard series, *Dead in the Pumpkin Patch,* will be released in October, 2000. Thorn and I will be back again to update you on the goings-on in Vamoose. Considering my condition, things might be a bit more complicated while pursuing my investigation, but rest assured that I will never falter in my quest for truth and justice in small-town America.

*Expectant*ly yours,
Amanda Hazard-Thorn, CPA

P.S. If there are those of you out there who can convince Hazard to take it easy for the next few months, please contact my headstrong wife. I will appreciate all the help and support I can get.

Yours truly,
Nick Thorn, Vamoose PD

P.P.S. Please disregard Thorn's request. Expectant fathers are not rational.

Yours truly,
Amanda

The Amanda Hazard Series
By Connie Feddersen